VOW OF JUSTICE

Books by Lynette Eason

WOMEN OF JUSTICE

Too Close to Home
Don't Look Back
A Killer Among Us

DEADLY REUNIONS

When the Smoke Clears
When a Heart Stops
When a Secret Kills

HIDDEN IDENTITY

No One to Trust
Nowhere to Turn
No Place to Hide

ELITE GUARDIANS

Always Watching
Without Warning
Moving Target
Chasing Secrets

BLUE JUSTICE

Oath of Honor
Called to Protect
Code of Valor
Vow of Justice

VOW OF JUSTICE

LYNETTE EASON

Revell

a division of Baker Publishing Group
Grand Rapids, Michigan

© 2019 by Lynette Eason

Published by Revell
a division of Baker Publishing Group
PO Box 6287, Grand Rapids, MI 49516-6287
www.revellbooks.com

Printed in the United States of America

Library of Congress Cataloging-in-Publication Data
Names: Eason, Lynette, author.
Title: Vow of justice / Lynette Eason.
Description: Grand Rapids, MI : Revell, [2019] | Series: Blue Justice Series ; 4
Identifiers: LCCN 2018052131 | ISBN 9780800727208 (paper)
Subjects: LCSH: United States. Federal Bureau of Investigation—Fiction. | Protective custody—Fiction. | Murder—Investigation—Fiction. | Man-woman relationships—Fiction. | Police—Fiction.
Classification: LCC PS3605.A79 V69 2019 | DDC 813/.6—dc23
LC record available at https://lccn.loc.gov/2018052131

ISBN 978-0-8007-3622-4 (casebound)

19 20 21 22 23 24 25   7 6 5 4 3 2 1

Dedicated to Jesus—
justice seeker, abundant forgiver,
and passionate pursuer of his children.
Thank you for allowing me to do what I do.

LAW ENFORCEMENT
Oath of Honor

★ ★

On my honor,
I will never betray my badge, my integrity,
my character, or the public trust.
I will always have the courage
to hold myself and others
accountable for our actions.
I will always uphold the constitution,
my community, and the agency I serve.

★ ★

1

LATE APRIL
VLADISLAV NEVSKY'S HOME
COLUMBIA, SOUTH CAROLINA

FBI Special Agent Allison Radcliffe fingered the key in her apron pocket, debating whether she could break into Vladislav Nevsky's office without getting caught. "Are you there?" she asked, her voice low. She stood inside the vast kitchen pantry with the door shut. With listening devices all over the house, this little bug-free area was the one place she could verbally touch base with her fellow agents without fear of being overheard by enemy ears.

"Always." Linc St. John, her partner, answered immediately through her earpiece.

"I think this is my chance."

"You're sure?"

"Somewhat."

"That's not good enough. We've waited this long, we can wait a little longer."

"I don't think so." She rubbed her palms together. "My Spidey senses are tingling and telling me time is running out. I think he suspects me." Nevsky's keys had gone missing and mysteriously turned up under his favorite recliner. His eyes told her he was gauging her reaction when he asked her about it.

"Then forget it and get out."

"No way. My whole life has been leading up to this. I'm not leaving without getting in that office. Soon."

"Your whole life?"

She bit her lip. "In a manner of speaking."

Eighteen months ago, Russian Mafia head Vladislav Nevsky, also known as the *Pakhan*, had moved part of his New York–based organization to South Carolina, and the outfit had proceeded to grow like a cancer. The team had all agreed that taking out Nevsky was the only way to start the process of eradicating the worst of the disease. Allie had her own reasons for wanting the man stopped. Personal reasons.

They had met to brainstorm a way to infiltrate his home to find the evidence they needed to do that.

"He likes to eat," Allie had said, slapping the conference table covered in surveillance photos.

Linc blinked. "Huh?"

"Look at these pictures. What do you see?" She jabbed a finger at the nearest one. Then another and another. "Nevsky is eating in just about every picture. Well, guess what? I like to cook. Not only that, I'm good at it. Very good, thanks to a college roommate studying to be a professional chef. I'm going undercover as Nevsky's personal cook."

Supervisory Special Agent Henry Ogden and Linc had exchanged glances, shrugs, and finally nods. Only they hadn't known who else she'd seen in one of those pictures.

Gregori Radchenko—the man she wanted almost more than Nevsky.

So, here she was. Looking for a way to take down Nevsky and settle an old score with Radchenko.

Only time was running out and Radchenko was nowhere to

be found. It was better to get what she could on Nevsky and get out—and live to fight another day. "Right now, there are no guards in the hallways," Allie whispered, "and none in the kitchen."

The study, accessed from the hallway or from the master suite, had been her goal since entering the home. Unfortunately, finding a way in had proved impossible, since Nevsky had almost as many surveillance cameras inside his home as he did outside and no way to disable them without setting off alarms. The time had come to take her chances, then pray he didn't have any reason to look at the footage before she could slip out of the house once and for all.

While her mind grappled with when to act, she swung open the pantry door, then turned back to grab the flour, along with a bag of apples, cinnamon, and everything else she needed to make a mouthwatering apple pie. Nevsky's favorite dessert next to baklava.

"What are you making today?"

Allie swallowed a startled screech and popped out of the pantry to find Nevsky's seventeen-year-old daughter, Daria, perched on one of the stools at the kitchen island. "You scared ten years off of me," Allie said, pressing a hand to her beating heart.

"You're young, you can spare them."

"Ha. No one can spare ten years. Are you looking for another cooking lesson?"

"Nope."

Allie lifted a brow. "Okay." Usually Daria showed up about this time after school, and the two spent the afternoon preparing dinner. As long as her father wasn't home. If Nevsky was home, Daria sketched or painted. But today was supposed to be different. "What are you doing here? I thought you had that field trip to the museum downtown." She glanced behind her. "And where's Gerard?" Daria's bodyguard was usually ten paces behind her.

"He'll be along soon enough. I gave him the slip." She rolled her eyes. "And I did."

"Did what?"

"Have a field trip. I canceled it—or at least my participation in it."

"Because?"

"Because life is short and it's time to live, take the bull by the horns, and chart my own course," the girl said. "Or something along those lines."

"I'm sorry, what?" The teen was forever speaking in riddles—or saying one thing and meaning another. Usually, Allie could follow along, but today, she'd been caught off guard by Daria's change of plans.

Daria grinned, twin dimples peeking at Allie as she swept her long blonde hair up into a ponytail, then hopped down to turn on the sink. She stuck her hands under the water. "I'm going to do the whole thing by myself." She paused midlather to frown. "Unless you don't think I can?"

"I totally think you can. It's just . . ."

"What?"

"Well, it's my job. It's what your dad pays me for, remember?" Allie let out a little laugh. She grabbed a few ice cubes from the freezer, dropped them in the blender, and flipped it on. She leaned in close to Daria's ear. "You and I both know he wouldn't approve—and if he finds out, which he will if he looks at the security footage he has going 24/7—then he'd probably fire me."

"And I don't really care—about the approval and finding out part, not the firing part." Daria's eyes darkened for a fraction of a second. She lowered her voice, just enough that Allie could hear her above the blender. "He does plenty of things I don't approve of."

"Oh?" Allie said, keeping her own voice casual and soft while she pulled measuring spoons from the drawer to her right. "Like what?" she whispered. She cut the blender off and dumped the ice into a glass.

Daria shrugged. "Doesn't matter."

"Of course it matters."

She gave a small, curiously unreadable smile. "Let's just say"—
she motioned to the blender again and Allie refilled it with ice and
turned it on—"he's not as smart as he thinks he is."

"How so?"

Daria pursed her lips and her eyes flashed. "He thinks everyone
and everything can be bought," she said, her voice so low Allie
had to move even closer to hear her. "More than that, he thinks
I'm stupid and therefore I'm invisible to him. If I was a boy, I'd be
his favorite person. Like my brother."

Allie blinked. "You don't have a brother."

"Actually, I do. He's older and he doesn't live here. I never see
him. I think I've been in the same room with him maybe four
times that I can remember." She doodled on a napkin in front of
her. "Truthfully, I'm not even sure he knows I exist. Which is fine
since he's just as evil as my father."

A brother? There'd been nothing about Nevsky having a son
in their copious amounts of research.

"But I'm just a girl," Daria said. "A stupid, worthless, invisible
girl." On the napkin, a unicorn emerged beneath her skilled strokes.

"I hope you realize you're none of those."

"Hmm. I'm beginning to, thanks to you," she said, her voice soft.
She cleared her throat. "But I did something he'll notice. Something
he definitely won't approve of." A giggle slipped from her.

"Daria?" Allie wanted to shake her. "What'd you do?"

"It's funny how such a smart man can be so very foolish." At
Allie's blank stare, she sighed. "You know what they say about
the foolish man who builds his house upon the sand."

"No, what do they say?"

"'When the rains come down and the floodwaters rise, the house
built on the sand will meet its demise.'"

"You're talking in riddles again."

Her smile flipped. "It's the only way I can talk around here so
I don't get into trouble," she whispered.

13

Allie avoided glancing at the camera in the far corner of the room. "What are you really trying to tell me here?"

The teen laughed and waved a hand in dismissal. "Nothing. I want to make a pie. You've got the roast in the slow cooker. I can handle the other veggies just like you've taught me. I've got this, so you can take the afternoon off. And that's no riddle."

"But—" Allie turned the blender off. She'd already left it on long enough for Nevsky to be suspicious should he decide to watch or listen in on the footage. "Seriously, Daria—"

"No, no, no. No buts allowed. Literally. So remove yours from the premises and go read a book or something. But first, pass me the apron and then I don't want to see you until six."

Allie's adrenaline flowed a bit faster. "You're sure? I really don't want to get you in trouble," she said, handing over the apron after slipping the key from the pocket.

"One hundred percent." The girl's face softened. "You've taught me so much. I love to cook, and since Papa's not going to be here for dinner, this is the perfect time for me to put my new skills to the test." She bit her lip, then gave Allie a quick hug. Then looked at the blender. "Then maybe I can surprise him one day with something he loves, and he'll be glad I took the time to learn." She sighed. "Then again, probably not."

"Daria—"

The girl waved a hand. "Forget it. It's not important."

But it obviously was. "All right, then. Holler if you need me."

"Will do."

Allie slipped from the kitchen and hurried down the hallway toward the study, located past the circular stairwell and the massive living room. The house spanned twelve thousand square feet, and at first, it had taken her a good two days to find enough time to sneak away from her duties in the kitchen and learn her way around. The only thing she liked about the place was Daria's artwork subtly displayed in various rooms.

The teen was hands-down talented when it came to creating unique pieces using any medium she chose. Although she did seem to favor using everyday items from ChapStick tubes to measuring spoons in her creations.

After spending a little over four weeks undercover and sleeping in the guest room on the second floor across from Daria, Allie now knew the place as well as her own twelve-*hundred*-square-foot apartment.

"Allie? You there?" Linc's voice came through the earpiece.

"I'm here," she said softly. Low enough that any mics wouldn't pick up her words. "Did you get all of that?"

"Most of it. There were some spotty places because you were whispering, but I got the gist of it. I'd give my right arm to know what Daria doesn't approve of."

"Same here. I'd also like to know who this brother is that she's talking about."

"Ask her."

"I will when I get the chance."

"You've gained her trust."

"I know." A flash of guilt hit her. From the beginning, she'd played on Daria's desire for a mother figure and had Daria's adoration within days. At least she thought she did. Unless the girl was playing her as well as she played everyone else in her life.

Allie slid the key into the lock and gave a quick sigh of relief when it turned. She slipped inside the office and shut the door behind her. "I'm in."

Without wasting any time admiring the luxurious décor, since she knew the money used to outfit it had been gained via the deaths of good people, she strode to the desk, to find the laptop right where she'd last seen it. Next to it were two new EpiPens. The man was terrified of bees even though he had no allergy that they were aware of. "Is Annabelle ready to do her thing?"

"She is. And if she hears you calling her Annabelle, she'll probably shoot you."

Allie inserted the flash drive that would allow Annie, their IT genius at Quantico, to take over the laptop as long as she could crack the password. Once she was in, she'd copy as much of the hard drive as she could. Depending on how much was on the laptop, even with Annie's high-dollar technology, Allie wasn't sure she'd be able to get it all before she had to pull the device.

While the machine worked, Allie opened the top drawer and found a stack of file folders.

"Annie's in," Linc said. "That was almost too easy."

"He keeps this place locked up 24/7 and he's got guards all over the place outside. As far as he's concerned, no one's getting in."

"As long as you can get out."

Allie set the folders on the desk and opened the first one. It looked like legitimate business information, but she took pictures of it anyway and sent those while she went to the next folder. More pictures. Not what she was looking for, but one never knew what would come in handy.

"Hurry up, Allie, you're taking too long."

"I'm fine. According to Daria, Nevsky's not due back for a while." Finally, at the last folder, she opened it and gasped.

"What is it?" Linc asked. "Are you okay?"

"Yes, but you're not."

"What do you mean?"

"They're watching you." Quickly, she worked her phone's camera. "And sending pictures to Nevsky."

"Me? Why would they be watching me?"

"I don't know." She paused and bit her lip. "Unless my cover is blown and they're trying to figure out who I'm communicating with."

The next picture sent her reeling. "He's got a picture of us together. The date stamp is from a week ago. It's when we met with Henry at the hotel in Irmo."

"You need to get out of there."

Allie's stomach twisted. "He's got pictures of your family too," she whispered.

"What?"

"You and Brady and Chloe playing basketball in your parents' drive. The dates on the pictures are from last Sunday afternoon." Terrifying, but still not what she was searching for.

And another picture of her and Linc sitting on his parents' back porch swing. Stomach in knots, she shoved everything back where she found it and went to the next drawer. Locked.

"He probably thinks we're a couple, Linc. And he most likely knows who I am." Or at least that she was there under false pretenses. So why was she still alive? Something was off.

"Allie—"

She slid the specialized knife from her front pocket and opened the tool that would give her access to the lock. Within seconds, it popped and she pulled the drawer open. More files. She opened the one on top. "Oh my," she whispered.

"Allie." Henry's voice came through her earpiece this time. "Put everything back now and leave."

"He's got a whole list of military equipment for sale," Allie said. "Where would he be getting that stuff?" She snapped pictures, then shoved everything back where she found it. She stood there for a moment while she sent the pictures to Henry.

"Get. Out. Of. There. Now," Linc said. "Walk out of the house and head to the van."

"Working on it."

The door to the office opened.

Allie jerked her head up. "Uh-oh."

2

U h-oh?" Sitting in the command van a short distance from the estate, Linc felt his heart take a nosedive. "Allie, there's no 'uh-oh' in undercover work." He paused. "Allie?"

"Daria," Allie said.

"What's she doing?" Henry leaned in with a frown.

Linc shook his head.

"What are you doing?" the teen asked.

"I was just looking for—"

"Looking for what?"

"Good question, my daughter."

Linc froze at the second voice.

Henry snapped his head around to lock eyes with Linc. "That's Nevsky."

"I know."

"He's not supposed to be there."

"I know that too. He must have slipped in the back somehow."

"What, may I ask," came the deeply accented voice through their earpieces, "do you think you will find to cook in here?"

Henry went to work, ordering a team into place in case they had to go in and get Allie.

"Hello, sir," Allie said. "The door was open and I thought—"

18

"You thought?"

"Well, that I might find some cash in your desk."

Silence.

"You admit you were going to steal from me?"

Linc flinched at the outrage in the man's voice. If he hadn't been so worried about Nevsky's unpredictable nature, he would have rolled his eyes at the irony.

"Steal?" Allie squealed. "What? No way! No, no, no. I wanted to make a surprise dish for you tonight, but I used all the grocery money you gave me for this week because you have that big party coming up, so I thought I might find some in your desk. I was going to leave you a note. I'd never steal from you, I promise."

"I told her you kept some cash in your desk, Papa," Daria said.

"I see. How did you get in?"

"The door was cracked," she said. "Like it wasn't shut well when someone left. I was truly surprised to find it open because it never is, and well . . . I guess I just decided to check your desk as a spur-of-the-moment thing." A pause. "I'm sorry. I know how this looks. I'll . . . I'll go pack my things." The utter dejection in her voice shot Linc's admiration level rocketing upward.

"No!" Daria cried. "Papa, she wasn't going to steal. She wouldn't do that. She's only here because of me. Please, don't send her away."

Henry raised a brow at Linc. "Allie's talent is wasted with the FBI. She should be onstage somewhere."

Silence. Then, "Fine. You will stay," Nevsky said.

"His accent just got a lot stronger," Linc murmured. He also had his mic on mute. "What does that mean?"

"He's undecided," Henry said. "He's not quite sure what to do." He slammed a fist into his open palm. "This isn't the way this was supposed to go down."

"I know, Henry, I know. Just hold tight."

"I—I don't understand," Allie stammered. "You think I was going to steal from you, but you want me to stay?"

"I'm not sure, but Daria says you were not."

"Since when has he put any stock into what Daria thought?" Linc muttered.

A pause. "What were you going to cook for me?" Nevsky asked.

"Daria said you loved a well-done baklava," Allie said, "but that no one ever gets the crust flaky enough for you. I can do that and wanted to do so as a surprise, but I didn't have any money." She paused. "I'm terribly sorry." Linc heard the tears in her voice.

"Then do it," Nevsky said. "Order what you need and have it delivered. I'll have James pay for it."

"Of course."

Linc leaned back and rubbed a hand down his face. "No way he's letting her off. I'm not buying it."

"Me neither. We've got to get her out of there."

Allie followed Daria back into the kitchen, slipping the flash drive into her pocket. She'd barely had time to pull the device and slap the laptop shut before Nevsky appeared in the doorway. But Daria had seen her do it. The girl went to the counter, opened the slow cooker, and stirred.

"Thank you," Allie said softly, keeping her voice low enough so that it wouldn't trigger the voice-activated recorder on the cameras. "Why'd you lie for me?"

For a moment, she wondered if Daria would answer her. Finally, the teen turned and the look in her eyes chilled Allie. "Because," Daria said, her voice barely there as well, "if he believed you were stealing from him, he would have killed you right there."

All traces of the happy, childish teen were gone and goose bumps pebbled Allie's skin. "I wasn't stealing from him. Exactly." Unless one counted taking information as stealing.

"Then you were looking for something."

"I . . ." Allie paused. For some reason, her instincts were

telling her not to lie. And yet, that's what she should do. "I'll have to explain later." Nevsky knew who she was. It was time for her to find a way out.

With a frown, Daria checked the food in the oven and Allie pulled the kitchen laptop in front of her, praying Daria wouldn't push for more. She scrambled for something normal to say. "Can I ask you a question?"

"Sure."

"I couldn't help noticing. Why does your dad have so many EpiPens?" The teen laughed, a sincere chuckle that sent Allie's brows up to her hairline. "Why is that such a funny question?"

"I think bees are the only thing he's actually scared of. When he was ten, his older brother, my uncle who was fourteen at the time, thought he'd be smart and knock down a hornet's nest. He was stung several times and died."

"Oh, how awful!"

"Agreed. My mom told me the story before she died. But now my dad thinks every bee is out to get him and refuses to be without at least two EpiPens within reaching distance—just in case one doesn't work, you know. All of his bodyguards are required to carry them. There are two things my father is OCD about . . . his EpiPens and his privacy." She rolled her eyes as only a seventeen-year-old can do.

It made sense. Allie turned back to the laptop. Except . . . Nevsky hadn't had a password on the laptop in his office.

"What are you doing now?" Daria asked, her voice at normal volume.

"Ordering the supplies for the baklava."

Daria's jaw sagged. "You mean you're not leaving?"

"Not at the moment. Not until I make sure you're okay with everything that just went down." But Nevsky would know *she* knew that he knew. Maybe. Regardless, the clock was ticking and she had to leave.

The girl rushed over to hug her, and just like that the teenager was back. Daria glanced toward the hallway, then at the kitchen door that led to the ten-car garage. "Come with me," she whispered close to Allie's ear.

"Where?"

"To the pool house. I want to show you something—then you're going to have to leave."

Daria started to lead Allie from the kitchen when one of Nevsky's bodyguards stepped into the room. "No one leaves the house for now."

"Why?" Allie asked. Okay, definitely time to get out.

"The groceries will be here shortly, remember?"

"I think we'll hear the bell," Daria said. "It rings in the pool house too, *remember?*"

Her sarcasm didn't faze him. "Nevertheless, she doesn't leave the main house."

Daria crossed her arms and stuck out her chin. "It's just the pool house, James."

James Killian. Bodyguard to Nevsky and suspected assassin when Nevsky needed someone dead.

Like her?

"No. Your dad's orders. Sorry." He sounded anything but.

Daria placed her hands on her hips. "Where's Gerard?"

"On business for your father."

A chill swept over Allie. It had probably only been Daria's presence that kept Nevsky or Killian from shooting her on the spot. That, and it would have messed up his nice Oriental rug. He was biding his time. When she and Daria went their separate ways, things would get ugly.

"Fine." Daria rolled her eyes. "We'll go up to my room."

James's hooded eyes glittered ice.

Daria gripped Allie's fingers and pulled her from the kitchen. "Daria—"

Daria's grip tightened and she held a finger to her lips.

Allie went silent.

When Daria led her into the bedroom on the second floor, Allie shut the door behind her. Not a typical teen's room, her walls held maps and navigational paraphernalia she'd collected while traveling with her school or her mother before the woman had died. A picture of Daria with her crossbow standing over a deer sat on her dresser. The cabin in the background reminded Allie of the one she and her family had stayed at one summer.

Another frame held a photo of her and Gerard. And then the artwork. The girl was seriously talented. "Daria, what are you—" Allie tried again.

Daria shook her head and grabbed her laptop from the desk, then crooked her finger to Allie, motioning her to follow. She went to her window and shoved it open. She climbed out and Allie followed her onto the small balcony.

"Now we can talk," Daria said after shutting the window.

"What's going on?"

"I know things."

"Like what?"

"Like how to get around the cameras and listening devices all over this house. Along with the fact that my father is a murderer and someone needs to stop him. I think you're trying to do that."

Allie stilled. Could Nevsky have put his daughter up to this to smoke Allie out? But he hadn't been alone with her since the office incident. Still . . . "I don't think you should say those kinds of things about him."

"Why not? It's true. Aren't you an undercover fed?"

Allie gaped. Linc's strangled gasp echoed through her earpiece.

A huff of impatience escaped Daria. "You feds. You're smart, but you're not invisible." She nodded to Allie's ear. "Your friend—partner? He's listening in, watching your back, right?"

Another nod from Allie. She wouldn't admit anything out loud.

"And you're investigating my father, looking for something to use against him, right?"

"Uh . . . wow."

"I'm young, I'm not stupid."

"No, you're definitely not stupid."

"The blender in the kitchen convinced me. My father's a murderer and I can prove it."

"Daria . . ." Allie drew in a deep breath. It was time to take a chance and pray it didn't get her—and Daria—killed. "How?"

"I know the code to access the security footage. I have him on camera committing murder, and I've got still shots of every person who ever walked into this house. Easy for your facial recognition software. Everything around here is recorded. Audio, video. Everything."

"Including me in the office?" Allie asked even while she processed what Daria was telling her. This child could take down her father's entire organization and send him to death row. What the girl had *done*. If Nevsky found out . . .

"No. That and his bedroom are the only rooms he keeps 'bug free.'" Her fingers wiggled air quotes around the last two words.

Then Nevsky wouldn't know what she'd been doing in there. Or that she knew he was aware of the reason she was in his house. Unless Daria was wrong. "What about my bedroom and yours?" She'd swept hers when she first moved in and hadn't found anything.

"I don't know. I don't think so, but I didn't want to take a chance by talking inside."

But Allie using the key to enter the office would prove she'd lied about the door being open. Linc and Henry were right. She needed to get out of the house, and soon—and she needed to take Daria with her. "We need to get out of here."

"I can't leave. Not yet."

"Why not?"

"Because if I leave, he'll kill Gerard," Daria said. "He's been more of a father to me than Vladislav, that's for sure. And for all his loyalty to my father, I won't let that happen."

Allie groaned, conflicted about what to do next.

Daria opened the laptop and clicked her keyboard with all the confidence and skill of a professional.

"What are you doing?" Allie asked, still trying to formulate a plan that ended with her and Daria somewhere safe.

"I can erase the footage of you going into his office," the teen said. "He'll know you didn't find the door open. How'd you get the key?"

The girl continued to stun. Allie shot her hand out to stop her. "I finally managed to make a copy from your father's. Would have been easier if he'd just left it in the plant next to the door like I do," she muttered.

Daria raised a brow, her expression slightly bemused. "You're an agent with the FBI and you keep your spare key in a plant? You couldn't be more creative than that?"

"It worked for the moment." Allie hesitated. "If you ever need a safe place to go, remember this address." Breaking every rule in the book, Allie gave it to her—ignoring Linc's soft protest—and Daria repeated it back to her. "Good. Use the key and let yourself in."

"Okay. Thank you," Daria said.

"Now let's focus."

The girl frowned. "I still think I should take the footage off."

"No. I can guarantee you that your father's going to go back and look at that footage, and if it doesn't show me entering, he'll realize something's off—and he may suspect you."

"But he'll see."

"It doesn't matter. He knows who I am anyway," she said. "It's the only way to keep you safe. Please. Don't touch it."

Daria dropped her hands from the keyboard. "I've had the evidence for a while. I've just been waiting for the right person to give that copy to, the right person to trust." The old eyes in her young face met Allie's. "I think that person is you."

"Who did you see him kill?" Allie asked.

Tears sprang into Daria's eyes, but her expression never wavered from cool indifference. "A guy I liked. We ditched the bodyguards and went dancing. My father didn't appreciate it."

"What was his name?"

"It doesn't matter."

Sick certainty curled in the pit of Allie's stomach. "He made you watch, didn't he?"

Daria didn't answer. She didn't have to. "From that point on, I decided to do everything I could to make sure he landed in prison."

Allie's heart broke for the girl.

"Allie?"

Linc's voice in her ear startled her. "Yes?"

"Things are mobilizing at the house. Activity outside is picking up. Get out now."

Allie caught Daria's confused look and pointed to her ear, silently confirming Daria's earlier guess that she was a fed.

"Allie, you need to run!" she said, her eyes on the window.

"Allie!" Linc's voice had a stronger edge. "Get out of the house or I'm going to have to come in."

"They're in the bedroom," Daria hissed.

Allie looked over the side of the balcony. It was a long way down. Three long stories down. The landing would most likely include some broken bones—or death. But it would be better—and quicker—than being killed by Nevsky's hand.

Daria's hand gripped hers and tugged. "Go up."

"What?"

"On the roof. Use the chair and pull yourself up. You can go to the other side and drop down to each roof covering the balconies and then land in the grass by the pool. That's when the cameras will pick you back up. The gate code is 4786 to get out. It's the same for both gates."

"Done that before, have you?"

Red tinted the girl's pale cheeks, but she gave Allie a light shove. "Hurry. When they finish checking the bathroom, they're going to look out here." She settled herself back against the wall, slid the laptop to the side, and picked up a book.

Still, Allie hesitated. "I can't leave you."

"I'm out here all the time in all kinds of weather. It's my favorite spot and they won't think anything about it. But if you're with me, they'll tell him. Go! Please!" She flicked an anxious glance at the window. "It's James and Gerard. Gerard will protect me."

"The evidence?"

"I'll get it to you later. Go!" The hysteria in Daria's voice propelled Allie to the chair and up onto the roof.

She knelt, ignoring the adrenaline rushing through her, and listened. There was no way she was going to leave if Daria was in danger.

"Daria?" A harsh voice reached her. Gerard.

"Yes?"

"Where is she?"

"I don't know." A rustling reached her. Daria standing? "I was just getting ready to go check on the food. It should be done by now."

"She came up here with you," Gerard said.

"Yeah, then went to her room. Did you check there?"

A long-suffering sigh came from the man. "Get in here, kid. Let's not tell your dad about this, okay?"

"Fine by me."

"And no giving me the slip this time, Daria, understand?" His low voice held a lethal warning.

Gerard had taught Daria everything she knew about escaping

from her watchdogs, and she had a feeling he'd done it for a reason—only now it could backfire on him.

"Sure, Gerard. I won't give you the slip today. I promise."

The window shut and Allie let out a slow breath, thankful it had been Gerard with James and not one of the other bodyguards. One thing greatly concerned her, though. If Gerard watched the security footage and realized Allie had *not* gone to her room, he'd know Daria was lying. She eased across the rooftop, anxious not to make any noise that would attract attention. "Linc? You there?"

"I'm here. I've got you spotted on the roof. Be careful."

She only had a few minutes, possibly less, before they realized she wasn't in her room. "I'll be coming down by the pool. Can you have the gate open so I can dart out?" He'd have heard the code.

"I'm on it."

Over the COMMS, she heard the van door slide open, then close. Allie continued to the top of the roof, grateful she had no fear of heights—and that the slope, while steep, wasn't impossible to climb. However, as she started down the other side, her foot slipped and a shingle broke away and hit the ground with a thud. She caught her balance and kept going.

If they heard it, they'd come investigate, which meant time was short. Shorter. At the edge of the lowest part of the roof, she held on to the gutter and swung her legs over to settle her feet onto the shingles that covered the balcony roof below. And on she went until she dropped and rolled to the grassy area.

When she stood and turned, a man she'd never seen before stepped out from behind one of the thick columns. "Nevsky would like to see you in his office."

The weapon he held on her dared her to argue with him.

A flash of movement came from behind him and a golf club connected with the back of his head. Allie caught a brief glimpse of Daria before she disappeared back inside the media room. No doubt she'd slipped away from Gerard once more.

The man staggered. Allie charged, slamming a shoulder into his chest, and his weapon fell to the smooth stone surface surrounding the pool.

"Allie!"

Linc. Near the pool gate.

Allie heaved herself up and away from the groaning man.

"Hurry!" Linc said. "More are heading this way!"

A burst of speed propelled her toward him. She slipped out of the gate and he let the heavy metal slam behind them. He grasped her hand and they raced across the field of green grass.

A gunshot cracked the air, then another. They ducked instinctively but didn't slow.

"You're dead!" Nevsky's voice rang across the property. "I'll find you and end you and everybody you love!"

Allie turned to see the man in the upstairs window of the bedroom she'd used, one hand gripping the sill, the other taking aim once more with his pistol. Her eyes locked on his for a nanosecond before Linc yanked her through the final gate and into the waiting van.

3

ONE WEEK LATER
ON THE COOPER RIVER NEAR THE JOINT BASE CHARLESTON
CHARLESTON, SOUTH CAROLINA

Seated under the shade of the oversized umbrella on the deck of the forty-five-foot catamaran, Allie lowered the binoculars and frowned. "I've got nothing but regular comings and goings from the base."

After finding the pictures in Nevsky's desk, Henry had worked quickly, putting together a raid to go down the next time Nevsky appeared on the base. Today was reported to be that day. How the man had clearance to enter was beyond her. Had to be some kind of forged or faked identification card. But agents were on base as well, ready to snatch him the moment he arrived. Henry had insisted they take the water surveillance. They'd move in and dock as soon as they got the signal.

Linc, lounging in the antigravity chair next to her, ran a hand through his wind-tossed dark hair, then ran his fingers over the five o'clock shadow that Allie begged him on a regular basis not to shave. She liked it. His blue eyes focused on her. She liked his eyes too. In fact, there weren't too many things about Linc St. John she didn't like.

He turned to Henry. "You're sure this is good intel?"

"I'm sure." Henry grinned. "Come on, you have to admit, this isn't the worst assignment you've ever had. Eighty-two degrees on a first-class boat floating on the river?"

"True," Allie said. "But I've got to say I've had enough of the sun for now. I'll just stay here under this nice bit of shade."

"Have you ever heard of the pea aphid?" Henry asked.

"Uh-oh," Linc said, "here it comes."

"Humor him," Allie drawled. "No, Henry, I haven't." Henry did like his insects. A former forensic entomologist, he took great pleasure in educating those who didn't know—or care—nearly as much as he did about the subject.

"A pea aphid is interesting for all kinds of reasons." Henry pulled his keys from his pocket and spun them on his forefinger, a habit that seemed to help him think. "But most recently it's been discovered that it's possible they grow their own carotenoids. No other creature can do that. They have to get them from their diet."

"That's just fascinating," Allie said.

Linc smirked. "You have no clue what that means."

"And you do?"

"Nope."

Henry laughed. "It basically means they're the only creature that's able to harvest energy from the sun. So, all that to say, be like a pea aphid and soak it in while you can. You may need the energy later." He drew in a deep breath. "Smell that fresh air? Feel the sun? It beats climbing out of windows and racing from the home of a killer, I would think. Are you really going to complain?"

Allie smiled. "I've definitely been on worse assignments." It had been a week since her adventure in escaping from Nevsky's home, but her adrenaline still hadn't calmed down. Her smile faded. "But where'd this intel come from, Henry? We moved to get out here so fast, you didn't have time to explain how you arranged everything with the Charleston office."

"Boyd Jackson, the SSA here, is a good friend. I told him we'd been chasing this guy for months, that you'd been on the inside and had managed to get information about the stolen military equipment. Then he received intel that Nevsky was coming today. He was stretched a bit thin with some extensive training exercise and an ongoing wiretap, so when I offered to do this, he took me up on it. Backup is waiting in the wings as soon as I give the order." He paused. "He knows how bad I want to be in on taking Nevsky down."

That made sense. "How's Daria?" she asked.

"She's fine—just like she was the last time you asked. We've got eyes on her."

Allie had insisted that the girl needed protection—or at least someone watching her. Henry had agreed. For now.

"Mark got a glimpse of her at school," Henry said, "but Nevsky is definitely keeping close tabs on her."

"As long as she's safe," Allie said. "And that means we need to make sure Nevsky doesn't know what a threat she is to him." She'd been trying to find a way to get back in touch with the girl that wouldn't endanger her. She could text her, of course, but was afraid Nevsky might be monitoring Daria's phone activity.

The fact that Daria hadn't texted Allie had her nerves in a twist. She should have heard from her by now. So why hadn't she? Because Daria *couldn't* text or call? Or because she was just afraid to?

Nevsky's last threat still echoed in her head. *"You're dead! I'll find you and end you and everybody you love!"*

Fortunately—in this case—the people she loved were few and far between. She didn't let many people get too close. Her eyes slid to Linc. Except her partner. He'd snuck under her emotional walls with very little effort. And Nevsky knew that. But how? How had he even connected the two of them? They'd been so careful.

Obviously not careful enough.

A low hum above the catamaran snapped her attention skyward. She frowned. "What's that?" She walked to the side of the vessel, tracking the object with her eyes. Because of the Air Force base, it wasn't unusual to have airplanes occupying the airspace over the ocean, but that was too small—a mere dot that was growing bigger and coming closer.

Linc joined her and raised his binoculars to the sky. "A drone."

Henry snagged his phone. "Keep an eye on it."

While Henry barked questions at the person on the other end of the line, uneasiness crept up Allie's spine and she slowly followed the rail around the side to keep the drone in sight.

"Get it out of the sky," Henry said. "This is restricted airspace. Allie, come here a sec. Linc, see if you can get any identifying marks off it."

Linc continued to monitor the drone while Allie slipped up next to Henry.

"What is it?" she asked.

He lowered the phone, then handed her his binoculars. "Who do you see sitting in the Hummer next to the dock? Tell me that isn't Nevsky."

Allie spotted a man who looked similar to the Russian Mafia boss, but she didn't think it was actually him. "No, I don't—"

"Get down!"

Linc's cry from the other end of the vessel jerked Allie around. The drone was coming in fast, aiming right for them. "Linc, jump!"

A hard hand clamped on to her arm and pulled her over the side and into the water.

When she hit, the breath whooshed from her lungs. She threw her arms out, scrambling to stop the descent. She slowed, got her bearings, and kicked toward the surface, desperate for air and the need to know what was going on—and that Linc was safe.

A loud boom sent a shock wave through the water, rolling her over twice. Stars danced in front of her eyes while her body begged for air. She kicked, aiming for the surface.

When Allie broke through, she filled her starving lungs, treading water and waiting for the blackness that had been so close to sucking her under to fade. When her eyes focused, they settled on the catamaran, now burning with great orange and blue flames. "Linc! Henry!"

"Allie! I'm here," Henry called. He grasped a life jacket in one hand and swam toward her.

Sirens sounded from the base. They were mobilizing rescue boats. She turned in the water, debris knocking against her. She took a hard hit to the back of her head, bringing back the stars. Allie swept a hand up to feel the wound. A knot had already started to form, but the stars were fading.

"Henry, I don't see Linc!" She swam toward the burning vessel, ignoring Henry calling her name. She aimed herself toward the stern, where Linc had been watching the drone. "Linc, where are you?"

Allie pushed aside a piece of plastic and tried to go forward. Then stopped. Smoke surrounded her, burning her eyes, filling her lungs.

Henry reached her. "Put this on." He shoved the life jacket at her.

She slid the head opening around her neck and had to back away from the burning boat. Something jabbed her shoulder and she spun to find Henry shoving away debris. He caught her arm. "You're hurt!"

"I'm okay." Tears clogged her throat. "Linc," she whispered. Dizziness hit her and she blinked as her vision wobbled.

Rescue boats arrived and Henry waved one over. "Get in the boat, Allie."

"No, we have to find Linc." The rescuers blurred. Her muscles refused to cooperate and her head throbbed.

Henry slid an arm around her and towed her to the nearest

rescue boat. Within seconds, she was on the hull, fighting to stay conscious. "Linc . . ."

"Heart rate is dropping," someone said, the urgency in the voice making Allie frown. Who was he talking about? "Pulse is slow and thready! Let's go!"

And then Allie let the blackness swallow her.

4

Thirsty. Had he ever been so thirsty in his life? Linc pried his eyelids open and instantly regretted it. Squinting, he registered the monitors next to his head with their incessant beeping.

Probably what had pulled him from his deep sleep.

Sleep? What . . .

Last thing he remembered was being on the boat.

The explosion.

That explained the hospital, but . . .

Allie! Henry!

Heart pounding, he pushed himself into a sitting position. The sheets puddled at his waist and he shivered at the chill in the room. But that was the least of his worries. He lifted a hand to the bandage over his left ear. A head wound. That explained the pain jackhammering at his skull.

The door opened. "Linc!"

His sister Ruthie rushed at him. Dressed in operating scrubs from head to toe, she looked like she'd just come from surgery.

"Hey."

"What are you doing?" The question came from his left. His mother rose from the chair next to him and placed a hand on his bare shoulder. "Lie back down."

"Can't." He cleared his throat. "Water. Please."

Ruthie shoved a straw between his lips and he drank until she pulled it away. "Not too much."

"There was an explosion. Where's Allie? And Henry?" The two women exchanged a look.

The door opened again and his father entered, followed by his other two sisters, Izzy and Chloe. He caught a glimpse of Derek and Brady, his brothers, hovering behind them.

"The room's too small for all of you," Linc said. "I'm fine. You can all go away for now. After you tell me where Allie and Henry are." He sounded grumpy and rude even to himself, but fear had taken hold of him. That look between his mother and sister when he'd asked about Henry and Allie . . .

"Fine?" Ruthie asked. "I hardly think so."

"Where's Allie?" he asked softly.

Ruthie looked away.

"She didn't make it, Linc," Izzy said, stepping forward, tears in her eyes.

Paralyzed by the words, Linc could only stare while he tried to get his brain to process. "Yes, she did." *She had to.*

Chloe bit her lip. His mother squeezed his shoulder. His dad cleared his throat. They'd known her about as long as he had and they'd fallen in love with her just as fast. His partner. His best friend. His future—

"No, she didn't," his mom said. "I'm so sorry, honey." A tear slid down her cheek. "Henry said she died on the way to the hospital."

"Henry? Henry survived?"

"Yes." She nodded.

"But Allie—?"

"No. They life-flighted you both to the Medical University in Charleston. You know they've got some of the best doctors in the state. The country even. But Henry said the wound to her head was just too great. It caused her brain to swell—" She broke off and Linc closed his eyes. "When you were stable, we had you transported here to Columbia so we could be with you."

"How long have I been out?"

"Since yesterday."

"I want to see her."

"You . . . can't," Izzy said. "Henry said she had express wishes that she be cremated. She didn't want a funeral."

His mind rewound to one night after a touchy raid.

"No funeral," Allie had told him.

"What?" He'd looked up from his steak to find her staring at a landscape of the Australian Outback on the wall of the steakhouse.

"I don't want a funeral. Just cremate me and scatter my ashes over the ocean."

"Why are we talking about this?"

She shrugged. "You're the only person who'd come to my funeral anyway. Well, I suppose your family would, but yeah, that's what I want."

"Allie—"

She held up a hand. "Promise me. No funeral if I die first."

"Fine. No funeral. Now, pass me the salt." She did so. He looked up to catch her eye. "I'm going to need dessert after that depressing topic."

Allie threw her head back and laughed and ordered them the largest molten chocolate cake he'd ever seen. They ate every bite and stumbled from the restaurant in agony. "Never again," he grunted as they lounged on his sofa in front of one of the classic movies they shared a love for.

She agreed with a groan. "We made a very bad choice."

"But it was worth it," he'd said and grinned at her before grimacing and downing another antacid.

"Linc?"

He blinked and realized his mother had said his name several times.

Linc rubbed his eyes. "I need some time alone. Please." He didn't recognize the rough hoarseness in his voice.

"Honey—"

"Alone, Mom. Please."

His mother looked up to meet his father's gaze. His dad nodded.

"I went looking for Allie's family," his mother said.

He froze. "She doesn't have any. You know that."

"Well, I thought there must be *someone*."

As the chief of police, she'd have the resources to find someone if they existed. "And?"

"No one. And no record of Allison Radcliffe before her sophomore year of high school."

"What? That can't be. I know her. I know everything about her and . . ." No, apparently he didn't, because his mother had never lied to him, so if what she said was true . . . He pressed fingers to his eyes and tried to think past the throbbing in his skull—and realized that every time he'd brought up Allie's past, she'd skillfully avoided talking about it—or told him just enough to satisfy him. "I need some time."

"Don't cut yourself off from us like you did before," his mother pleaded. "You need us."

Before. When he'd been betrayed by the woman he'd loved—and thought loved him. But she'd just been playing him, pretending to fall for him so she could gather information to use to further her own criminal career.

Cops weren't the only ones who could go undercover.

The only thing that had made being played for a fool bearable was the fact that he'd been the one to set up the sting that had finally taken Regina and her gang down. She now sat in prison for the next twenty years, and Linc felt like he'd somehow managed to redeem himself.

And then he'd been partnered with Allie last year—and started to fall for her. Only now he'd never get the chance to tell her.

No, not Allie. *Please, God, not Allie.*

He wanted to rail, to shake his fist at God, but numbness had set in and all he could do was stare at the wall.

"Linc?" his mother said.

He let his gaze meet his mother's pained and fearful one—and his heart softened. "I'll call you," he said. "I promise. Just let me deal with this the way I deal." Alone. "Please."

"Sure. Okay, then." She leaned over to kiss his forehead like she used to do when she tucked him into bed at night. The action brought a lump to his throat.

The rest of his family filed out one by one. Each stopped to hug him or offer a sympathetic "I'm sorry." They'd liked Allie too.

Linc let them go without comment and soon found himself in the empty room. Alone. With the lump in his throat growing to unmanageable proportions.

The sob ripped from him and he closed his eyes as his brain processed what his heart wanted to deny.

Allie was gone.

Allie groaned at the sound of . . . what? She cracked her eyes open, then frowned as she let her gaze scan her surroundings. A hospital? Oh, right. She'd awakened once before and thought she'd been dreaming.

Shadows, created by the lights on the monitors, danced on the wall, causing a creepy sensation to shiver up her spine. Silly. Gently, she turned her head to one side, expecting to feel a rush of pain. Surprised at the lack of discomfort, she turned her head to the other side. Henry sat in the chair next to her, eyes closed, face drawn, looking like he hadn't slept in a while. He was spinning his keys. Spin, *clink*. Spin, *clink*.

She lifted a hand to her head and felt the bandage just below her shoulder blade pull. The IV in her arm itched, a minor annoyance she ignored as she processed where she was.

"Allie?"

"Henry. What happened?"

At her voice, he sat forward and tossed the keys onto the table beside him. "Someone blew up the boat. Don't you remember?"

"The drone."

"Yeah."

"Linc!" She sat up. This time lightning bolts of agony shafted through her head. She lay back, pressed her palms to her eyes, and fought the wave of nausea. Finally, she looked up.

Henry's face made her forget the pain and everything else.

"What is it?"

"You can't talk to him just yet, Allie. We need to think this through."

"But he's alive?"

"Yes."

"Then I need to talk to him." She ran her tongue over her dry lips. "Please. Bring me a phone."

"You can't."

"Why not?" Another wave of nausea swept through her and she drew in a sharp breath. "He's dead and you're not telling me. Is that it?"

"No, Allie—"

"I don't believe you." Tears ran down her temples. The pain in her head was no match to the torment shredding her heart. "No," she whispered. "No."

"Give her something to sleep," Henry said to an unidentified person. "She needs to heal more before dealing with this."

A woman stepped from the corner of the shadowy room and inserted a needle into the IV port. A rush of coolness hit her vein. Sleep approached. But she needed to stay awake. "Linc," she whispered just before the darkness closed in.

Allie wasn't sure how much time passed before awareness returned but was grateful the pounding in her head had eased. However, her mind went immediately to Henry's words.

Linc! Grief clawed at her and she moaned. A hand clasped hers. She gasped and opened her eyes. "Henry."

He held a straw to her lips and she drank. When she finished, he set the cup within reaching distance and sat in the chair next to the bed. "How are you feeling?"

"Okay. I think. But Linc . . . ?"

"He's alive. I promise."

"How did he survive?" she asked.

"I don't know. It's a crazy miracle. The drone hit the stern where he was. We were on the opposite end. *You—we—*almost didn't survive, but all three of us did."

The fact that she was alive should thrill her, but all she could think about was that she wanted to see Linc and then possibly return to the dark, pain-free abyss of unconsciousness. No, she needed to stay awake. "How long have I been asleep?"

"Four days."

"Four days!"

"We had to keep you sedated. PT has been in to work with you, and you got excellent nutrition through the feeding tube."

She touched her nose. "What?"

"Dr. Forsythe took it out when he decided it was time for you to wake up."

It was all too much to process. She needed Linc.

Allie reached for the phone that all hospital rooms had and found the table empty. "Where's the phone? I need to call him. I need to—"

A knock on the door interrupted her. She swallowed the sobs that threatened to erupt and pressed a hand to her lips. "Come in," she finally said.

The man who stepped into the room took everything in with a single, sweeping glance of his dark eyes. "Glad to see you're awake and coherent."

"Who are you?" she asked.

"This is Dr. Nathan Forsythe," Henry said. "He's the doctor who's been tending to you for the past four days."

"How's the head this morning?" Dr. Forsythe asked. In his mid-forties, he was tall with a smooth olive complexion.

"Fine." She needed to get out of there so she could find Linc and make sure Henry wasn't lying to her.

A smile tilted one side of his lips and a dimple flashed briefly. "Why do I think that's not a completely accurate description?"

She grimaced. "Because you're probably pretty good at what you do." A sigh slipped from her. "It hurts, but not terribly."

"Fortunately, the hit on your head wasn't that bad. Not even a concussion. You've got four stitches in your back, thanks to a piece of the debris, but that shouldn't give you too much trouble other than some itching while it heals."

"Okay, when can I get out of here?" The doctor and Henry exchanged a glance. "What?" she asked.

"Well," Dr. Forsythe said. "You really need at least a few more days."

"No way. I need to get out of here and find Nevsky."

"Listen to him, Allie," Henry said. "If you go after Nevsky half healed, you might not live to finish the job. You're still weak." He rubbed a hand down his face. "Besides, Nevsky's not going anywhere. He'll be there when you're ready."

She sighed, loath to admit he was right. She *was* weak. And so very tired. "Where's my phone?"

"It was lost in the explosion."

"I need you to get me a new one then and I need to talk to Linc." She nodded to the hospital end table. "Why isn't there a phone in here?"

"We took it out," the doctor said, "to keep you from being disturbed."

She gave a light snort. "There's no one to disturb me." At least no family to care if she was alive. A few fellow agents would want to know how she was doing, but Henry had no doubt informed them.

Weariness tugged at her. Her back ached and she vaguely remembered getting hit with a piece of the boat. Stitches, the doc had said. Wonderful. Her eyes drooped. "Henry?"

"Yeah?"

"How'd he know we were there? The guy with the drone. How'd he know?" Allie forced her lids up.

Henry rubbed his chin. "I don't know. I've wondered that myself."

Of course he had. "You promise he's okay?"

"I promise."

"I don't believe you. Why won't you let me talk to him?"

"Later, when you're better, we have a lot to discuss. And it involves protecting Linc."

"Protecting him?" Her words slurred and her lids drooped. "He's dead. I know you're lying to me."

The last word came out on a squeak and Henry moved to sit on the bed next to her. "Allie . . ."

But the sobs took over and he held her, promising her that Linc was alive. However, she'd traveled this road before and they wouldn't trick her again. Doctors, even her mother, had told her that everyone was alive, and once she'd healed, they'd finally told her the truth. Her father and her sister. Dead. They were dead.

Just like Linc was now.

Sleep crept in as the sobs faded and she fought it. She needed to stay awake and go after the man who'd killed yet one more person she loved.

5

Linc sat on the boat and stared at the water where he'd last seen Allie. His brother Brady had gone down fifteen minutes ago. "Anything?" He wore the earpiece that would allow him to communicate with Brady while he searched.

"No, sorry, man. You know I'll tell you if I find anything."

He was five days post-release from the hospital. It hadn't taken too much pleading to convince Brady to journey back to Charleston and go to the bottom of the river to search for anything that might lead him to the people who'd bombed the boat and killed Allie.

Thirty minutes later, Brady surfaced. Linc helped him into the boat and Brady pulled the mask off. "That's it, Linc. I'm sorry. All the evidence has already been collected. There's nothing down there and I need to get back to work."

Guilt swamped Linc for dragging Brady out there, but . . . "You weren't on the team. They might have missed something."

"I really don't think they did. We've gone in a full circle. Everything's gone. All traces of the boat have been swept up and are most likely being processed."

"And yet, so far no one's figured out where the drone came from, who built it, or who was flying it."

"No. At least not yet. The good thing is, I think they got every last piece of it that was around to get."

"It's connected to Nevsky. Somehow he knew about the surveillance."

"Maybe so," Brady said, "but you're not going to find the evidence down there—and neither am I."

A heavy sigh escaped Linc. "Fine." He paused, thinking, while Brady stripped out of the wet suit and pulled on his street clothes. "I know who has some evidence," Linc said, "I just don't know how to go about getting it."

"Who?"

"Daria Nevsky."

"The daughter?"

"Yeah."

Brady frowned. "Then bring her in and talk to her."

"It's not that easy. We don't know where she is."

"Thought you had eyes on her."

"We did."

"Did?"

Linc groaned. "They lost her."

"How?"

"No idea." He shook his head. "One minute she was there, the next she was gone."

"He knew you were watching her," Brady said.

"Apparently. And staged a way to make her disappear. She hasn't been in school since the attack on the boat."

"You think she's still alive?"

"I don't know, but I think I owe it to her to find out." He paused. "Allie had formed a special bond with the girl. She'd want me to look out for her." Grief pierced him as it did every time he mentioned Allie's name or thought about her. Which was almost every minute of every day.

"How are you going to do that?" Brady asked as he raked his

fingers through his hair several times, trying to tame it into some semblance of order.

Linc allowed the familiar action to distract him from the grief and refocus. "I've been searching for everything I can find on Nevsky and I keep coming back to something," he said.

"What? You found something some of the best in the business—including Annie—couldn't find?"

"Maybe, but only because I had some insider information no one else was privy to."

"Like what?"

"Something Daria said when I was listening in on her and Allie the day her cover was blown. At least I tried to listen in. Allie had the blender going while she was talking to Daria, but she also had her head close to the girl's lips, so I was able to pick up most of the conversation."

"What'd she say?" Brady settled into the seat next to the captain's and pulled on his shoes.

"Something about a foolish man building his house on the sand and when the floodwaters rise, the house would crash down."

"Sounds like a song we sang in Vacation Bible School," his brother said.

"And I think that's why Daria used it. I think she was trying to send a message. She said that she could only talk in riddles around her house in order to stay out of trouble. I'm sure it's because Nevsky was listening in on everything."

"So, what was the message in that cryptic piece of dialogue?"

"I did a little research this morning while I was waiting on you to come pick me up. Nevsky has an office building. Kind of like a small warehouse with space for offices. He's got it under a shell corporation name, but it's definitely his. I located it with Annie's help. It's a new build and was just finished last week."

"Okay. How does that help?"

"The construction company's name is Sands and Sons Construction."

Brady stilled. "Sounds like a bit of a long shot, but I'm listening."

"What if Daria was telling Allie she needed to look into it?"

"Guess it won't hurt to check it out."

"You and me and a couple of others for backup just in case. I don't want to spook the guy." Linc rubbed a hand across his eyes, thinking. "I can't believe that, as involved as he is in everything that goes on in the operation, we can't get him on something. I want this guy to go away for life. I want his organization wiped off the face of the earth. And I want him alive." He blew out a low breath. "Death's too good for him. He needs to live every day locked up with nothing but his memories of what it was like to be free."

"Then let's head back to the office and figure out a way to make that happen."

Two days later, Henry still hadn't brought her a phone and she was getting mighty irritated—and Henry had to know that. Which was probably why he'd escaped her room for a while. He'd been there every time she woke up and every time she closed her eyes. He'd convinced her that she needed to stay in the bed to recuperate while cooperating with the physical therapist who'd come in the room to work with her.

Frankly, Henry had been like a mother hen, and Allie had to admit, she'd vaguely enjoyed the attention and having someone else take care of her. However, that had worn off quickly and now she was smothering, anxious to get back to work and, this time, put together a fail-proof plan that would enable her to find and arrest Nevsky—and anyone who worked for him.

They'd started her on a pill regimen. She had probably needed the stronger drugs but hated them because they made her feel so woozy and light-headed. Yesterday after Henry had left, she pulled out the IV to make them transition her to pills. The way Henry had been fussing over her, if he thought she wasn't getting pain meds, he'd harangue her to death. This way, she could prove she was fit to be released. Today.

Allie slipped out of the bed, wincing at the tug on her back where the stitches were still healing and the general aches and pains that came with almost getting blown up. She'd yet to leave the room per the doctor's and Henry's orders, but she was done with lying in a hospital bed.

Her floor exercises and trips to the bathroom weren't enough, and now, with the drugs out of her system, she didn't get weak-kneed and nauseated when she got out of bed. She needed to move.

And to grieve without an audience, because Henry had not been able to convince her that Linc was still alive.

That meant quitting her job and getting away from Henry. Because how would she be able to continue working with a man who lied to her?

If Linc was still alive, he would have called or come to see her by now. So the only conclusion she could draw from his absence was that he was dead and Henry had lied.

So she was done.

In the closet, she found several outfits in her size hanging neatly. Enough for at least a week. Upon closer inspection, she found a bag containing toiletries and everything she might need for an extended stay away from home.

"What in the world, Henry?" she whispered. She dressed as quickly as her wounds would let her, then opened the door and stepped into the hallway.

And gaped.

Luxury greeted her, from the dark hardwoods covered in Oriental rugs to the greenery-filled atrium to her left. Allie wasn't in the likes of any hospital she'd ever seen before.

Twenty feet in front of her, a woman dressed in green scrubs looked up. "Hello. Well now, you're looking great. It's good to see you up and dressed. I wasn't sure I'd get to see you up and around before you were released. Did you need something?"

"Yes. Who are you and can you tell me where I am? Because I don't think I'm in Kansas anymore."

The pretty woman grinned. "I'm Catherine Hayworth. This is a rehab facility, but your friend Henry and Dr. Forsythe go way back. You're not the first agent Henry's brought here to recuperate because of a threat to her life."

Allie's racing heart slowed a bit. "Okay. That answers a couple of questions. Am I still in Charleston?"

"No, Hilton Head Island."

"I see." She drew in a steadying breath. "And where's Henry?"

"He stepped down the hall to the restrooms, then was heading down to the cafeteria to grab some lunch, I believe. Would you like anything to drink? A snack?" She walked to the cabinet behind her and opened it to expose an array of healthy foods and drinks.

"Not right now, thanks. I need a cell phone. Is there a gift store or anything where I can purchase one?"

Catherine bit her lip. "I'm afraid not. Some clients do bring their phones and laptops, but we don't provide them."

"All right, how about a business center? I need to check my messages."

The woman sighed and a flush crept into her cheeks. "Again, no, I'm sorry. I know you're not our usual clientele, so I'd be happy to see if I can round up a spare laptop somewhere so you can get online."

"That would be lovely, thank you. I'll just wait here."

Less than a minute later, the kind nurse returned with the promised laptop in her hands. "Here you are. Do you need me to call IT to help you with anything?"

"No, I can handle it from here, thanks."

While the woman reached for the ringing phone, Allie took the laptop to the small seating area at the end of the hall and settled herself onto the leather sofa.

The wall-sized window in front of her offered her a soothing view of the Atlantic Ocean. She closed her eyes, picturing Linc on the catamaran, his smile flashing in her direction when she'd come from below in her modest one-piece swimsuit. His grin held a teasing appreciation, reflecting his attraction, yet never once did he display anything that she would consider to be disrespectful toward her.

She could honestly say her intense like for the man might have slipped over the edge into love at that moment.

And then he'd been snatched from her less than two hours later.

A sob built and, with effort, she choked it back. She opened the laptop and easily connected to the Wi-Fi. She wasn't a technical genius, but she knew enough to get what she needed.

Access to her emails and text messages.

She swiped an escaped tear and began to type. First her texts. It didn't take long to follow the steps to retrieve her texts and find she had one. From an unknown number.

> **Unknown**
> He knows and he's going to kill me. Maybe not
> today, but soon. Pls find me! At his new office
> bldg on Montro—

The text had been cut off as though there'd been no more time to type, and Allie's blood chilled. It had to be Daria. Who else?

She lurched to her feet, ignoring the shooting pain in various parts of her body.

"Allie?"

She spun to find Henry striding toward her, a frantic look on his face. "What is it?" she asked. "What's wrong?"

"What are you doing?"

"Checking my text messages, why?"

"Are you sure you should be doing that?"

She frowned. "Yes. We have to go. Daria's in danger and I have to get to her. Then find out how to get Nevsky and make him pay for killing Linc."

Henry gripped her arms. "Allie, I told you. He's alive."

She searched his eyes, pushing memories of that other time to the side. Could he really have been telling her the truth?

With her emotions in such turmoil, it was hard to pull her next move to the surface. Finally, she sucked in a steadying breath. "Then why hasn't he called or texted? Or emailed? Why isn't he here? He wasn't just a passing acquaintance, Henry. If he's alive, then where is he?"

"Still on medical leave from the Bureau, but he's doing fine from what I understand. I've been out of the office and here with you since you were brought here, so I haven't seen him, but I promise, word is he's practically back to new."

"Wow." She raked a hand over her messy ponytail. "All right, then. Good." But that didn't explain why he hadn't contacted her. "He can help us find Daria."

"No," Henry said, "he can't."

She frowned. "I don't understand. You said he was doing fine."

"It's not that." Henry paced behind the couch, coming back to stop in front of her. "He thinks you're dead."

"What!"

"Allie, there was mass chaos on the water. You and Linc were both hurt and it was just . . . crazy. By the time everything calmed down, I actually thought Linc was dead at first. By the time we were airlifted out of there, they hadn't located him. I just assumed . . ."

"Assumed? Henry!"

"I know, I know. But can't you see how that could happen?"

Unfortunately, she could.

"Allie, no matter how much it hurts you, he can't know you're alive."

52

She began an agitated pace from one end of the area to the other.

"Just listen for a second, okay?"

She paused in front of him and gave him a short nod. She'd hear him out, but there was no way she wasn't going after Daria.

"You know as well as I do that Nevsky was going after you and threatened the people you loved. He knew you and Linc were partners."

"And even had pictures of his family," she murmured.

"Exactly. But as long as you're dead, they *should* be left alone."

"How can you be sure?"

"Because he has no reason to go after them now. I think he'll watch them for a while longer, just to be sure, but you're the one he has the personal grudge against. *You* infiltrated his home, *you* befriended his daughter—and *you* betrayed his trust."

Allie sucked in a breath. "He'll hate me, Henry. I can't do that to him. Not only will he hate me and never forgive me, he'll be terribly hurt. I know I would be. We were just beginning to develop something . . . personal."

Henry frowned.

"Oh, come on, Henry, you're not blind. I know you noticed."

"I did, but that's not my business. My business is doing what's best for my agents."

"And what's best is for Linc to think I'm dead? Let him grieve when there's no reason to? To one day find out that I deceived him on purpose? I can't *do* that to him!"

"You have to. At least until we have a plan."

"What kind of plan?"

"That will depend on Nevsky's next move."

"Which is?"

"I don't know!" Henry paced to the window and raked his hands over his head. "I . . . don't know. But there must be some advantage to having Nevsky think you're dead. And if there is, I want some time to think about it and plan accordingly."

"Nevsky, yes. Linc? No!"

"If Linc finds out you're not dead, Nevsky will know. He's got people watching him around the clock. There's no way to tell Linc without telling Nevsky." Henry's flat, no-nonsense statement stopped her.

"I need a chance to think about it," she finally said. "And I can't do that right this second. I can't think past anything other than the fact that Daria texted me that she's in trouble and begged me to find her. I need to get out of here and figure out a way to help her."

"When did she send the text?"

"Yesterday." She pressed fingers to her suddenly pounding head. "We may be too late." Allie narrowed her gaze on Henry. "You got me here by chopper, didn't you?"

"Yes."

"Then get that chopper back, please, so it can take us home. I've got to go after Daria."

"I'll call in a team—"

"No. It's got to be me."

"Allie—"

"Just do it, Henry, or I'll find my own way!" The shout reverberated between them and she swallowed at his stunned expression. "I'm sorry. I know you're concerned, but the heavy meds are out of my system." A flush heated her cheeks. "I'm off opioids. I took the IV out yesterday."

"You what?" Anger flashed.

"So there's nothing keeping me from doing this. Now, will you help me, or am I on my own?"

Henry gave a slow nod. "There's no talking you out of this, is there?"

"No. I need my weapon."

"Fine, but no contacting Linc, understand? Not until we talk about this more. After we have a plan in place to keep him and his family safe, you can let him know you're alive."

"Understood. I have no desire to do anything that would throw him back into the path of danger." She grabbed the laptop. "I need to give this back to the nurse, then I'll be ready to go."

Fifteen minutes later, she sat in the helicopter with her headset on. Medication had eased her headache and she was able to ignore the rest of the aches and pains.

And lo and behold, Henry had placed a brand-new cell phone and weapon in her hand as he'd climbed into the seat beside her.

"Thank you, Henry."

"Of course. Let's go rescue Daria."

6

Allie adjusted the earpiece a little deeper into her ear canal. "You're sure she's still there? In the same place? Alone?"

Even though Daria's text had been sent yesterday, it hadn't been hard to find the building, even with the partial address. A quick reconnaissance of the structure with thermal imaging had given them a picture of the inside.

Five men gathered around a table in a conference room. The smaller form sitting on the floor in a separate part of the building looked like it could be female. She was going on the educated guess that it was Daria.

"I'm sure," Henry said. A pause. "You don't have to do this, Allie."

"Yes, I do. She said they were going to kill her." If she was honest, Allie hadn't expected her to still be alive. She'd almost wept when she realized she wasn't too late. "She's got evidence against Nevsky that will put him behind bars forever, remember? I want my life back, I want Linc and his family safe, and Daria's the key to making that happen." She wanted a lot of things back. Like Linc. "But the most important thing is making sure she's safe. She's the priority, understand?"

"Of course. But if you get caught, they'll kill you too. Will make it kind of hard to get your life back."

"Then let's make sure I don't get caught." She placed the flat-head ax and Halligan bar tool against the exterior exit door that led to Daria's room and pulled, popping the flimsy lock. Normally, SWAT would be the one making the dynamic entry, but she didn't want to waste time waiting on them to organize and get over here.

Bars on the windows and a ten-dollar lock a five-year-old could snap. She'd take it and be grateful for it.

Waiting to see if anyone burst outside to investigate the noise, Allie gripped her weapon, breaths coming in slow, measured puffs. Senses sharp, adrenaline on high, she held still.

When seconds passed and nothing happened, Allie crouched and slid her tactical mirror through the broken lock. She angled it to see a closed door across the small room. A glass window separated it from the outer area—and the girl sat on the floor working on a laptop, eyes darting from the exit door to the window every few seconds.

Daria held herself in a strategic position that allowed her to watch the window, but anyone looking in wouldn't be able to see the laptop screen. The kid was smart with good instincts, and Allie intended to ensure that she stayed alive to see that potential unfold.

Rotating the mirror once again, Allie decided she could open the door and anyone on the other side of the privacy window wouldn't notice. Not unless they were right up against the glass and looking into the office.

Allie adjusted the mirror down and saw Daria's leg shackled to a steel loop attached to the floor. The girl shot furtive glances at the interior door, then back to the mirror, then at the door once more.

Still kneeling, Allie pushed the exit door inward and lowered herself to all fours. She let her gaze meet the teen's. Daria's eyes widened and hope flared. Finger to her lips in an unnecessary warning, Allie shoved the mirror into one of the pockets of her tactical vest.

"Daria," she whispered.

"Allie, I'm so glad to see you."

"If I can get you loose, can you run out the door?"

"Yes, please!"

Allie shut the damaged door behind her as much as possible, then army-crawled the short distance to the desk, using it to stay out of sight of anyone who looked into the room. Her stitches pulled and she grimaced at the shooting pain but refused to let it slow her down.

She removed the handcuff key from her pocket and released the teen's leg. "Don't move yet," Allie whispered. "As soon as I tell you, go. There's a guy on the other side who'll be looking for you. His name is Henry, midforties, tactical gear on. Get to him and he'll keep you safe until I can get there."

"My father's gone crazy," Daria hissed. "Or crazier. Somehow he knows what I've done and he's going to kill me as soon as he figures out where the evidence is. I've got to get out of here." Hysteria tinged her words.

"I know. Hold on a second," Allie said.

"How could he know, Allie? You're the only person I told."

Allie shook her head. "He must have heard it on a mic we missed or something."

"I guess."

"We'll figure that out later. Right now, we're going to go out the way I came in." She stole a glance at the window and noted the silhouette on the other side of the privacy glass, cloudy but still clear enough to see through. She wondered exactly how she was going to get her out.

"The guy at the window is watching me," Daria murmured, slowly closing the laptop and sliding it under the desk. "I don't think he can see very well, but he can see enough to know if I'm here or not—and if I'm alone."

"Okay, just stay still." Allie's gaze went to the backpack against the wall. Whoever had locked Daria in the room hadn't bothered to search the backpack? Interesting. Weird. Stupid? Or for a reason?

Using the desk to hide behind, much like Daria had done, Allie maneuvered so she could see the window. She could make out the profile of a large man to the side, eyeing Daria, who sat with her forehead resting on the knees she had drawn to her chest.

"Henry? How's it looking outside?" Allie asked.

"SWAT is here."

"What?" she hissed. "Why didn't you say something?"

"They just got here. I didn't know about it. I've been a bit out of the loop lately, if you'll recall."

Because he'd been hiding her away from the world, letting everyone think she was dead. For many valid reasons, she'd admit, but still . . . "So, now what?"

"There's a guard on the perimeter near the door," he said. "Stay put while I get rid of him and let SWAT know you're here."

The knob rattled.

"Someone's coming," Daria hissed. "We need to get out now!"

Linc held his weapon ready as SWAT surrounded the office building. As always, when he was about to enter enemy territory, his adrenaline pounded and his nerves twitched, but the hand that held the weapon was rock-solid steady.

Blood humming, he drew in a steadying breath and tried not to think about what he would do once the mission was completed—meaning Nevsky was either dead or behind bars. While he wanted him alive, if he had to die, he decided that was fine too. He just wanted him unable to hurt another soul.

But after that . . . He tried not to picture life without Allie. The black hole of grief would swallow him up if he wasn't careful.

His earpiece came to life. "Thermal imaging shows four live ones in the front, two in the back office, and one standing near the two in the back but not in the office with them," the voice said. "The two in the office look like they could be female, the others are all male. SWAT team is in place. We're a go on command."

Two females? Daria and who? A guard?

Linc had positioned himself to be the first one in the door. The team member with the battering ram stood prepared and Linc nodded. "Go!"

The ram slammed into the wooden door, knocking it open. Linc swept inside, weapon in front of him. The chopper thumped above. Other agents poured in behind him, commands echoing. "FBI! Hands in the air! Keep your hands where I can see them! On the floor! On the floor!" The four men who'd been gathered around the table full of white powder and cash scattered.

Two obeyed the agents' orders. The others ran. While his coworkers went after them, Linc vaguely registered the shocked expressions of the two on the floor as their hands were cuffed behind them. The raid had been a complete surprise. Good to know.

The man who had been by the office in the back darted for the nearest exit.

"Got another runner," Linc said.

He wouldn't get far. The helicopters hovering above would take care of tracking the guy. Linc continued his journey farther into the building, his goal the back office where the women were. Daria especially. Hope pounded. This was it. At the door, he stood to the side, then kicked it in.

And came face-to-face with a dead woman.

———

"Linc!" Allie gasped. "Behind you!"

She grabbed his forearm and pulled. He stumbled into the room.

"Look out!" Daria shoved the rolling chair toward the man who was raising his weapon behind Linc. The chair clipped him, throwing him off balance, and Linc turned, swiping his weapon across the man's temple.

He crumpled, rolling and swearing. Linc dropped a knee into his back. "Be still!"

When the groaning man finally complied, Linc cuffed him.

Allie stepped to the door and scanned the outer area for any more immediate danger while her mind churned with what she was going to tell Linc.

"Clear!"

"Clear over here!"

The calls came in. Everyone was in custody. Allie lowered her weapon and turned back to find Linc staring at her—and Daria gone. Henry stood at the back door, his eyes swinging back and forth between her and Linc, pure frustration stamped on his features. "Well, I guess the cat's out of the bag now."

"Where's Daria?" Allie asked.

"I got her in the van away from the reporters that are on the scene," Henry said. "I swear, they show up faster and faster." He eyed Allie. "Everything okay in here?"

"Yes," Allie said.

"No, everything's *not* okay," Linc countered. "Mark!"

Mark King stepped in and Allie quickly turned her back, not wanting to be recognized yet.

"Yeah, what you got?"

"Take care of this vermin for me, will you?" Linc said. "I've got something to deal with."

"Got it."

Once he had his prisoner in capable hands and the three of them were alone, Linc swung back to Allie and Henry, jabbing a finger at his supervisor. "You knew she was alive all this time?"

"Yes."

He reeled back, the single-word answer as effective as a sucker punch.

Allie winced and stepped forward, hand outstretched. "Let us explain."

"Explain? You let me think you were dead and you want to explain? There's no explanation. None!" He backed toward the door.

"There is! I had no choice! At least, I thought I didn't."

"There's always a choice, Allie. Always. I guess you've got Daria now. That means you've got the evidence, so you don't need me anymore." And then he was gone.

Allie resisted the urge to crumble to the floor in a puddle of tears. Instead, she shot Henry a black look, masking her hurt behind the anger. "You go after him while I go see Daria and get that evidence."

Henry caught her arm. "You can't."

"What do you mean?"

"You're dead, remember? You have to stay that way for the moment. Even with this raid, no one's seen you except Linc, and he'll keep his mouth shut once I explain things to him. The minute you show your face outside this room, Nevsky will learn about it."

She slapped her sunglasses on and pulled her baseball cap over her head. "I'm going to make sure Daria is all right." She waved off his protests. "I'll make sure no one recognizes me."

"Fine." She could see Henry gritting his teeth. Finally, he shook his head. "Just let me get Smythe out of the van and you can talk to her alone. Then I'll track down Linc and explain everything. I'll tell him it was my idea and I ordered you to go along with it."

"Do it. Please." She tacked the last word on the end. After all, he was still her supervisor.

Henry left and Allie paced the floor of the small office, impatience edging her closer and closer to stepping out the door.

Finally, Henry reappeared, jaw tight. "She's not there."

"What? Then where is she?"

"Smythe said she asked to go to the bathroom. He escorted her to the one next door and she . . . left."

"Left!" Allie stared. "What do you mean she left? How did she just leave?"

"Climbed out of the window."

"And no one saw her? The media? Anyone?"

"No."

"Unbelievable." Allie curled her fingers into a fist and barely managed to keep from slamming it into the wall. "She's in danger, Henry."

He winced. "I know. I told Smythe to keep an eye on her, but she slipped away from him. Who'd have thought she'd run from our protection after we rescued her?"

Allie pinched the bridge of her nose as her stomach twisted in a knot. Had Daria been snatched again, or had she run? If she'd run, why? She'd been safe. Had the gunfire scared her into bolting? Maybe, but that didn't sound like her. She'd risked her life to get evidence against her father. Had lived in the same house with the man who could have killed her at any moment and she had hardly blinked an eye. And she hadn't hesitated to help Linc take out one of the goons. So, either she'd been taken again or something major had spooked her into running.

"See if you can track her down. Please, Henry. We've got to find her before her father does."

Henry got on his radio. A minute later, he met her gaze. "Okay, agents are combing the area. It doesn't look like she was snatched. One agent said he saw her walking away from the scene toward the road."

"That makes no sense," Allie said. "Why?"

"I don't know, but we're looking for her."

"I've also got to go talk to Linc, then I'm going to join in the search for Daria."

"Now, that's not a good idea," Henry said.

"Maybe not, but it's what I'm going to do. I need a uniform to blend in," she said. "Can you get me a vest?"

Henry's jaw tightened, then he gave a shrug of resignation. "Wait on me. We've both got to talk to him."

"No, I want to talk to him alone first. He's furious, Henry." And hurt. As well as betrayed. And he was justified in all of it.

"I know. He'll cool off. Stay here and I'll get that vest."

She sighed and hoped he was right about Linc cooling off, but she had a feeling it was going to be a long process.

7

Linc sat behind the wheel of his new SUV and desperately tried to get his seething emotions under control. He honestly couldn't think of a time he'd been so hurt, so angry, so filled with uncontrollable rage that he was actually tempted to do something violent. Like punch his supervisor in the face.

Not even Regina's betrayal had stirred such rage.

And Allie . . .

Resting his palms against his eyes, he ignored the organized chaos still going on at the scene. He needed a moment. Several actually.

The moment he'd seen Henry and Allie together, he'd known faking her death had been Henry's idea. But for Allie to go along with it?

"How could you, Allie?" he whispered.

He needed to be asking her those questions instead of the empty space in his SUV. But while he was overjoyed that she was alive, he wasn't ready to face her yet. "Let us explain," she'd said. *Us.* Meaning her and Henry.

What possible excuse could they have to keep her "dead"?

Well, if you'd let them explain, maybe you'd find out.

Linc wasn't interested in listening to the part of his brain that was still able to think rationally. He just wanted to be mad.

Right now.

Eventually, he'd want to hear what they had to say.

A knock on the passenger door jerked him from his thoughts, heart pounding, sweat breaking across his forehead. He couldn't make out the figure on the other side of the tinted window, but saw it was female and wearing the standard FBI baseball cap.

He rolled the window down and Special Agent Donna Sims turned. "I need to check out your vehicle."

"Why?"

"I have no idea. I was asked to do it and told not to question why. I've already done four others and you're the fifth." She pulled a mirror from one of the pockets on her vest and started going over the underbelly of his dash.

Linc stepped out and took the mirror from her, carefully using it to clear the interior. "Nothing," he said. "You find anything on the others?"

"No." She took the mirror back and started on the outside of the SUV.

At the back, she paused, then finished the walk, then returned to show him a small disk about the size of a dime. "Found it under the license plate. Someone's tracking you," she said.

He curled his fingers into a fist. "You'll take it to the lab? See if they can get any info from it?"

"Of course." She dropped it into an evidence bag, labeled it, then passed it off to another officer, who signed the tag noting that he'd received it. "Pull around the covered area behind the building, will you?"

"Why?"

"Again, I don't know. I was just asked—in a very strange way, I might add—to pass the message along." She handed him a sheet of paper with those instructions ending with the initials HO.

"Henry gave you this?"

"Nope. Another agent, but I didn't get a good look at her. She passed it and kept walking, so I figured she was trying to get a message to you without anyone else knowing—including me. It was fast and she was slick."

"She, huh?"

"Yeah. You need any help? Backup?"

"No, but thanks."

Not convinced, she stared at him and started to protest when Linc climbed back into the driver's seat, his mind whirling. He twisted the key and the engine roared to life. Anger and curiosity burned a path through his brain as he began the slow trek to the back. Having done a reconnaissance of the building before entry, he knew exactly the spot Donna meant.

Once under cover of the loading area, he glanced around, hand on his weapon. No Henry.

The door that connected the loading area to the office building opened and a woman stepped out. Dressed in her FBI khaki slacks, blue shirt, and vest, she kept her head down. The baseball cap covered her hair and dark sunglasses hid her eyes. She knocked on the passenger window and he lowered it.

"We need to talk," she said as she opened the door and slid into his passenger seat, keeping the ball cap pulled low.

"Hop in and have a seat," he said. "Make yourself comfortable."

"Save the sarcasm, Linc. I know you're hurt, or just plain angry. Put whatever emotion you want to on it, I don't blame you."

"You have no idea."

"Yeah, I do, just in reverse."

He started to bite off a response, then stopped. He faced her. "What does that mean?"

"Can you drive? I can't let anyone see me with you." She moved the seat as far back as it would go, then scrunched down onto the floorboard, shoulders against the door. Fortunately, the floorboard of the large Suburban was roomy enough to accommodate her.

For some reason he couldn't put his finger on, he didn't bother arguing with her. Instead, he shifted into drive and pulled away from the still-busy scene. "What did you mean?"

"I understand because I've been there."

"So you said. What are you talking about?"

"I'm talking about when someone shot my parents and me and my little sister and left us for dead."

Linc gave a harsh gasp. "What?" The word came out garbled, strangled, and he stared at her a bit too long. He jerked the wheel to keep them on the road. He'd thought he knew most everything about her. An only child whose parents had died when she was a teenager. "You never said a thing about that. You never said anything about siblings."

"I don't like to talk about it. A teenager by the name of Gregori Radchenko shot my parents while they were sleeping, then killed my eight-year-old sister in the hallway when she came out of her bedroom. I saw him shoot her, and when I screamed at him, Radchenko turned the gun on me. He fired once and missed. I turned to run and he shot me in the back. My dad and sister died right there. I remember seeing Gregori run for the stairs and heard the front door slam."

Speechless, he stared at the road instead of her, his jaw working, but unable to get any words out.

"My mom and I survived because our next-door neighbor was a surgeon and was out walking his dog at three in the morning when it happened," she said. "He called for help while he worked to save me. I remember him yelling into the phone that I was going to bleed out if someone didn't get there. And then I blacked out."

Linc didn't know what to say. She spoke without emotion, staring somewhere in the vicinity of his legs, her rigid shoulders and white-knuckled fists resting on her knees the only indication that telling the story troubled her.

"Allie—"

"When I woke up in the hospital, I started screaming for my little sister. They told me she was in ICU and I could see her after I'd healed. They told me my dad was fine and he'd be in to see me later."

"How old were you?" He nearly choked on the question, trying to breathe around the shock.

"Fourteen."

Linc raked a hand over his head. "I don't even know what to say."

"There's nothing to say. They lied. The doctors, the nurses, everyone. Even my mom."

"She lived?"

"She was hit by one bullet. A flesh wound, so she recovered fairly quickly. She told me everyone was fine. Of course, as I healed and grew stronger, it was more difficult to continue to put me off. Finally, when I insisted on someone taking me to see them or I was going to find them myself, she had to tell me the truth. I was livid. Hysterical. They had to keep me sedated for two days." She shook her head. "I thought you were dead until about four hours before I saw you in that raid," she said.

He blanched. "Henry told you I was dead?"

She gave a short laugh. "No, he told me you were alive. I was high as a kite on painkillers and I was . . . messed up, flashing back and forth between crashing drones, exploding boats, and the moment when I realized my mother had been lying to me for two weeks. When Henry told me you were alive and that I just needed to concentrate on getting better, I didn't believe him."

"Because of what happened with your family," Linc said.

She looked away and nodded and he thought he saw tears in her eyes. But when she turned back, her eyes were clear, hard, with no sign of emotion.

Finally, he exited the highway.

"Where are we going?" she asked.

"Someplace we can talk without worrying about being followed or overheard."

Unsure where he thought they could go that would afford them the privacy they needed, Allie clamped her lips shut and let him drive while she grappled with her emotions, wrestling them into submission. "I'm sorry Henry let you believe I was dead," she finally said past the lump in her throat, "but after he explained some things to me, I . . . understood that it might be for the best. Although, to be honest, if the shoe was on the other foot, I'd be reacting exactly like you are."

Without answering, Linc made several more turns, the last one leading him down a long cement drive to a ranch-style home set well back and out of sight from the main road. He pulled into the garage and cut the engine. "I'll listen," he finally said.

He'd listen. Well, that was better than she'd expected. "Where are we?"

"A safe house."

"How come I don't know about this one?"

He shrugged. "Because it belongs to the Columbia PD, not the FBI. I helped Brady out with a case a while back and we used this place."

"Emily?"

"Yes."

Emily Chastain, now Emily St. John because she'd married Linc's brother, Brady, four months ago.

Once they were inside, Linc motioned to the sofa, and she dropped onto it with a wince. The stitches in her back still bothered her, but she figured they were the least of her worries at the moment. Linc took the recliner near the large wall of windows that overlooked the lake.

Allie drew in a deep breath. Might as well get this over with. "Henry said you and your family would be in danger should Nevsky learn I was alive. Because of the pictures in his office, I was inclined to agree."

"Maybe so, but is there any reason that I couldn't know you were alive?"

She gave a halfhearted shrug. "If Nevsky even had a whiff that I was alive, I don't know what he might do. I took a huge chance arranging this at the last minute and getting in the car with you. Henry's going to be livid when he finds out, but I couldn't let you just leave, thinking that I'd deliberately set out to hurt you." She looked away. If someone had followed them, she couldn't tell. She'd had to quickly come up with a plan to get Linc alone, and the best she could do was take advantage of the controlled chaos at the scene to slip into the loading area and into Linc's vehicle. But a chance was still a chance.

"Wait a minute. What do you mean when he finds out? I got a note from Henry arranging this."

"No, that was me. I suggested to Henry that someone should check the vehicles for tracking devices so if anyone was watching it wouldn't be obvious yours was the focus of the search. I wrote the note, signed Henry's initials, and slipped it to Donna with a whisper to pass it on to you. She and I have rarely talked or worked together, so I didn't think she'd recognize me."

He blew out a breath and shook his head. "She didn't."

"You need to check everything for tracking and listening devices. Your family does too."

"I've already warned everyone that it's possible Nevsky was watching them, but no one's seen anything—or found any devices that I know of."

"Probably because he thought I was dead and had no reason to go after them now. Or you."

He shook his head. "I don't understand. Why go after me and my family if it's you he wants dead?"

Allie couldn't sit still another minute. She rose to pace. "I've thought about that, and the only thing I could think of was that with him watching us so closely, he would notice that things were . . . developing . . . between us."

Linc raised a brow. "Developing?"

She flushed and hated the heat. Linc was the only one who could do that to her. "We haven't advertised the fact that we were hanging out, maybe behaving like we were a little more than just friends, but we didn't try to hide it either."

"Hanging out?"

"What do you call it?"

"Dating."

"Dating?"

"You asked what I called it. I call it dating." He slid a glance at her. "Although I'll admit, I've picked up on the conflicting signals. Every time I would think we were getting closer, you'd back off."

She flinched and wondered if she should change the subject ASAP. Unfortunately, she didn't speak fast enough.

"I've never made any secret how I feel about you, Allie," he said. "I thought you were starting to feel the same."

"I . . . I mean, yes, of course, I care about you."

"Ouch."

Allie groaned. "I can't deal with that discussion right now. Maybe we should get back to the topic of Nevsky."

"Fine."

The word and his laser look conveyed the distinct message that they weren't done with the previous topic.

She cleared her throat. "If Nevsky wanted to hurt me, he'd go after the man he was under the impression that I was building a relationship with . . . as well as that man's family, right?" She clasped her hands together and dropped her gaze to them. "Because going after what's left of mine wouldn't have any leverage."

"Tell me more about your family. You said they were dead."

Linc's soft voice drew her eyes to his. Only to find she couldn't read him.

Thrown, she hesitated. He'd never hidden anything from her. She'd been the one with secrets. The past haunted her and she'd be the first to admit it. However, most of the time, she could keep the memories and the nightmares at bay. Talking about it always brought everything surging to the surface, making it hard to stuff it all back into the little compartment in her brain that allowed her to function.

Unfortunately, now that she'd unlocked those emotions and memories, she had a feeling the lid wasn't going to shut as easily this time.

"Allie?"

She jerked her gaze back to his.

"You said they were dead."

"They are." She huffed a small laugh and went to the window. The view was beautiful, peaceful. A direct contrast to her emotional state right now. "I owe you an apology."

"For what?"

"For trying to live a life I was never meant to live."

He frowned. "Don't talk in riddles."

"Sorry, Daria's worn off on me." She sighed and rubbed her palms together. "Look, we don't have time for this. We need to figure out a plan to find Daria. She's smart, but she's still young and running scared from a father who won't hesitate to torture her for the information she has on him."

"And then kill her when she gives it to him."

"Yes."

He sighed. "Okay, we'll table the personal stuff for now."

"Thank you."

"But we're coming back to it."

She gave him a tight smile. "I never thought otherwise."

"As far as locating Daria, how did Nevsky find out about the evidence?"

"He had to have heard us talking. Daria thought she was safe outside on her little balcony, but I'm guessing there was a mic out there—or Gerard told him. I know the guy is crazy about Daria, but it's very possible he's more concerned about his own neck and told Nevsky what Daria had done." She sighed. "She shouldn't have trusted him."

Linc nodded and rubbed his head. "So, how are we going to find Daria if you're dead? In order to work this case effectively, you've got to come back to the land of the living."

For a moment, she simply thought. "I don't know," she finally said. "I don't know what to do. I think I need you to help me figure that out—and fast."

He blew out a low breath. "Let's talk to Henry and see what the three of us can come up with together."

"You're speaking to Henry?"

He shot her a dark look. "Strictly on a professional level. But he's not out of the doghouse yet."

8

Linc pulled a chair up to the conference table at the temporary safe house and settled into it. Allie took the one opposite him, and Henry aligned himself next to Allie.

Probably figured it was better to continue to keep some distance between him and Linc until things cooled off a little. At least he'd brought some decent food. Linc opened his box and pulled out half of his club sandwich. Allie did the same.

"So," Henry said with a sigh, "let me get this off my chest." He glanced at Linc. "I'm sorry I let you believe that Allie was dead. I truly thought it best for you and your family, in addition to the fact that it would give us an advantage over Nevsky. As long as he believes she's dead, he won't see her coming."

Linc jerked a nod at the man. "I get that, but I wasn't just grieving a partner." He locked eyes with Allie and she swallowed, but at least she didn't look away. Linc shook his head. "You're my supervisor, Henry. I have to believe you have my back and my well-being in mind with every decision you make that's related to me. This time I think you erred in judgment."

"Noted."

"Good. In spite of that, I think we both still have the common goal of bringing down Nevsky and his organization. So I can put aside my personal feelings." Maybe. Truthfully, he wasn't sure, but he'd give it a shot. For now.

"I can do whatever it takes," Henry said.

Allie shoved her sandwich aside, stood, and paced. "Guys, our main objective is Daria. To bring Nevsky down, we need her—and we need to find her before her father or one of his assassins does."

"Absolutely," Linc said. "But let's be honest, if we find Daria, Nevsky—or one of his assassins—probably won't be far behind."

"Assuming we get to her first," Henry said.

"We have to." Allie's hands opened and closed at her sides, the only indication that she was stressed.

"Exactly." Linc leaned forward. "We're going to need help."

"No help," Henry said.

Allie frowned. "Henry, we can't do this with just the three of us."

"We have to. If word gets back to Nevsky that you're alive, there's no telling what he might do—or who he'll do it to."

"You really expect that the three of us are going to take down Vladislav Nevsky when an entire task force hasn't been able to do it?" Linc crossed his arms and glared at his supervisor, wanting to be petty and take back his words of being able to put aside his personal feelings. "I don't mean to be insubordinate, but that's not happening."

Henry's gaze bounced between them until he finally sighed. He swung his keys around his forefinger, then dropped them on the table with a clunk. "I gotta stop doing that," he muttered. "I'm going to leave them somewhere one day." He put the keys back in his pocket and raked a hand through his hair. "Okay, you're right. I'm just worried about tipping Nevsky off when we finally—through circumstances I wouldn't have wished on anyone—have an advantage over the man. And since we're here, I don't want to lose that."

"Neither do we, but we don't want to get killed either," Linc said.

"Of course not. You know me. I'm open. What do you suggest? Do you have a plan?"

"Of sorts," Linc said. "It needs some refining, but yeah."

"Refining how?"

"I want to bring my family in on this. Since they're the ones who'd be threatened, they should have a chance to go on the offensive, be a part of the plan to go after Nevsky and his organization."

Henry was shaking his head before Linc finished.

"Yes, Henry," Allie said. "That makes sense. But we'll do all of this under the radar."

"How? You just said you wanted to bring in other people."

Allie rubbed her forehead and Linc wondered if hers was pounding as hard as his. "Okay," she said, "what if I stay dead for the time being? That way Nevsky isn't as alert as he would be if he knew I was alive and he'll hopefully leave Linc's family alone. We'll still have to keep agents watching their houses and make sure they have escorts to and from work, that sort of thing. At least for a while until we're sure they're not in danger."

Henry nodded.

"And," Allie continued, "being dead will allow me the opportunity to look for Daria without Nevsky looking for me."

Henry shook his head. "I really think you need to go underground and let Linc and me handle going after Nevsky."

"Not a chance."

He huffed a breath of impatience. "How are you going to be a part of looking for Daria without someone finding out you're alive?"

"Simple. I'll use a disguise. I've changed my appearance before, I can do it again. Granted, it won't include plastic surgery this time, but . . ." She winced.

"What's wrong?" Henry asked.

"Just these stupid stitches. They're driving me crazy." She rubbed her shoulder. "Anyway, yeah. I can do a disguise. No one will ever recognize me."

Henry leaned forward, conceding with a slow nod. "Like the *Paraplectana coccinella*."

Allie rolled her eyes. "Yes, exactly like . . . that." She paused. "You're going to tell me what that is, right?"

"It's a special spider that uses its ability to look like a ladybug—which can be toxic to some predators—to scare them away." At her blank look, he lifted a hand. "Just saying it's a good defense mechanism."

Allie nodded. "Thank you, Henry. I've learned more about insects in the last year than I ever thought I'd need to know."

"Forget the bugs," Linc asked. "What do you mean, plastic surgery?"

At his question, Allie's shoulders tensed. "The shooter punched my face. He broke my jaw, nose, and one cheekbone. I look quite a bit different than I used to."

Linc blinked.

Henry glanced at Linc, then back to Allie. "You really think you can pull this off? Staying dead?"

"I think I have to in order to protect Linc's family and find Daria. And to keep Nevsky off guard."

"So, no telling Linc's family then? We're agreed?" Henry asked.

Allie nodded. "For now. If we find that we're going to need more help, then I'm fine with letting them in on it. And don't forget, Daria knows I'm alive."

Henry dropped his chin to his chest. "That's right."

"As do Dr. Forsythe and one nurse at the rehab place in Hilton Head," Allie said. "But they wouldn't have any connection to Nevsky or any reason to be in contact with me."

Linc frowned. "Rehab place?"

Allie waved a hand. "It's a long story. I'll explain later."

Henry ran a hand down his face and blew out a deep breath.

"Yes, later. Okay, so Daria's on the run for whatever reason. It's not like she's going to go looking for you." He paused. "Or will she?"

"I have no idea."

"But it's a good question," Linc said softly. "She knows where you live."

"I'm not sure that's an issue," Henry said with a wave of dismissal. "She ran from the scene, meaning she ran from you. Why would she go looking for you?"

Allie bit her lip. "I don't know, Henry. She hates her father. She's smart and resourceful and I don't want to underestimate her."

"Okay, I can put some people on your apartment. If she shows up there, I'll get a call. But let's deal with that later. For now, we need to assume that she's not going to come looking for you. How are we going to find her?"

"How about this," Linc said. "I can enlist the help of my family and ask them to all be on the lookout for Daria without knowing all the details—or that Allie's alive. They're grieving her loss too, and will be happy to be involved with anything that's going to get justice for her." He wanted to berate Henry for his deception, but the truth was, he was beginning to see why the man had decided it might be the best route. In the end, when it all came together, Nevsky would be kept off guard and wouldn't be constantly looking over his shoulder for Allie.

"Now that we've got that settled," Henry said, "let's talk about where we might be able to find Daria. Where would she run to?"

"I'm actually more interested in why she ran at the moment," Allie said. "She was safe. She knew I was there and would take care of her. And yet she ran. Why?"

"We've already been over that," Linc said. "Something spooked her."

"But what?"

"There's no telling." Linc looked at Henry. "Is there any security footage we could pull from that building? We noticed the outside cameras before the raid. Can we get into his system?"

"I've already requested the footage," Henry said. "Interestingly enough, there weren't any cameras inside."

"Good. Then we don't have to worry about Nevsky seeing me on the footage," Allie said.

"Exactly." Henry rubbed a hand over his tired face. "When I have the footage from the outside cameras, I'll let you know and we'll take a look at it."

"Great," Linc said. "So, for now, where's Allie going to stay? She can't go home."

"She can stay with me," Henry said, turning to her. "I mean, if you want. Otherwise, we can do a hotel or something."

"No," Allie said, her eyes shadowed. "I have to go home."

Linc frowned. The way she said it held more meaning than she just wanted to go home. "Why?"

"I'm assuming that if I'm dead, someone's going to clean out my apartment at some point. I have files and other things related to a case that I can't have anyone else seeing."

"I can clean that out for you," Henry said.

"No."

Henry blinked at her whip-snapped word.

She cleared her throat. "Thanks, but no. I can get in and get out and no one will know I've been there. Trust me, I had to figure that out unless I wanted to get stuck talking to one of the residents every time I walked out my door."

Henry laughed—short and humorless. "Absolutely not. If you enter the apartment and someone notices—regardless of how sneaky you think you are—you'll cease to be dead."

"I'll go with her," Linc said. "I'll make sure I'm visible. No one would question her partner being there and taking care of things for her."

"No one would question her supervisor either, probably." Henry pulled his keys from his pocket, spun them on his finger, then slid them back. "But you do it your way."

Allie gave a slow nod. "That'll work, especially if you run into Mr. Carter—which you will. He's a retired police officer and makes no secret he keeps an eye on everything that goes on at the complex. And, if you don't live there, once he has a description of you, the whole place receives an email with every last bit of information he can pull about you."

Henry groaned. "How did I wind up supervising the two most stubborn agents in the entire Bureau?"

"You must have made someone mad," Allie deadpanned.

"Yeah, who's got it in for you?" Linc asked.

Henry scowled. "Get out of here, you two. Just be careful and make sure Allie isn't caught rising from the dead."

Allie stayed in the shadows of the trees behind her apartment, watching. Linc would enter through the front door, talking to anyone he saw on his way in to make sure there was no reason for someone to question him being in Allie's home.

When she'd picked the place, it had been for its convenient location near the office, but she had to admit, she'd very much enjoyed her nightly habit of slipping out onto the screened porch and letting the stresses of the day roll from her shoulders as she stared out into the wooded area.

On the porch, wrapped in the blanket of darkness, she'd found she didn't mind being so alone in the world. And it was there she'd had some of her most intense discussions with God. Okay, arguments, if she was honest. And begging. Lots of pleading for God to let her find Radchenko and Nevsky—and answers to questions that had been burning a hole in her mind for fifteen years.

But apparently God had gone deaf, because her desperate requests had gotten her nowhere. Or maybe he'd just gotten tired of her whining and was ignoring her.

Allie focused on the kitchen window, awaiting the all clear from Linc. Finally, the shade went up and she bolted across the grassy area to the six concrete steps. Taking them two at a time, she reached her screen door, then opened the back door and slipped inside her first-floor apartment. She shut the door behind her and threw the dead bolt. When she turned, she found Linc studying her hallway. Every so often he'd take a step to the left and continue his perusal. In silence, she joined him.

For the next four minutes, he went from picture to picture, until he reached the end, then met her gaze. "Your own personal crime scene wall?"

"Yes."

"Your family?"

"Yes."

"And you look at these every day?"

He was referring to the pictures of her father and sister, dead. Her father lay in the bed he'd shared with her mother, on his face, hands above his head and a bullet in his skull.

And her little sister, sprawled indignantly on the hall floor, the back of her head bleeding from the bullet the killer had put into it without hesitation.

"No. Not every day." Just most days. She didn't miss her father, but her baby sister . . . She cleared her throat, pushing away the grief that was never far away. "Did you see anyone on your way in?"

"Just the guy you warned me about. Roland Carter."

She nodded. "Then the whole complex will know within the hour that you're here."

"I thought for sure you were exaggerating."

"He's very protective of his residents, and if there's a stranger in the midst, then . . . yeah. And he has a group text he moderates."

"That's a bit much, isn't it?"

"He's a retired cop with a lot of time on his hands."

"Right." He pointed to a picture of a smiling young man holding a football under one arm. The name Gregori Radchenko had been written across the bottom of the photo. A bull's-eye had been drawn on his face. "The teenager who killed your family?"

"Yes."

"Why'd he do it?"

Allie sighed and shook her head. "I don't know."

"Did you know him?"

"Yes." She didn't want to get into it. Not now. Thankfully, he didn't press for more details.

"Tell me about the night they died before the actual shooting took place. Anything unusual happen?"

She closed her eyes and heard the argument, remembered curling into herself as the harsh words bounced off the walls.

"There was a screaming match between my parents that night. Which wasn't unusual. They often argued. But this seemed more intense. When I demanded to know what was going on, Mom ordered me to my room and Dad looked like he had a loose grip on his rage. Since I'd been on the receiving end of that rage more than once, I didn't ask any more questions. I pretended to leave, but hid around the corner to hear what I could."

"What'd you learn?"

"My father was livid. He demanded to know how my mother could betray him by going to Nevsky and asking him for money."

"Whoa."

"Yeah. And then he said, 'You've done it now.'"

"Were you all having a difficult time financially? I mean, obviously you were, but . . ."

"Not that I specifically recall, but . . ." Allie walked into her spare bedroom with Linc on her heels. The walls looked much like her hallway, but it was the large farmhouse table in the center of the room that she aimed for. "This says differently." She snagged a thick manila folder and pulled it toward her. Linc stood beside her and looked over her shoulder. His nearness unexpectedly caused her heart to ache, and she had to battle the desire to turn and bury her face in his chest, to seek comfort and reassurance that everything was going to be okay.

Instead, she edged to the right, putting some distance between them and opened the folder. "My parents' bank statements, investment accounts, everything I could find. They were flat broke, and the house was getting ready to go into foreclosure."

"Where'd the money go?"

"I'm not sure. There were a lot of cash withdrawals in large amounts."

"Blackmail?"

"I've wondered about that, of course, but haven't found any evidence to support it. Or evidence that would allow me to toss the possibility aside. However, I did find an invoice from a travel agency, and they said an airline ticket had been purchased but travel hadn't been completed. The name on the ticket wasn't my father's name, but he could have been using an alias." She bit her lip. "I think he knew things were going south and decided to bail. He just never had a chance to. As for the money"—she shrugged—"who knows? I have my theories, though."

"If he was going to leave you all, he could have been socking that money away in an offshore account somewhere."

She blinked. "That was one of my theories, so it wouldn't surprise me."

"So your parents were fighting because your mother went behind your father's back to Nevsky for help bailing them out of financial trouble."

"That's what it sounded like to me."

"How did your mother even know Nevsky?"

"My dad and Nevsky were both from Moscow," she said. "They

left to go to college in Brooklyn the same year and met there, drawn by the things they had in common—like their country and language. From what I can figure out from digging into my parents' records and looking at old yearbooks, my mother, father, and Nevsky were good friends. Then Mom and Dad got married and Nevsky disappeared."

"Wait a minute, Moscow? Radcliffe isn't a Russian surname."

"No, my mother legally changed it after the shooting and we went into hiding for a while, afraid the shooter would come back once he learned we'd survived."

"Okay, so Nevsky disappeared because he became part of the *Bratva*?"

"I think so," she said, not surprised he knew the slang term for the Russian Mafia. "I'm not sure when exactly, but it appears to have happened sometime shortly after my parents' marriage, and I think that's when the friendship dissolved."

"Your parents didn't want to have anything to do with Nevsky once they found out?"

"I don't know." She rubbed her eyes, fatigue hitting her. "I don't know a lot of things. Most of the stuff I've come up with is speculation based on the information I've got and a few scattered memories."

"And you think he's responsible for your family's deaths?"

"Yes. I know that he convinced Gregori Radchenko to be his hit man," she said softly. "I just don't know why."

"Which is why you were so eager to go undercover as his cook," Linc said.

"Yes. And he still slipped away from us." She narrowed her eyes. "Doesn't it make you wonder?"

"Wonder what?"

"Nevsky keeps close tabs on his operations. He's not the best delegator, which makes him slightly more vulnerable in some ways than others who pass everything off to their minions and keep their own hands clean. But while we can seem to track him down, physically, when it comes to actually getting him into custody, it's like he's a ghost."

Linc narrowed his eyes. "So, what are you saying?"

"I've wondered if he has someone in his pocket."

"Like who?"

She shook her head. "There's no telling. I mean, I don't want to think that, of course, but guys like Nevsky have their ways of finding the weak spots in some cops. Could be anybody. Could be several anybodies. His net is cast wide and he has a whole lot of money."

"I can check with my mother and see if she's heard any rumors about any cops working for Nevsky. Although, if she has, I'm sure she's got her own investigation going."

Allie nodded. "Wanna help me pack all this up?"

"Where are you going to stash it?"

"I don't know."

"I can take it to my place if you want."

She bit her lip, then gave a short nod. "You have room for it all?"

"I've got a closet it'll fit into."

For the next hour, they packed the boxes the information had originally been in and Linc carried them down to his truck while Allie continued to stay out of sight. When he returned for the last time, he shut the door behind him. "Your Mr. Carter is an interesting guy. I wish I had more time to trade stories with him."

She smiled. "I like him too. Did he grill you?"

"Absolutely. If I wasn't really your partner who knew all the right answers, I think he would have had me in cuffs and waiting to be picked up."

"Once a cop, always a cop."

"He likes you. Teared up when I told him I was your partner. Said he was really going to miss you and your shop talking."

A lump formed in her throat, and she forced it away, along with the guilt of her necessary duplicity. "Yeah, well, it's not forever. I hope."

"It's definitely not. Now, where are we going to park you so we can work this case without risk that someone's going to recognize you?"

"I think if I cut and dye my hair, use glasses, wear a hat, and pad my clothing a bit, I can do whatever I need to do without worrying about it."

"Carter would recognize you."

She huffed a short laugh. "Probably, but he'd keep his mouth shut until I could tell him what was going on."

"Probably. So," he said, "what's your suggestion on making this transformation happen?"

9

Linc waited for Allie to leave the way she'd entered. Once she'd merged into the woods behind the complex, he grabbed the last box that contained a few changes of clothing and toiletries and hefted it onto his shoulder, then locked the door behind him and pocketed the key.

A short walkway took him to the parking lot. He looked up to see Allie's neighbor sitting on his second-floor balcony.

"All finished in there?" Mr. Carter asked. He leaned forward in the rocker, his arms crossed, blue eyes intense.

"Yes, sir, all finished."

"How long were you and Allie partners?"

"A little over a year."

"That's a good amount of time to get to know someone."

"And miss them," Linc said, trying not to rush.

"Sure is. I lost a partner my first year on the job. He shoved me out of the way of a bullet and took it himself. Left behind two teenagers and a wife." Grief flashed. "That was fifty years ago, and I still think about him every day."

Linc hesitated. "I'm sorry."

"Me too. You'll think about her and you'll miss her, but I knew Allie pretty well. She wouldn't want you to stop living just because she's gone. Ya hear?"

"I hear. And you're right. She wouldn't." He shook his head, anger at the deception sweeping over him once more in spite of the benefits he could see in it. The most important one to him being that it kept her safe from Nevsky. He supposed that should be enough to satisfy him. However, Linc still wasn't completely convinced it was the best plan Henry had ever come up with.

"I'm going to get this in the car and head home. I'll probably be coming back for a few more things, so I imagine I'll see you again soon."

"Yes, I imagine you will. Take care, son, and stay safe."

"Thank you, sir. I'll do my best."

Linc walked away from the man with the strangest feeling that Mr. Carter had seen through the whole charade. He frowned. There was no way. Linc was just being paranoid.

Wasn't he?

He loaded the box into the back of the Suburban, then climbed behind the wheel. However, he couldn't help one last glance in the rearview mirror. Mr. Carter stood there, chewing on his toothpick, hands shoved in his front pockets and watching with that eagle-eyed vision he seemed to have.

"Stop it," Linc muttered to himself. "He's a retired cop. He's going to see something suspicious whether it's there or not."

But it *was* there. Linc growled and cranked the vehicle. He called his mother, using the Bluetooth.

She answered on the first ring. "Linc, good to hear from you."

"Hi, Mom. I can't talk long, but I've got a question for you."

"Of course."

"Have you heard any rumors of any officers who might be on Nevsky's payroll?"

A sigh slipped through the line. "Why do you ask?"

"I need to know."

"Just between you and me?"

"Absolutely."

"Then, yes. There've been rumors. We've done an internal investigation, of course, but nothing solid has turned up."

"So, you're finished with the investigation?"

"I didn't say that."

"Right." He paused. "Could you let me know if you do find something?"

Another pause. "Off the record? Yes."

"Thanks."

They said their goodbyes and Linc drove to the convenience store Allie had instructed him to go to when he'd finished with her apartment. He pulled into the last parking spot on the right, facing the building. Allie slipped around the corner, climbed into the passenger side and shut the door. "Thanks."

"Sure."

"What is it?" she asked.

He raised a brow. "What do you mean?"

"Something's bothering you. You have that little crease in your forehead that means you're thinking or something's nagging at you."

Linc let his eyes linger on the woman who'd been the first one in a very long time to turn his heart and his world upside down. A woman he'd started to lower his guard with and now regretted it. Sort of. "I talked to my mother. No cops officially known to be on Nevsky's payroll."

"Unofficially?"

"The investigation is ongoing."

"Okay. Good to know, I guess. What else?"

He laughed. "It's scary how you can read me."

"It's a gift."

"It's your neighbor."

"Carter?"

"Yeah. He's definitely one to watch."

"I know. I told you he would talk your ear off once he found out you were law enforcement."

90

"No, there's something else about him. Something I can't read."

"Like what?"

He sighed. "I don't know. That's the problem. I think he suspects something is wonky and is trying to figure it out. He's a cop. His instincts are shouting."

"Well, they're just going to have to shout. We have a teenager to find before her father does."

He nodded, but only because he couldn't do anything about her neighbor at the moment. "Let's get the stuff you need for your disguise and I'll think about it. I'm also going to check in with Annie and see if she can get busy tracking down Daria."

"Henry's working on that."

"I know, but Henry's also working other cases that have his attention pulled in different directions. I want Annie on this."

Allie nodded. "Works for me. The more people looking for her, the better. And Annie's got the resources at her fingertips." She frowned. "Although I've got to say, I'm not so sure even Annie's resources are going to do us a whole lot of good with Daria."

"Why not?"

"The girl's got skills. As long as she's not held captive somewhere, I think she'll be a challenge to track down."

"What kind of skills?"

"She's got street smarts, including how to make her phone untraceable. She ran away from home when she was sixteen because she was mad at her father. Gerard, her bodyguard, finally found her three weeks later and brought her home."

"Not much of a bodyguard if he lost her in the first place."

She gave a low chuckle. "He's actually a good one. Daria is just genius-level clever. And I'm not even kidding when I use the word 'genius.' Her IQ has got to be off the charts. You heard some of the conversations we had. You know what I'm talking about."

"I missed the one where she mentioned running away. How'd he talk her into coming back home?"

"She didn't go into details on how he found her, but basically, she got word that her father threatened to kill Gerard, so she got a message to Gerard, telling him where to find her."

"Oh."

"Yeah."

"So, where was Gerard when she was being held at the office building we raided?"

Allie shook her head. "I don't know. I have to admit, I've been wondering that. I'm actually wondering if the man is still alive—or if he's just more loyal to Nevsky than to Daria after all."

"Would she run to him for help?"

She raised a brow. "We may have only been working together for a year, but we sure are on the same wavelength." He smiled and Allie nodded. "I've come to the conclusion that he would be her first choice to turn to for help—as long as she doesn't feel like he betrayed her in some way with her father. Then again, she knows that I know she may run to him and avoid him altogether if she really doesn't want to be found."

"Why not run to you?" He shook his head. "I keep coming back to that."

"I don't know," she said quietly. "I had her trust. She was glad to see me in the office. But something sent her running. If she thought I was in danger because of her, she'd stay away. If she thought I betrayed her somehow, she'd stay away. If she saw someone she *thought* would betray her, she'd stay away."

"So, it's possible she could think she's protecting people she cares about by running."

"Yes, she's that type. She sure didn't get her father's genes."

At the nearest superstore, he pulled into a parking spot off to the side. "Duck down and keep thinking. I'll be right back."

"And get cortisone cream for my stitches, will you? They're itching me to death."

Allie stayed hunkered down on the floorboard of the Suburban. Not exactly the most comfortable spot she'd ever been in, but not the worst either. While Linc shopped, she texted Henry and filled him in.

He texted back:

Where are you going to stay?

> Haven't figured that out yet. Will let you know where I land.

My offer stands.

> I know. Thanks, but I don't see that working. You live in a very tight-knit neighborhood. People would notice. LOL

Yeah, I thought about that. I have another place that would work for you.

> Really? Where?

It's kind of my getaway man cave thing. I go there to wind down and de-stress. You're welcome to it. It's about thirty minutes outside of Columbia.

> You're not married and have no kids. Why do you need a man-cave?

Do you want it or not?

Ouch. Touchy subject? She considered it. And couldn't say she wasn't tempted. But she didn't want to be that far away from where she figured Daria was probably hiding out. On the same streets she ran to a year ago.

That's okay, Henry. Thanks.

If you change your mind, let me know. What's the next step?

Finding Daria and the information she has on her father.

Do you have a lead?

Did she? Not really. But . . . she did have an idea.

Maybe. I'll let you know how it pans out.

Details?

Will let you know when I figure them out.

I'll be waiting to hear.

Once I find Daria—or the information she has on her father—or hopefully both—we can grab him and put him away for good.

Until then, we brainstorm. Keep me posted.

Allie set the phone on the floor beside her and closed her eyes. What was taking Linc so long? It was funny, but seated on the floorboard with the doors locked, she felt safe. Probably the safest she'd felt in a very long time—like since the night she'd watched her family be slaughtered by a seventeen-year-old kid.

Hate for the shooter welled and she stuffed it down, drawing on years of training to control her emotions. This had to end. She needed to find her family's killer in order to gain closure once and for all. And ask the burning question that had haunted her for the last fifteen years.

Why?

If she could just find out why, then maybe she could finally put her family—and her own restless spirit—to rest. Unfortunately, that was proving much harder than she'd anticipated when she joined the Bureau.

The key, of course, was Nevsky, but the man was as elusive as smoke. And while she'd been in his home and cooked his meals, she'd had very little interaction with him. Certainly not enough to glean any useful information about anyone working for him. He had a handful of assassins at his disposal. Other than what she'd found in his office about the military equipment he was stealing and selling to the highest bidder, she was loath to admit she hadn't uncovered anywhere near as much as she'd thought she would. And Annie hadn't gotten back to Henry about what she'd found on the laptop.

But at least it was done and nothing else would disappear from the base to wind up who knew where. Henry would have taken care of that situation and arrests of involved military personnel had already been made. At least at that base. The others would be on high alert and double-checking their inventory logs.

But Nevsky was still out there working his evil. Once again, he'd slipped through the net without breaking a sweat. It was infuriating. However, she'd have to come back to him later—and Radchenko.

The big question was Daria. Where would she go?

She sent the girl another text.

> Daria, please let me know you're safe.

> Daria
> I'm safe. Quit texting me. I don't want anything more to do with you. I'm turning off my phone now so don't bother trying to track it.

She texted Linc.

> Daria texted! See if you can track her phone.

Linc

On it.

To Daria:

Please, tell me where you are. How can we help?

Two minutes passed without another answer from the teen. The door locks clicked up, jerking her from her thoughts, and her fingers curled around her weapon as her adrenaline chased her fatigue and sense of safety away.

When the door opened and Linc slid into the driver's seat, Allie relaxed her hold on the gun with a slow sigh. "Did you ask Annie to try and track Daria's phone? I don't know how long we've got until she goes dark again."

"I did. She's working on it and will let me know if she gets a hit. What about you? Everything okay?"

"Yes. Quiet. It's actually been peaceful for a few moments."

He raised a brow when she didn't bother to elaborate. "Got your stuff. Hope it's the right kind. I'm not used to shopping for hair color or makeup—even with three sisters."

"I'm sure it's fine. As long as it will turn me from a blonde to a brunette, we're good."

"It'll do that."

An hour later, Allie stared in the cracked mirror. If she passed herself on the street, she wouldn't look twice. He'd thrown in a pair of scissors and she'd cut about four inches off her hair so the dark ends barely brushed her shoulders.

Add the black-rimmed, nerdy-looking glasses, the subtle makeup, and an extra layer of clothing, and the disguise was the best she was going to do without professional intervention.

She took another look and decided she was okay with that.

When she returned to the truck and climbed in, Linc looked at her and blinked.

"Well? How do I look?" she asked.

He gaped. "Allie?"

"Guess that answers that question."

"You don't look like you. At all."

She shot him a wry smile. "I think that's the whole point."

"Yeah. Right. Of course. Good job, though."

"Thanks." She buckled up. "So, I've got an idea."

"Tell me while I hit that drive-thru next door. I'm starving."

He drove through a Steak 'n Shake and parked while they ate their burgers and fries.

Allie took a sip of the chocolate shake. "I want to go back to Nevsky's house."

He paused, a french fry suspended midair. "You what?"

"Just listen."

"Okay."

"Daria was going to show me what she did with the evidence. I feel like it's hidden in the house. Most specifically, the pool house."

"Why's that?"

"Because that's where she wanted to go after finding me in her father's office, but we were stopped by James, one of the bodyguards, and rerouted."

"That's when you went up to her room?"

"Yes. Daria's out there somewhere. Maybe we can find the evidence she was hiding. Or maybe there's something that will tell us where she ran to."

"All right. But how are you planning on getting into the pool house to search?"

"I don't know if I can, but I want to go by there and do some recon. Then maybe consult with Henry and see if we can come up with an idea for a distraction or something to get Nevsky out of the house."

"Want to set off Nevsky's fire alarm?"

She gave a light snort. "Don't think that would work." A pause.

"What if we have a massive police presence around his house? Think that would chase him out?"

"Might, but it could just shut him down instead and he could decide to hibernate."

She groaned, then narrowed her eyes. "No, I just thought of something even better."

"What?"

"You remember that case where that guy took his family hostage and we learned he was terrified of snakes?"

"I remember Mark shoving a few inside and the guy ran out screaming."

"Right."

He shook his head. "That could have gone way south. I still can't believe it actually worked."

"Me either, but it did."

"Yeah, but remember the chewing out we got, and it wasn't even our idea. I'm not ready to go there again."

"Well, I'm dead, so I'm not really worried about that. My point is, Nevsky's afraid of bees."

"Is he allergic?"

"I don't think so. He's phobic because that's how his brother died. He carries two EpiPens on him at all times and keeps one in every room of the house. The man spends a fortune on them."

"Okay, so what are you thinking?"

"Can we pump some bees into his bedroom? Or even just his house. I guarantee you he'd be out of that house so fast it'd make your head spin. And he'd probably put it on the market the next day."

"Are you even serious?"

"Not really, but do you have a better plan?"

"I'm working on it."

10

So," Allie said, "no bees."

"Nope. I'm not saying we should do nothing, I just think we should do smart."

"I'm all for doing smart."

"Then it's time to call in reinforcements."

"Your family?"

"Yeah. Izzy at least. Chloe could bring Hank if we had something for him to sniff out." His sister Chloe had married Blake MacCallum five months ago and loved working with her K-9 partner, Hank. She'd be happy to help if she could. "Brady and Derek can tap into their resources. I'd have to see who was available."

"Why don't you text them and see?" She looked away. "I still need to get inside tonight, though. I don't know how much time Daria has left. If any."

After sending the group text, Linc drove the twenty miles to Nevsky's home while Allie described the best way to get in if they were able to disarm the alarm. "He probably changed the code to the gate and the house," she said.

"Maybe."

"Let's take a look and see what we can see."

After a drive-by sweep of the front, Linc rolled to a stop at the

99

back of the house. The same spot he and Henry had parked the surveillance van two weeks ago. Had it only been two weeks? Darkness had fallen about fifteen minutes ago, and Linc had to admit he welcomed it, even as music blared from the pool area.

"Well, that changes things a bit, doesn't it?" Allie asked.

"A party. He's throwing a party. Celebrating how many lives he's ruined?" He wanted to race into the midst of it and arrest them all. Fortunately, restraint edged out the disgust.

"Probably."

For a moment, they sat in silence, eyes on the house in the distance, easily discernible thanks to the floodlights. "Sitting by the pool, you'd never know it was dark outside unless you looked up," Linc muttered. "I'd hate to have his power bill."

"No kidding."

Linc lifted the binoculars he'd grabbed from the console. The wrought-iron fence topped with spikes encased the large expanse of grass. Beyond that lay the pool and the pool house—Daria's destination the day Allie's cover had been officially blown. Music blared, people milled, guards walked, caterers paid close attention to empty glasses and plates.

"Wait a minute," Allie said, "something's weird."

"Weird how?"

"There wasn't a guard at the front gate."

"I noticed that too." He swept the binoculars to the front gate. "We can get onto the property without being noticed, I think."

"How many people do you see around the pool and is anyone near the pool house?"

With the binoculars held to his eyes, he counted. "I'd say there are around fifty people at the pool. In all manner of dress. From bathing suits to shorts and T-shirts to more formal attire."

"So, we'll fit in."

"Yeah, we'd fit in. I'm just not sure it's wise to do this without backup."

"I think it's time you had a makeover," she said.

"What?"

"Time for you to change your appearance too. If Nevsky's in there—and I'm assuming he is—he knows what you look like, thanks to his spy's pictures."

For the next fifteen minutes, she transformed him, using the scissors and the makeup. "Where are your glasses?"

He flinched. "I don't need them."

"Now's not the time to be vain. Take the contacts out and use your glasses."

With a heavy sigh, he obeyed, only because she was right. The fact that she knew him well enough to know he kept a lens case and solution in his console sent a pang through his chest. But he didn't know her nearly as well as he'd thought he did. And yet . . . he did.

She slipped out of the SUV and shut the door. Linc did the same. For a moment, she stood still, rubbing her palms down the sides of her jean shorts. "You're probably right. This is very likely the worst plan in the history of worst plans, but . . . I'm ready when you are."

"This isn't like you, Allie," he said softly.

She turned hard eyes to his. Then gave an involuntary shudder before looking away. "I've always done things by the book," she said, her voice as quiet as his. "This time, it's a little different."

"Because of Daria?"

"Yes. Mostly. But also because it feels like the rules have changed. Like I'm off-kilter or for some reason, I'm playing with a partial deck—or someone is stacking the deck to make me look like the fool."

"Nevsky?"

"He's one of them."

"Who else?"

A shrug. "That's a conversation for another time."

The mysterious nature of her words perplexed him, but he let it slide.

"You ready?" she asked as she started for the gate without waiting for his answer.

"Allie, hold up."

She stopped. "If you keep calling me Allie, you're going to blow my disguise," she said softly.

"What should I call you then?"

"Nina." She said the name with a soft smile.

The nickname meant something to her. Interesting. He'd have to ask her about it. At some point. Like when they weren't looking for missing teenagers—or chasing killers.

Which would probably be never.

So, he'd ask her about it soon—assuming he lived to do so. He tried to ignore the fact that she'd just revealed one more piece of information that he hadn't known about her. "Call me Rick."

"Any special reason why?"

"First name that came to mind."

"Ah." At the gate, she punched in the code, then let out a low laugh. "Unbelievable. He didn't change it."

"He didn't think you'd live long enough to warrant going to the trouble." Linc thought about pulling his weapon as he followed her through the gate, but supposed that would defeat the attempt to fit in.

Under cover of darkness, they ran across the grass, halting just before they'd step into the area illuminated by the floodlights.

"Why didn't we call Henry about this?" he whispered.

"Because he'd talk us out of it—or simply order us not to do it."

"Right."

"Hey, you two, are you coming to join the party? Hey! Who are you?" They both froze for a split second.

"We need a better plan," Linc said. "And fast."

102

"I have one." She turned her face to his, wrapped her arms around his neck, and kissed him.

For a moment, Linc stilled. He hadn't forgotten how much he enjoyed kissing her, but it had been a while since he'd done so—and considering that she'd allowed Henry to talk her into deceiving him, he wasn't too sure it was a good idea.

Mostly because kissing her made his brain turn to mush.

Not exactly the safest thing when they were crashing a Mafia head's party. Only the fact that Nevsky wanted to kill her and he needed to be alert allowed him to keep his eyes open and on the people around the pool.

The person who'd called out to them stood waiting, watching.

Allie pulled away and started walking. He noticed her attention was also on the figure at the edge of the pool's concrete. Laughter, followed by a squeal and a loud splash, reached him.

And then they were at the gate. Allie fake-laughed. "We're here. Let the party begin!"

Cheers erupted from the tipsy partiers. The guard shook his head and walked away.

Allie's shoulders rose and fell—the only sign she was battling nerves—then she grabbed his hand and pulled him toward the pool house.

No one stopped them. No one even seemed to notice them at that point.

He followed her, feeling too exposed in the brightly lit area with no COMMS, no one watching his back, and no immediate rescue operation available.

At the pool house, Allie twisted the knob and Linc placed a hand over hers, stopping her. "You realize if we do this, any evidence we find won't be admissible," he whispered and nuzzled her ear in an attempt to keep up the charade. Or so he told himself.

She hesitated. "Yes, it will."

"How's that?"

"Exigent circumstances. Daria's life is in real danger. We're looking for her. She could be inside and be hurt for all we know. Whatever else we might come across is a bonus."

"Hmm . . ." He paused mid nibble. "It might slide. Is anyone else in there?"

"I don't think so, but I'm ready to find out if you'll stop kissing my ear."

"I like kissing your ear." And he did. He just wished he could focus on that instead of making sure no one was going to stop them from entering the pool house—or kill them. So far, they'd earned a few glances, but no one offered to interrupt or question them.

"Linc . . ."

"Rick."

"Right. *Rick*. Anyone watching?"

"Not that I can tell." He released her hand and she let herself inside. He glanced back over his shoulder, expecting to hear the shout of a guard at any moment.

Instead, the music played on. Someone had started a rousing game of limbo, and attention had focused on the ones brave enough to participate.

He followed Allie into the two-story pool house that was slightly larger than his small home.

"Since the party's being catered," Allie said, "it looks like they're not using this tonight for any kind of food prep."

"But there's no guarantee someone won't walk in at any moment for a bathroom break."

"There are closer bathrooms in the game room. They'll probably use those, but let's get started and get out of here."

Allie parted the blinds a fraction to allow some light in, and with his hand on his weapon, Linc swept his gaze around the room to make sure it was truly unoccupied. "Looks clear down here," he murmured. "Let's see what's upstairs."

His phone vibrated. A text from Brady.

Are you all right for the fifth time? I'm outside
the property and Izzy just pulled up. If you don't
answer within twenty seconds, we're coming in.

We're fine. Stay put unless I tell you otherwise.

What have you gotten yourself into?

Will explain later.

He paused.

If you hear gunshots or I don't answer your
texts within sixty seconds of you sending, then
bring in the cavalry.

Gunshots??

Later. Just be alert.

Linc took a moment to note the luxury. With a mother as the chief of police and a lawyer for a father, he'd not grown up doing without. Quite the opposite, in fact. However, this kind of wealth took his breath away—and nauseated him at the way it had been achieved.

Nevsky wasn't the first rich man Linc had gone after who thought he was above the law, but he was the one he wanted most to catch. Probably because the man had tried to blow him up, and caused Allie to change—almost overnight—into someone he barely recognized. She'd grown harder and more closed off than when he'd first met her—and that was saying something.

It hurt, but he shouldn't be surprised by her betrayal. No, not betrayal, but . . . something close. Clamping down on his emotions, he focused. They cleared the second floor, then returned to the first.

Allie's gaze bounced and he could almost hear her brain working.

"See anything that looks like something Daria would use as a hiding place?" he finally asked.

"Not yet." She went to the computer on the desk. "You don't think she'd store it on here, do you?"

"You know her better than I do."

"She wanted me to come to the pool house that day for some reason." Allie rummaged through the desk contents and found nothing. "Can you get into that computer?"

He wiggled the mouse. "You have the password?"

"No, but I do have a flash drive." She handed it to him. "Can Annie work her magic once more?"

"Can't hurt to try." He stood guard at the door while he put the call in to Annie. She answered in spite of the late hour. "Are you at home?" he asked.

"Yes. What do you need?"

"I've got that flash drive that allows you to do crazy things with a computer. Can you get into this one?"

"Sure. Hold on. I just need to get to my computer."

"This is your night off, huh?"

"Night off? What's that?"

Linc chuckled. "Exactly. You need a vacation."

"And you don't?"

"Hmm."

The keyboard clicked. "All right," she said, "what am I looking for?"

"Security footage that's been downloaded from a camera."

"Okay, that narrows it down a bit. I'm going to copy the hard drive and do some searching."

"Anything on the other laptop Allie found in Nevsky's office?"

Silence.

"Annie?" A huff from the other end reached him. He frowned. "Annie?"

"No," she finally said. "And I'm embarrassed about that."

"About what?"

"That I haven't found anything!"

106

"Annie?"

"What?"

"If you haven't found anything, then there's probably nothing to find." More silence. "Right?"

"Yes. That's the conclusion that I've come to," she said in a rush. "But I know what Allie risked to get the information off that computer, and I thought for sure there'd be something on there and . . . there's not. I mean, I keep checking, trying different things, but there's nothing."

"Then we'll find something somewhere else. Examine this one and see what turns up."

"Getting access right now. I'll keep you updated."

He hung up and turned to find Allie with her hands on her hips and her brow raised. "Nothing on Nevsky's office computer?"

"No."

"How is that possible?"

"He's a very smart man. Even though he keeps his office locked up, I can see that he wouldn't take a chance and leave things on a laptop that could incriminate him." He shrugged. "We knew it was a long shot."

She rubbed her eyes. "This computer isn't going to be any different, is it?"

"Probably not. Unless you're right about Daria wanting to show you something on it."

"Well, while Annie's working on that end, let's finish up in here."

They worked in silence before Linc stopped to examine one of the paintings on the wall. The name in the bottom right-hand corner lifted his brow. "Daria? Wow. She's talented."

"Very." Allie looked up from her search of the sideboard behind the dining table.

"This seems to indicate that Nevsky is proud of her," Linc said. "That doesn't jibe with the man who wants to kill her."

"Those were done when her mother was alive. She hung them."

"Ah. What happened to her mother?"

"Car wreck two years ago."

"That's right. It was ruled an accident?"

"That's what the report said." Allie stood and joined him to study the painting. "She was married to Nevsky, so who knows?" She sighed. "How are we on the game?"

"I'll check." He slipped to the window and glanced through the parted blinds. "Looks like it might be wrapping up," he said.

"Do you want to watch the door while I search upstairs?" she asked. "There are two bedrooms and two baths. It shouldn't take long."

"I'm right behind you. It'll go faster if we're both looking. And besides, we'll hear if someone comes in."

She led the way and quickly had their search of the second floor turn up void. Back on the first floor in the kitchen area, Allie frowned. "Nothing."

"What if she had it with her at the office building and Nevsky already got it?" Linc asked.

"She didn't."

"How do you know?"

"Because she hadn't been tortured and she was still alive."

True.

"I think we got there before Nevsky did," Allie said. "I know she'd been there at least a day before I got her text message. I think Nevsky was letting her sweat it out, using psychological warfare, so to speak. She knows what he's capable of and he was letting her think about that."

"Then we got her out just in time."

"Yes, but if he gets his hands on her again, he won't hesitate to start right in with the physical stuff."

"And we can't let that happen."

"Right. We're going to have to slip into the main house and into Daria's bedroom."

"That's going to be tough. No one's looked at us twice out here, but inside . . ." He blew out a low breath.

"I know."

He nodded. "I've got your back."

"Do we have a plan?" Allie murmured.

"To not get killed."

"I'm good with that."

Instead of a plan, they had an opportunity and were going to go with it. It wouldn't be the first time. From the pool house, they made their way around the edge of the sparkling aqua water, nodding and smiling as though they were supposed to be there. Allie snitched a glass of champagne from one of the trays and lifted it in a toast to the couple next to her. They grinned and did the same, then sipped.

Without taking her eyes from the milling people, Allie set her glass on the edge of the table and grasped Linc's hand, her heart still trembling from the kiss and ear nuzzling, no matter how much she tried to act unaffected. She missed him. Missed sharing laughter, movies, and pizza nights. Missed their in-depth conversations about faith and God. He always made her think.

But . . . she had to do what she was meant to do. Take down Nevsky and find the one who'd murdered her family.

Linc gripped her fingers and pulled her toward the open door that led to the game room. Inside, the crowd thickened, if that was even possible, but Allie was grateful. Sweat dripped from her brow and she dabbed at it, hoping it didn't run through the heavy foundation base she'd applied.

He put an arm around her shoulders. "So, which way?"

"Up the stairs to the next floor, then up the next set. At least we don't have to worry about the alarm."

Linc dropped his arm and took her hand, threading through the crowd.

Allie led them up the stairs, and as they reached the first floor, just off the kitchen, she heard treading on the steps behind them. A quick glance back gave her a glimpse of black clothing.

"Behind us." She dove for the pantry door and yanked Linc inside with her.

He swung the door closed and pulled her toward him. "Ready for another kiss?"

"Wha—?"

And then *he* was kissing *her*. She was going to have a hard time sticking to her resolution that she was completely wrong for him if they didn't stop with the kissing.

The door opened.

Lips still connected with Linc's, Allie glanced up to find James Killian, the bodyguard she'd seen the most while employed as Nevsky's cook. His eyes met hers for a fraction of a second before she dropped her lids and slid her hand to her Glock sitting snugly in her shoulder holster. Linc reached for his as well, his hand grazing her hip as he wrapped his fingers around the grip.

Killian was still lasering them with his dark gaze.

Linc lifted his head and pressed Allie's face against his shoulder.

"Get a room," Killian muttered. "You're not supposed to be up here. The party's at the pool and in the game room only."

"Right," Linc said. Allie stood still, her weapon snug against her palm, waiting, ready to act if Killian decided to play rough. "Give us a minute and we'll be right down."

"You've got sixty seconds," Killian said. "I'll be looking for you. If you're not there, I'll find you and escort you off the property myself—and it won't be pleasant if you make me do that." Confident that they would obey him, he shoved the door wide open and spun around.

"He's an arrogant one, isn't he?" Linc whispered.

"Yes." When Killian had disappeared down to the game room again, Allie stepped back and sucked in a lungful of air. "Hurry," she urged.

"That was James Killian," Linc said. One of Nevsky's most trusted bodyguards and suspected assassins.

"I recognized him." She stepped into the kitchen and motioned for Linc to follow.

"Did he recognize you?"

"No. At least I don't think so. He makes my teeth itch, though." He shut the door behind them.

Allie led the way through the familiar kitchen. Three of the caterers were working at the island, their movements efficient and well rehearsed. They earned a glance from each of the workers before being dismissed as no one important—or no one they should speak to. She motioned for Linc to follow into the living area.

And stopped. One entire side of the room was windows that faced the pool. She turned to Linc. "If we keep going," she whispered, "we're going to be completely exposed in front of those windows. If Killian's out there, he may see us. And I don't trust him not to just shoot through the windows. It's not like anyone here would say a word about it."

"Is there another way to the second floor?"

"Not without passing a lot of windows."

Linc glanced around the column. "Yeah, I see him. He's got his eyes on the game room door." Which was right below the windows they needed to pass to reach the stairs. "We'll have to wait for him to turn his back. I'll go first."

"Why? So you can draw fire if Killian's watching?"

He darted across the room and was on the other side near the stairs before she could blink. "You rat," she whispered. He held up a hand, palm facing her while he watched the windows from behind the cover of the large recliner. Seconds ticked past. Sounds from the kitchen intensified as her adrenaline made her nerves hum. Then Linc motioned to her with a flick of his hand.

She mimicked his example, ducking low and keeping as many pieces of the heavy furniture between her and the windows as possible. When she reached him, she looked up at him and found his gaze on the windows, weapon aimed.

"Killian's out there and he's facing this way."

"Did he see us?"

"I don't think so."

She punched his biceps and he frowned. "Hey, what was that for?"

"You went first."

"The opportunity presented itself and I took it."

"Always the protector, aren't you?" She refused to admit there was no heat in her words.

His eyes softened. "For you? As long as there's breath in my body—even if I am still mad that you and Henry let me think you were dead."

Allie ignored the last part of his statement and silently admitted she couldn't get angry about his protective instincts. She knew he trusted her skills as an agent, but as a man who believed himself in love with her, he saw it as his duty to protect her as well.

Having had a protector once upon a time—and then been betrayed by him—she'd set out to never need protecting. Ever. However, Linc had worked his way under her skin—and into her heart, if she was honest—and now she wasn't sure what to do with him. The truth was, she found the whole thing unsettling.

And comforting.

Which could prove to be a deadly distraction for him. And her.

She drew in a deep breath and led the way up the steps, gun still pulled, safety off. Now that they were out of the area where the party was, there was no telling who was in the house. With cautious steps, she rounded the corner at the top of the staircase.

And saw nothing and no one.

On silent feet, she slipped into Daria's room and Linc followed, shutting the door behind them. "What are we looking for?" he asked.

"Anything that could be used to store information from a security system. A flash drive, an SD card, a laptop?" She paused.

"What is it?"

"She had her laptop with her when we rescued her. Before she disappeared."

"You think she'd keep the evidence on there?"

"Unlikely. But even if she did, I think she'd have a backup somewhere. She's smart and thinks like an agent."

"Or someone used to living with a man she knows is a murderer," Linc said.

"Or that."

Allie picked up the picture she'd noticed that last day here. Daria's face still held the same smile, but Allie's attention zeroed in on the cabin in the background. And she knew. A laugh escaped her.

"What is it?" Linc asked.

"I know where she'd go," she said softly.

11

The door burst in.

Instinct sent Allie diving for cover behind the bed.

Less than a second behind Allie, Linc hunkered down as a spate of bullets hit the wall behind them.

"You think I don't know who you are?" the shooter spat. "FBI Special Agent Linc St. John? You think you can hide behind some makeup and glasses?"

Another round of bullets flew over the bed and slammed into the wall behind them and the mattress in front of them.

Rolling, Linc swung his weapon around the end of the bed and fired back. Over the ringing in his ears, he heard a grunt, then running footsteps.

Allie beat him out the door by a nanosecond. He snagged her arm and pulled her back inside, slammed and locked the door. She yanked away from him. "What are you doing?"

"We're outnumbered and outgunned. We're not going after him."

"Right. So letting them trap us in here is a better idea?"

"You got out once, we can do it again the same way."

"True. This way." Allie went to the window and shoved it up. Just like when she'd been with Daria, she climbed out and pulled herself up on the roof. Linc followed and she placed a hand on his arm and motioned for him to sit beside her.

His phone buzzed and he realized it had been going off for quite a while. "Brady and Izzy are on the way in."

"Tell them to stay back unless they've got help. They'll get slaughtered."

He tapped in the text and pushed send. Allie walked up the roof, déjà vu hitting her hard. When she reached the top, she looked out. "Whoa."

Linc crested the roof. "What is it?"

"Come look."

He made his way to her and drew in a deep breath. "Well, I should have known this might happen."

"Why?"

"I didn't answer my texts."

"Your brother and sister called in the reinforcements?"

"Yep."

Flashing blue lights from more vehicles than she could count lit up the night. Partiers, realizing their good time was coming to an abrupt ending, scattered. Only to be stopped by the advancing army of law enforcement who'd drawn their weapons and were yelling orders.

"Well, this didn't go as well as I'd hoped," Allie muttered, watching the scene play out.

"This was an off-the-charts no-no. We're going to be in so much trouble," he said.

"We? You mean you. Not me."

"What do you mean?"

"I'm dead, remember? I believe that makes me exempt."

Linc rolled his eyes, then narrowed them, focusing on the scene below. "The shooter's still around somewhere."

"With an automatic weapon."

"I'm going after him."

"The officers know he's still here. They'll be looking for him."

"I'm going to help. Stay here until I let you know it's safe for you to come down without anyone seeing you."

He started down and she caught his forearm. "I'm doing the right thing, aren't I?" she asked when he met her gaze. "Staying dead is very deceptive, and while I get why Henry wants me to do it, I . . . I . . ."

"Yes?"

"I don't know. I can't put my finger on it, but something's bothering me about it."

"You know what bothers me?"

"What?"

"We never did see Nevsky tonight."

She nodded. "I noticed that. I also noticed that Killian recognized you but didn't seem to know who I was."

"He might suspect."

"Even though he thinks I'm dead?" She shook her head. "I doubt it. I'm safe for now. But you're not. Nevsky's going to come looking for you for sure now."

Linc rubbed a hand over his chin. "No, not if we get to Killian first and keep him from talking. He's probably still around here, because I think I managed to wing him with my shot."

"How are we going to keep him from talking to Nevsky? He could have already sent him a message or called him."

"Only one way to find out." Linc nodded to the chaos down below. "The place is surrounded. A few people might have managed to slip away, but not many. I'm going to see if Killian was rounded up."

"If you hit him, he's going to look for a place to lay low until everything dies down. He won't head to the hospital."

"No, he'll go dark. He may even be hiding in the house somewhere. Any ideas where? A hidden room or passage?"

"No, nothing like that. At least nothing that I ever saw."

116

Linc gave a low sigh. "We need to find him. I know what he looks like. I'm going to see if I can spot him, but I don't want to leave you alone."

"I'll be fine. I'm going to sit up here and observe. Just don't let Killian spot you first."

"Yeah." He paused.

"What is it?" she asked.

He glanced around, then shook his head. "The next time I'm part of a raid, remind me to check the roof first."

Linc made his way down off the roof as discreetly as possible and did a quick recon of the area.

Within minutes, all of the partygoers had been moved to a safe area out of range of anyone who might be inclined to start shooting again. A quick scan proved none of them were James Killian. Linc had flashed his credentials so much, he finally clipped his badge to his belt so he could move amongst the officers unencumbered.

Finally, he joined Brady and Izzy in Daria's bullet-riddled bedroom. He glanced at the floor. Blood. Not a puddle, but definitely a lot of drops.

Izzy frowned at him. "This is a crime scene. You can't be in here." Her eyes dropped to the badge on his belt. "Oh, sorry. FBI? You guys got here fast."

He'd forgotten about his disguise. "Izzy, it's me."

Her eyes went wide, and Brady blinked before he let out a guffaw. "Linc?"

"Yeah."

"What are you doing here?" Izzy asked, shooting Brady a "shut up" look. Brady ignored her.

"Working a case," Linc said.

"What? You're supposed to be on medical leave."

"I am."

"Right." She narrowed her eyes. "Are you here by yourself?"

Linc paused. "No, I had someone else with me, but she wasn't involved in the shooting—other than to survive it."

Brady and Izzy exchanged a frown. "We'll need to talk to her too," Brady said.

"You can't, and I can't explain why you can't. And if you have a problem with that, I'll give you Henry's number."

Izzy's brows rose high enough to sweep under her bangs. She and Brady exchanged another frown. "Can you talk off the record?"

"No."

"Wow. This have anything to do with Nevsky's bombing of Allie's and your boat?"

"Absolutely. Now, I've got to go find our shooter."

"We've got cops all over the place looking for him. Linc, what's going on?"

He ran a hand over his new haircut. "It's a long story. You'll have to work with the Bureau on this one." He pointed to the blood on the floor. "I've been looking for him and came back to get confirmation that I hit him."

"We saw the blood."

He met her gaze. "Did you find his weapon?"

"No."

"Which means he still has it with him." He hurried toward the door. "Can you radio and see if anyone's rounded up a guy with a bullet in him?"

Izzy put out the call and within seconds she nodded. "An officer said he thought he saw someone get into the back of the ambulance behind the pool house."

"Behind the pool house? The scene hasn't been cleared," he said, backing out the door. "He didn't check the ambulance?"

"He said he started to and was rerouted to another part of the house."

"By who?"

"I don't know."

"Can you find out?"

"Of course."

While Izzy worked on that, Linc raced down the stairs to the pool area. With a "shots fired" and an "officer needs help" call put out, every cruiser in the vicinity had turned out. Which would help with crowd control and taking statements and information. He then headed around to the back of the pool house and found the ambulance exactly where it had been reported to be.

From her perch next to the chimney, Allie had a good view of the activity below, near the pool house and beyond to where Linc's truck sat out of view beyond the wrought-iron fence. Why had Linc gone behind the pool house? More than once, she wished they had COMMS so she could hear everything going on.

Slowly, carefully, she made her way to the other side of the roof so she would be hidden from all the commotion on the pool side and ran to the point where she could surface and watch Linc. He'd exited the house and scanned the area, looking for the shooter, no doubt.

Just like she'd been doing since Linc had left her. The helicopter continued to make pass after pass, and she had to keep ducking behind anything she could find. Fortunately, there were several chimneys and turbine vents that shielded her. But it made for slow going.

Finally, she caught sight of him checking out the ambulance in semidarkness. With her weapon tucked against the small of her back, she took her time, making her way to the bottom edge of the roof. Hoping the gutter would hold her, she closed her fingers around it, then swung over and down to the ground.

She landed just in time to slip behind a bush as two officers walked past her, no doubt doing a perimeter check, still searching for the shooter. Fortunately, they weren't searching the bushes.

Any other time, she'd want to write them up for being slack, but tonight she was just glad.

Once they were out of sight, she opened her mouth to call out to Linc, but snapped it shut just in case anyone else was close by. She'd wait for Linc to finish with the ambulance, then let him know she was there.

Three other ambulances waited out front. So, why had anyone allowed this one on the property?

Linc glanced at the roof. Allie was nowhere to be seen, but he had a feeling she was still there. Probably behind one of the chimneys. At least he hoped so.

He turned back to the ambulance that was parked to the side with the lights off—his first clue to approach with caution. The pool lights illuminated his path to the pool house, but his trek down the side took out of sight of the main house and the stretch of public road that ran in front of the home.

The back door of the vehicle was closed, the interior lights off—his second clue that something was possibly off. The third clue was that feeling in the pit of his belly that compelled him to draw his weapon. He understood Allie's weird saying about her teeth itching.

With his back to the driver's side of the vehicle, he inched forward. Looked in the window. Nothing. He returned to the back and twisted the knob. The door flew open and a fist landed against his temple, sending him stumbling backward.

Pain ricocheted through him and he hit the ground, ears buzzing, spots dancing before his eyes. A gun rested against his head before he had a chance to react. "Time to collect my reward," a voice hissed.

Killian.

Linc bucked and rolled. The pistol fell away. A low *thwap* sounded next to his ear and the bullet buried itself in the ground much too close to his head.

Another weapon cracked and his attacker took off. Footsteps pounded away from him. A figure darted past him as he rolled to his feet, blinking. Allie?

His vision cleared enough for him to see the shooter and Allie disappear into the wooded area. "Hey!" With no time to grab his phone and call for help and no way to snag the attention of fellow officers, he spared a quick glance into the back of the ambulance to see two paramedics and one police officer. All three were dead with holes in their foreheads. No one had heard the shots because of the silencer on Killian's pistol. The automatic weapon lay on the floor of the ambulance. At least Killian wasn't carrying that too.

Linc bolted after the fleeing killer and Allie, his hand fishing his phone from his pocket. He hit the tree line and stumbled to a stop to listen. Which way? He narrowed his eyes, the darkness heavy, with only the slight light the moon offered.

A crunch to his left swiveled him around. He pushed through the undergrowth, his right hand wrapped around the grip of his gun, his left cradling his phone. One-handed, he texted Brady,

In woods. Help.

It was awkward, but he got it sent without slowing down. He could hear footsteps crunching branches up ahead.

A grunt and a sharp cry.

He put on an extra burst of speed, dodging limbs, pushing around bushes, not even bothering to try to disguise his approach.

He shot through the tree line and exited the wooded area to find Allie on the ground with the shooter, her fingers clamped around the man's wrist, doing her best to force the gun he held away from her head.

12

Allie's strength had just about ended when suddenly she was free. Linc had tackled the man on top of her and the two now grappled in the grass beside her.

She rolled, back throbbing, head pounding, her body screaming its reminder that she hadn't yet fully healed from the boat explosion.

She ignored its protests and scrambled to her feet.

Linc was losing the fight. Killian had the upper hand and was gradually moving the weapon toward Linc's head—just like he'd done with her. She took three steps and connected her foot with his chin. Exactly like she used to do to the soccer ball on the high school field.

Killian dropped like a stone, his weapon tumbling from his fingers.

Coach would have been proud.

Linc swiped up the gun and rolled away from the man, who now lay on the ground blinking at the night sky. Killian's jaw hung at an odd angle and pain-filled groans escaped him. Allie stepped over to Linc and took Killian's gun from him while he held his own Glock on the prisoner.

Breathing hard, she ordered her pulse to slow.

Sirens sounded, coming toward them. She shoved the weapon

into Linc's hand. "Wipe it. My prints are on it obviously, but we have to turn it in. Killian recognized me. Don't let him talk, please." She slipped back into the woods to watch.

With shaking hands—thanks to her still-rushing adrenaline—she dialed Henry's number.

He picked up on the first ring. "Allie?"

"Linc has James Killian in custody," she said, not bothering with a greeting. "And I imagine as soon as Nevsky finds out that one of his top assassins is going to be questioned and bargained with, he'll send someone after him."

"What? What did you do, Allie?"

"Explanations will have to wait."

"I'll get him into protective custody. Are you okay?"

"Fine. But, Henry?"

"Yeah?"

"Killian knows I'm alive. He saw me. If he tells Nevsky in some lame attempt to prove his loyalty—"

"We're toast."

"Well, I am, at least. Not sure how you are."

Silence. Then a low sigh. "I'll take care of it. Make sure he doesn't talk to anyone."

"He's got a broken jaw, so he's not going to say much, but he can still write. He's also going to need medical attention."

Another sigh. "Where are you?"

"Nevsky's house."

"What?" She flinched at his yell. "Tell Linc to bring—"

"Other cops are headed this way," she said. "I'm hiding. Call him and tell him where to meet you."

"Stay out of sight, I've got this." Henry hung up.

When Linc lifted his phone to his ear a second later, Allie pressed her palms to her eyes. This had been a ridiculous risk. But it had been beneficial. She now knew where to look for Daria. With one last glance at Linc, she hurried to his Suburban, climbed into the passenger side onto the floorboard, and pulled her phone from her back pocket.

> **Allie**
> Daria, text me. I need you to let me know you're safe.

Daria
I'm fine.

Allie caught her breath. A response!

> Where are you? Why did you run?

Leave me alone. You're just like all the rest. I can't trust anyone. Now stop looking for me.

> I don't understand. What do you mean I'm like all the rest?

Silence.

> Daria? What about the evidence against your father? I need that if you're ever going to have any kind of normal life free of fear. I need to put him in prison.

It is easier to forgive an enemy than to forgive a friend.

> What??

William Blake. I like him. Don't text me anymore, Allie. If that's even your real name.

> Please, Daria, tell me where you are.

After ten minutes of silence, Allie gave up hoping that Daria would respond again. And she couldn't even ask Annie to try to trace the messages. Because a dead woman couldn't make phone calls. Frustration pounded.

Soon, she heard the *whomp-whomp-whomp* of a helicopter and figured it would land in the large field where she'd tackled Killian.

The driver's door opened and Allie snapped her gun up. Then lowered it when Linc settled into the driver's seat. "You okay?" he asked.

"Yes. Henry got here fast."

"He's got a lot riding on making sure no one finds out you're alive. He didn't clear the decision for you to be dead with anyone, and if the powers that be find out, he could lose his job. So he's taking Killian back to a safe house where he can keep a muzzle on the guy."

"What about you? You fired your weapon. Don't you have a mountain of paperwork to fill out?"

"I talked to Henry and turned my weapon over to him. I've been released for now, but I'll have to talk to SIRG. I don't think it's going to be a problem convincing them that I complied with the Bureau's policy when it comes to using lethal force." He unlocked the glove box and pulled out a SIG Sauer P226. After he checked it, he slid it into the shoulder holster where his Glock used to be.

"Good, because I think I know where to find Daria."

"Where?"

"At that cabin in the woods."

"The one in the picture?"

"Yes. You remember when I said she had skills?"

"I do."

"Gerard used to take her hunting with him."

Linc raised a brow. "Nevsky approved of that?"

"He didn't approve of much of anything, but if Daria killed a deer, or any other animal, and brought it home, that's the one time Nevsky would offer his praise."

"Guess he's not going to win the Parent of the Year Award, is he? So, where's this cabin?"

"I'm not sure, but I think it may belong to Gerard. If not, he knows where it is."

"Then let's go find Gerard."

One thing they'd learned in their investigation was that Nevsky ran his operation like a legitimate business on the surface. Three shifts of a minimum of two bodyguards on his slow days, and more when he needed them—such as if he felt threatened in any way or needed muscle to convince someone of . . . whatever. All knew they were on call 24/7, but for the most part, they got to have personal lives. It didn't take Annie long to get the address for Gerard's personal residence.

Only it wasn't the cabin.

Gerard Lamb owned a large home near the city in one of the most prestigious neighborhoods. He'd purchased the property the same day Nevsky had closed on his. Both had been cash transactions. Both had bought the houses in their legal names. Both had used the same lawyer.

"He's been on Nevsky's payroll a long time if he's been Daria's bodyguard," Linc said.

"I'd say he warrants watching, but right now he's the least of our worries."

Linc grunted in agreement. "So, who could the cabin belong to?" He asked as he pulled to a stop just beyond Gerard's home.

"I don't know. I sure thought it was Gerard's. I guess he could have it under a bogus name. Or a relative's."

"Or a friend's," Linc said.

"Or it's a rental. Gerard never took Daria out there while I was in the house, or I would have had you track them."

"No, he didn't have much contact with her—other than to do his job and guard her—while you were there."

"Let's ask Annie to check relatives and see if any of them have a log cabin in their name," Allie said. "We can at least rule that out. Then let's get a warrant for Gerard's financials and see if he charged a deposit to a card in case it was a rental."

Linc shrugged. "It's a long shot and could be a huge waste of time."

"So? When has that stopped us?"

She had a point. Some of the best breaks in their cases had been long shots. But they had to measure said long shot against the time and resources it would take up and decide whether it was worth it.

He asked Annie to check, then requested the warrant.

For the next several minutes, they simply watched the house from the street. While the home was large, the front yard wasn't. At the end of a cul-de-sac, the lawn stretched to the curb while an abundance of trees lined the property, giving it the appearance of privacy.

"You see any cameras?" He handed her another set of binoculars and she pressed them to her eyes.

"Yes. On the house. I don't know how far they reach, though."

"I believe I'll just walk up there and knock on the door. You staying in the truck?"

"Think I'll meander around back. The house is practically hidden by the trees except for the front. I won't have any trouble avoiding the cameras unless I try to get in close." She shoved the COMMS into her ear and turned to grab a sweatshirt with a hood from the suitcase on the back seat of his truck. "I'll let you know where the cameras are."

"He might recognize you if he sees you," Linc said, mimicking her actions and placing the COMMS piece in his ear.

"I don't plan to let him see me, but you're not going in there without some kind of backup." She tapped her ear. "At least I'll be able to hear everything and be there if something goes sideways."

Linc gave a slow nod. He'd insist on the same if their roles were reversed.

Once Allie was out of sight in the dark around the side of the house, Linc approached the front door, stood to the side, and rapped on the glass window.

He waited.

When no one appeared after several seconds, he rang the bell. More seconds ticked past.

"Allie?"

"Yes?"

"Anything in the back?"

"No. Right now I'm just scoping the house, but there's nothing alarming. A swimming pool that would be a lot of fun on a warm day, lots of concrete with an outdoor kitchen that would do any chef proud, and landscaping better than Buckingham Palace. But that's about it."

"He's not answering the door."

"Any cars in the garage?"

"Can't tell. No windows."

A pause.

"Linc?" she said.

"Yeah?"

"The back door that leads to the kitchen is cracked open."

Linc tried the front door and the knob turned. "The front is unlocked."

"Does that seem weird to you?"

"Very."

"I'm going in."

"Allie—" He sighed. "Fine, I'll meet you in the kitchen. Be careful."

He pushed the door in with his left hand and swung around the edge, holding his weapon ready with his right. The chill in the house hit him immediately. "Guy likes his home meat-locker friendly," he muttered.

The large three-story foyer was magnificent and Linc noted it absently as he walked through it into the living room, his head swiveling, gun moving back and forth.

"I'm in the kitchen," Allie said. "It's clear in here. And you're right. It's freezing in here. Stepping into the dining room." She fell silent, then, "Talk to me, Linc."

"Heading to the other side of the house."

"How big do you think this place is?"

"Nine thousand square feet or something like that. Should have looked up the floor plan." And they still had three floors to clear. It took them another fifteen minutes to do all but the third.

They met at the bottom of the steps on the second floor and ascended back-to-back.

Linc had complete confidence in Allie's ability to protect his back, and that enabled him to focus on what was in front of him. Specifically, the body sprawled on the king bed in the master bedroom.

Allie stifled a gasp. "That's Gerard."

"No wonder he didn't answer his door," Linc said. He pulled his phone from his pocket. "I've got to call this in, so you're going to have to go if you want to continue being dead."

"Don't call it in yet. A couple of minutes won't matter."

Linc stepped over to the body and Allie almost joined him, but decided she'd better not. This was a crime scene and she was going to have to disappear. But from her position by the door, she had a perfect view of the man.

Gerard, dressed in silk pajama bottoms and no shirt, lay face-down on the bed, his hands clasped above his head, fingers linked. His position chilled her. "He has a bullet hole in the base of his skull, doesn't he?"

Linc shot her a sharp look. "Yes. How'd you know? You suddenly develop X-ray vision?"

"No. I've seen this killer's work before."

"You know who did this?"

"Yes. Gerard hasn't been dead long," she said. "Or he's been well-preserved by the frigid temps in the house."

"The autopsy will tell us—or a timeline of his activity." He paused. "The killer executed him."

Her stomach knotted and nausea churned. "Just like my father and sister," she said softly. "Gregori Radchenko did this."

He frowned at her. "I recognized his work from the photos on your wall, now that you mention it."

"He shot my father first, I think. Then he turned the weapon on my mother and shot her. Then went back to my father, turned him over, and finished him with a bullet at the base of the skull."

"And your mother?"

Allie shoved a strand of hair behind her ear. "I've thought and thought about that. He left her bleeding on the bed, but I think it was only because my sister distracted him and he bolted into the hall to shoot her. When she fell, he did the same thing, turned her over and shot her in the base of the skull. I screamed at him and he shot at me. The first bullet missed. I tried to run and the second one hit me. I went facedown to the floor. He stood over me and placed the gun at the base of my head . . ." She broke off and closed her eyes as the horror of that moment washed over her.

"Allie, you don't have to tell me."

"No, I want you to know. I should have told you long ago, but I just . . ."

"Just what?"

She shuddered, the images she kept buried pushing their way to the front of her mind. "I don't know. It's my past—and yet it's not completely. It's my present too. And even my future."

"Your future?"

"Well, it dictates my future. Because I won't rest until I find him."

"What if you don't find him?"

"Then I'm going to be very, very tired by the time I'm dead. For the second time." He frowned, studying her, and she forced a thin smile. "I'm only halfway kidding, but not finding him is not an option. I need to face him and ask him why. And I need justice for my parents and my sister. Otherwise, I don't think I'll ever have any peace."

"Peace isn't found in justice, Allie."

She rubbed her eyes. "Don't start preaching to me, Linc. I don't want to hear about God right now."

"I'm not preaching. I know you're a believer, so why the sudden distance between you and God?"

"I'm just . . . mad at him. Frustrated with him." She grimaced. "It would almost be easier if I wasn't a believer. Then I wouldn't have all of these emotions toward him."

"We've talked about this. If our peace is dependent upon justice for those who we say deserve it, then we're in big trouble. Trust me on that one." He paused. "Or maybe don't. You may have to discover that on your own."

"I know you're right, I just . . . it's hard with the past coming back at me like a tsunami."

How many times had they discussed God and their beliefs? How many times had she walked away, thinking about everything he'd said, her heart in turmoil because of his words, his absolute certainty in a God she was only just beginning to understand not only existed but loved her as well? In spite of herself. "And I do trust you. With my life. I just can't . . ." She blew out a breath. "You'd think it'd get easier after fifteen years, but some days it's like it happened yesterday."

"Easier? Are you kidding? A trauma like that? I don't know if 'easier' would be the word I'd use. Maybe come to grips with it or an acceptance of it, but not easier."

He gripped her hand and she pulled away. "You can call it in now," she said. "I'll meet you down on the street when you're finished."

"How did you survive the shooting?" he asked, even while he punched in the number that would bring the crime scene unit and detectives who would be assigned the case.

She fell silent while she waited for him to provide the details to the dispatcher.

When he hung up, she gave him a tight smile. "I fought back and I won."

"With a bullet in your back?"

"If I was going to die, I was going to take him with me. Fortunately, the bullet missed my spine. When he placed that gun on the back of my head, I went hysterical. I bucked and rolled fast. My hand came around and struck his arm. The gun flew out of his hand and slipped through the spindles of the balcony railing." She swallowed. "I blacked out after that. When I came to, my face was broken and my neighbor was beside me yelling at dispatch." She shook her head. "I think the only thing that saved me was the element of surprise. And I think it saved my mother a bullet in the back of her head. He had to run and couldn't return to finish the job."

"How do you know this guy?"

"It doesn't matter. What matters is stopping him." Sirens sounded in the distance and Allie darted for the stairs. "Text me. I'll be up the street." She tapped her ear. "Listening."

13

Linc watched her go with a pounding heart, then shook his head as though that would help to dislodge the images she'd planted with her horrifying words. It didn't work. He finally checked the room to make sure she hadn't left any evidence behind, but couldn't think of anything she'd done that might have contaminated the crime scene.

Since she hadn't even entered the bedroom, he thought it would be all right. Her shoes might have tracked in some dirt downstairs, but he'd been everywhere she'd been in the last few days, so he wasn't too worried someone would find anything amiss should they decide they needed samples for testing against whatever they found. Assuming they found anything.

His phone rang. Henry. "Hello?"

"Where are you? Where's Allie?"

"She's safe for now. I, however, am in the middle of a crime scene." Linc filled him in as local officers joined him in the bedroom, weapons drawn. Linc held up his badge and the weapons lowered. "Hold on, Henry." He introduced himself to the officers. Then Izzy and Brady stepped into the room.

"You guys caught this one?" Linc asked.

"Dispatcher told us it was you who called it in," Izzy said. "So we sort of felt obligated. You sure are making this shift extra long."

"Sorry." But not much. Izzy's comment about being obligated was just her being grumpy. There's no way she would have let this case go to someone else and they both knew it.

"What are you doing here?" Brady asked.

"Looking for that missing teenager. I thought this guy would have some information since he'd been seen with her a few times. When I came to question him, the door was open. I cleared the house and found him just like you see him."

Brady walked over to the bed. "Cold-blooded killer, huh?"

"An assassin," Izzy murmured. "Shot him in the base of the head." She leaned closer. "You know, a psychiatrist would have a field day with this one. Like the fact that he made the guy lie on his stomach so he didn't have to face him or some such thing."

"Yeah," Linc said, "I don't think he had any problem facing the guy. This just seems to be his signature."

Izzy shot him a sharp glance. "He's done this before?"

Linc mentally kicked himself for making such a stupid mistake. "Possibly. Excuse me a sec, I've got to finish this call."

"Mom wants an update from you," Izzy said to his back. "She's worried."

"I'll call her when I finish this one." He stepped out of the room into the hall. "All right, Henry, I'm back."

"Have you told them she's alive?"

"No, Henry, I haven't." His superior's question bothered him. "You know me better than that."

"You're right. I'm sorry. I just want this guy so bad and I feel like Allie's our best hope of getting him."

"I know."

"Where are you staying tonight?"

"My truck, with the way things are going right now. I'll let you know where we land."

"I don't like this. Why don't you both come over to my place if you don't want to leave her alone? It's secure and it will give us a chance to hash out the next move."

Linc frowned. "There's nothing really to hash out. We're looking for Daria. Speaking of Daria, do you have the security footage from the day of the raid when she disappeared?"

"I do, but it doesn't show much. I'll send it to you if you don't want to come over here."

Linc paused. Maybe staying at Henry's wasn't such a bad idea.

"Do you have a lead on her?" Henry asked before Linc could respond.

"Yes. At least we think so."

"Tell me."

He explained about Gerard and the cabin. "But we can't find it. Annie's working on it from her end."

"I'll see if I have any resources we can utilize to find it faster. Call me when you get settled. I need to know where you are. My job is kind of on the line here too."

A surge of anger swamped him. "That was your choice." He hung up. Then immediately regretted it. A sigh slipped from him. He had a feeling Henry wouldn't fire him, though. Not yet anyway. Linc would apologize later. Now for his next call.

His mother answered on the second ring. "What do you think you're doing, Linc?"

"Hi to you too."

"Linc."

He sighed. Whenever she said his name like that, he knew better than to be anything less than straight up with her. Still . . . "What do you mean?"

"You were almost killed. You're supposed to be taking it easy, and I find out you're chasing after Nevsky."

"Yes."

"And Henry okayed this?"

135

"In a sense, but I'm still not on the clock. This is my time."

"I know. Time for healing! What is Henry thinking?"

Linc took a silent inventory of his physical well-being. "Mom, my head hurts a bit. I've got some aches and bruises and I need a good night's sleep, but other than that, I'm fine." He paused. "And I'd be back at work already if the days off weren't mandatory until the doc gives me the all clear." He'd missed that appointment, he just realized. "But I can't sit around at home while I can be helping find a missing teenager."

"What's this about you breaking into Nevsky's home?"

"I didn't break in. I simply crashed a party." He heard her take a deep breath and knew she was doing so in an attempt to control her next words. Words he didn't want to hear. "Mom?"

"What?" She sighed.

"It's okay. I promise. I need you to trust me that I'm doing the right thing."

Another sigh. This one of resignation. "You always do the right thing, Linc. You always have, even as a child," she said softly.

"You and Dad are taking security measures, right? Turning on the alarm? Having extra patrols, et cetera?"

"We are. We've seen no sign of Nevsky or any of his hired killers, but we're not letting our guard down and neither is anyone else. We have 24/7 security on the house, and we have an escort to and from work. Extra marshals are on the courthouse when your dad's in court. Izzy and Ryan are staying here while their house is put back together. Chloe and Blake have Hank to warn them of any danger lurking around. Ruthie and Isaac are getting ready to leave for their Israel trip, and Derek is undercover."

"Again?" Linc asked. "He's going to burn out."

"He and Elaine are on the outs again. This is his way of coping."

"Does he have a death wish?"

"I don't know, Linc," she said, her voice heavy. "I just don't know. Call him and talk to him when you can, please."

"I will."

His phone dinged and he looked at the screen before holding the device back to his ear. "I've got to go, Mom. Annie just texted me some information I need to follow up on."

"Bye. Love you, son."

"You too, Mom."

He realized he still had his earpiece in. "Allie?"

"Yeah?"

"You just heard that entire conversation, didn't you?"

"Your side of it."

"Sorry."

"No worries."

"Where are you?" he asked.

"Hunkered down in the front seat of your truck."

"What? How did you get in there?"

"By being sneaky. Don't worry. No one saw me."

He closed his eyes a moment. "Okay, let me tell Izzy and Brady I'm leaving and I'll be there in a minute."

Once he was finished with his statement and said his goodbyes to his siblings, he walked out the front door and down to the curb. He climbed into the driver's seat and cranked the engine. Cool air blew from the vents and Allie looked up from her spot on the floorboard.

"Are you okay?" he asked.

"I'm so tired I'm feeling weak. As much as we need to find Daria, I need to sleep or I'm going to be worthless. Or worse, wind up making a stupid mistake that gets someone killed."

He nodded. "I'm punchy myself. I let it slip that the killer had a signature."

She shot him a swift look. "What did they say?"

"Nothing. I managed to dodge giving an explanation. For now. But let's go back to that safe house and crash."

"Perfect."

He pulled away from the curb and headed for the safe house while he called Annie back using his car's Bluetooth. When she answered in her usual chipper voice, he smiled. "I'm driving so didn't want to text. What have you got?"

"A cabin location. Got a hit on one of his credit cards."

"You're kidding. It's rented?"

"Yep. It's all his for a year. Well, three more months, technically."

Allie smirked at him, some of her fatigue fading from her eyes. "Give me the address," he said.

Allie was so tired her eyes refused to cooperate.

And her stitches throbbed and itched.

And her muscles ached.

And, and, and.

But she pulled herself into the passenger seat and buckled up. "Let's go."

"We should let Henry know." He palmed his phone.

"We can let him know after she's safe."

"Because he might insist on sending help, which might scare Daria off?"

"Something like that."

He paused and closed his eyes for a few seconds. "You realize we're probably killing our careers, right?"

"You want out?" Her stomach knotted. He was absolutely right. They were so far off the path of "doing things by the book" that she didn't know if she'd ever find her way back to it.

"No."

"I was hoping you'd say that."

"It's a two-hour ride to the cabin," he said. "Sleep for a while, okay?"

"Okay. I'll sleep an hour, then we'll switch." She eyed him. "Deal?"

"Deal, but I'm swinging through a drive-thru for coffee."

"If I wasn't dead, we could use a chopper." She yawned. And leaned her seat back.

The next thing she knew, a hand was shaking her shoulder. "Mm . . . what?" Reality crashed and she bolted upright. "My turn to drive?"

"No, we're here."

"What? Here where?" She frowned, scrubbed her face with a palm, and looked out the window. Trees surrounded her. Three cabins nestled into the area in front of her on about an acre of land apiece. Linc had parked off the road under a copse of oaks. Far enough off the lane that no one coming up the mountain would accidentally slam into the SUV in the dark. "You were supposed to stop and let me take over."

"I drank three cups of coffee." He nodded to the evidence at her feet. "I couldn't sleep if I wanted to."

"Where's mine?"

"The two in the cup holder."

She tried the first one and found it hot. "It's fresh."

"Made another stop. For a different reason than just the coffee." His lips quirked. "But since it was there, I got you some."

"Thank you." Once she'd worked her way through half the cup, the caffeine hit her system and, combined with the sleep, she felt like a new person. Except for the itchy stitches in her back. "I'll drive home."

"We'll worry about that later. The cabin is a hike up that hill. I didn't want to give her a heads-up we were coming. You up for it?"

"Of course. First, scratch my back over the stitches and reapply the cream, will you? They're driving me nuts."

He did so without hesitation and Allie again realized how much she'd missed him. Missed his touch. Missed *them*. Even though she'd fought so hard against the whole dating, falling-in-love thing.

Because for now, it wasn't to be. And, depending on a lot of things, might not be meant to be ever. Ignoring the sharp pang of regret, she pulled away from him. "Thanks. I'm ready when you are."

"Let's go."

Allie stepped out of the truck and shut the door with a soft click. She checked her weapon, then slid it into her holster. Together, she and Linc walked up the asphalt drive to the cabin at the top. This one sat on more acreage and was infinitely more isolated than the others they'd passed on their way up. Probably why Gerard had chosen it.

The moon cast enough light to make her nervous. There was no good way to approach without stepping into the open. Most likely another reason for Gerard's choice.

What if she was wrong? Then what?

"My shoulders are itching," she said softly.

"I thought your teeth itched."

"Those, too, but mostly the stitches." Her eyes skimmed the cabin. Lights off, except for a faint glow that came from the back.

"My nerves are twitchy too, but I'm not sure why. It makes me think of the time someone tried to blow up Brady and Emily."

She'd heard that story. Emily had a killer on her trail—in somewhat the same circumstances Allie now found herself—and Brady had stumbled onto the attempt on Emily's life and rescued her. Only to go on the run. "Well, Emily didn't know who was after her. I do, so hopefully that makes things a little easier."

"Who knows about this place besides Gerard and Daria?"

"No one," she said. "At least I don't think so."

"Are you sure about that? What about Nevsky?"

"Well . . . no." She paused. "I take that back. I guess it's possible. I mean, I suppose Gerard could have felt obligated to let Nevsky know where he was taking the man's daughter, but . . ." She shrugged and stopped walking now that they were right on the edge of the property with no real cover in sight. "Gerard could have let him know, even if Nevsky didn't care," she finally said. "Just because Nevsky's such a control freak."

"So, you might need to hide out a bit while I do some recon."

"I'm still in disguise. Let's just take it one step at a time."

He didn't like it, she could tell, but wouldn't argue with her. "Do you see any cameras?" he asked.

"No. You?"

"No, but that doesn't mean they're not there."

"I'm aware, but I think we have to chance it." She walked closer to the cabin, her nerves quivering. First, they walked the perimeter, watching for trip wires or booby traps, and cameras.

She saw nothing.

With Linc so close behind her, his back to hers, she could feel the heat radiating from him. She took comfort from it, silently admitting that she was extremely glad she wasn't doing this on her own.

The asphalt drive circled the home. Beginning in the front, it led to the full-length porch and branched off to continue down the side of the house and around the back to the opposite side and connecting back to the main entrance.

After the first lap around the cabin following the drive, she slipped behind a large shrub to gain access to the window nearest the front door. Linc joined her. She tried to see through the blinds but could only make out a sliver of a blue couch against the far wall. What she wouldn't give for some of the Bureau's equipment that she'd never take for granted again. She placed gloved hands on the window pane and pushed. Locked.

"Next one," she whispered.

Linc stayed between the shrubs and the side of the house as he moved over to the one she pointed to and tried to peer inside. He shook his head.

At the last window, once again, they couldn't see in, but it was unlocked.

Allie waited while Linc slid the window open just enough to stick a finger inside and shift the blinds slightly. He motioned for her to take a look.

While her view was limited, it was better than the first. In the dim glow of the night-light, she could make out the kitchen to her right and the living area to her left. Two glasses on the kitchen bar, two plates in the drying rack next to the sink. Allie pulled back. "Someone's here," she whispered. "Two someones, it looks like."

"No cars in the drive," he said.

"And if someone was staying here—" The low rumble of an engine caught her attention. "You hear that?"

"Yeah."

The crunch of tires against the asphalt crept closer. "No headlights," Linc murmured. "I don't like that."

"Me neither."

"If we move away from this window, we're going to be sitting ducks for whoever's coming up the drive."

Allie shoved the window open, found the cord, and pulled the blinds open. "Hurry. Inside." She hauled herself over the sill and into the room, then scrambled out of the way as Linc landed beside her. Linc shut the window and locked it. Then closed the blinds. Quiet echoed around them.

"I'll keep an eye on our visitors," he whispered. "You see if Daria's here."

Allie headed for the back of the cabin, grateful it was only one level. She'd use the term "cabin" loosely, though. Cabin implied rustic and small. This wasn't either. It had all the comforts of home, and she could see why Gerard liked to escape here. And Daria. At first, she'd been concerned about the relationship between the forty-year-old bodyguard and the seventeen-year-old girl, but once she'd been around them for an extended period of time, she realized Gerard looked at his charge as something between a daughter and his duty. Maybe even a little sister. Either way, she'd been relieved there hadn't been anything inappropriate between the two.

The investigation into Gerard's background had shown him estranged from his fifteen-year-old daughter, so Daria could have simply been a substitute for his own child.

Allie cleared the first bedroom and en suite bath and quickly moved to the second one next door. Also clear. In the media room, the French doors led to a deck off the back of the house. It dropped straight down into the woods below it. From there, she moved to the master across the hall and stopped at the open door.

Inside, someone lay sleeping in the king-size bed.

Allie's smothered gasp reached him and set the hair on the back of his neck on end. "Allie?"

"I'm fine. Someone's in the bed. I'm going to see who it is." He had to strain to hear her barely there whisper. He checked through the blinds one more time. The car had stopped just beyond the edge of the property, and the driver sat behind the wheel, not moving.

Just watching.

But watching what? The house. Monitoring. Calculating.

"Allie?"

No answer.

"Allie," he hissed a little louder.

A tap came over the COMMS and his heart slowed a fraction. Allie letting him know she was okay but couldn't talk. "There's a guy in the car," he said. "At least I think it's a guy. Can't really tell. And right now, he's just sitting there."

"I'm back in the hallway."

"Who's in the bed?"

"The ugly duckling."

"Huh?"

"A bunch of feather pillows made to look like someone was sleeping."

"That's an old trick."

"But effective." She gave a disgusted grunt. "And I fell for it."

"You're not the first." Linc glanced out the window once more, making sure not to move the blinds in a way that the guy would notice. "Where are you now?"

"Continuing the search. If she's here, she's well hidden." Allie's voice was once again so low he had to strain to hear it. The guy in the car opened his door and got out. He was dressed in black. Linc caught a glimpse of his profile for a brief second before he pulled a ski mask over his head. "Allie, this isn't good. He's heading this way. If Daria's here, we've got to find her. Fast."

She stepped back into the den. "She's not here. She may have been earlier, but she's gone now."

"Who or what tipped her off?"

"I don't have a clue. You think he's after her?"

"Has to be. It's not you. You're dead, remember? Nevsky probably sent him to grab her."

"But how did he know she was here?" she asked. "To come at this exact moment? To this place?"

"That's a very good question."

A loud thud came from the back of the house, and Linc jerked his gaze from the man heading their way to the ceiling. "The attic."

Allie bolted. Linc stayed to watch the approaching figure, who checked the weapon he held in his left hand.

A loud dong sounded and Linc jerked.

"What was that?" Allie asked.

"Gerard's alarm system and what tipped Daria off that we were here. As soon as we crossed a certain point on the property, she was alerted."

"Scared me to death," she muttered.

Linc pulled his phone from the clip on his belt and dialed 911. No way was he not calling for backup.

Allie approached the attic door with caution, but also with haste. The string dangled from the ceiling. She'd almost pulled it down earlier, then decided it would have been too hard for Daria to pull it back up. Maybe she'd ignored her own advice and underestimated the girl.

"He's approaching, Allie," Linc said. "I've called for backup."

"I heard."

"Yeah, but what you didn't hear was that they're at least ten minutes out." He sighed. "Brady and Izzy would kill me if they were to hear that call."

"They won't. They're two hours away."

"Exactly. I'm wishing they were here. I'd be willing to make the sacrifice," he muttered, "rather than deal with cops I don't know."

But if she happened to be seen by one of the local cops, no one would recognize her. "Where's our intruder?"

"Thanks to all the windows in this place, it's not too hard to keep eyes on him. Right now he's headed around toward the back of the house. We're running out of time, Allie. He's doing recon, but soon he's going to try to find a way in."

"Of course he is."

Allie had pulled the attic stairs down, staying well out of the way of the opening in case Daria was armed. The girl knew how to shoot and shoot well, but she was still seventeen and probably scared to death. She might shoot first and ask questions later.

"Daria?" Allie called softly. "You up there?"

No answer.

Of course, it could be someone—or something—else that had made that noise. "Hey, I'm friendly, okay? I'm looking for my friend Daria. Is that you up there?"

Silence. She supposed she could be talking to squirrels. Or rats.

Allie shuddered, bit her lip, and started climbing the wooden steps. When she reached the top, she glanced around the dimly lit

146

space. The moon filtered through the window opposite her, giving the area a creepy, shadowy appearance—and feel. "Daria? Please, honey, if it's you, say something. I know your father's after you and you're scared. Let me help you."

A clatter straight ahead of her to the right of the window. Allie hefted herself up and onto the wooden flooring of the attic. Tension threaded the muscles of her shoulders, up the back of her neck, and into the base of her skull.

She was going on the assumption it was Daria, but what if it wasn't? Her eyes landed on the object to her right. Daria's backpack.

"Allie?" Linc's voice in her ear.

"Yeah?"

"What's going on?"

"I think she's up here," she whispered, letting her eyes probe the shadows. "But she won't come out and I don't know why. What about you?"

"I'm watching him. I think he's trying to decide if she's here or not. He did his perimeter check and now he's looking for a way in. And he's going to find one shortly . . . or simply break a window."

Allie stepped over to retrieve the backpack when a hard hand landed in the middle of her back and sent her stumbling forward to slam her forehead against one of the roof's rafters. Stars spun and she went to her knees, head protesting this next round of abuse so soon after the explosion.

Someone scrambled down the steps behind her, and Allie whirled, hands grabbing. Her fingers raked the back of the person's shirt before the figure disappeared down the steps. But she caught a glimpse of the familiar high ponytail. "Daria, stop. Please!"

The girl never hesitated. Dizziness kept Allie on her knees.

"Allie? I heard a thud, you okay?" Linc asked.

"You see her?"

"No. I'm in the kitchen keeping an eye on our guy and wondering where our backup is."

"She just went down the attic steps and bolted. Stop her." Allie gritted her teeth against the spinning and clambered down the stairs after Daria just in time to see her open the front door. "Daria! No!"

Linc raced from the kitchen and dove for the girl as she hesitated for a fraction of a second at Allie's shout. His hand snagged her ankle and she went down. Daria landed on the floor with a thud. Linc kept his hold on her ankle with his right hand. In one move, he pulled her out of the open doorway, then reached to slam the door with his left.

Three bullets splintered the wood as the door swung on the hinges. The fourth whizzed above them. Daria lay on the floor and covered her head. Linc finally managed to get the door fully shut and locked. He spun back to Daria, who scrambled to her knees.

Another hail of bullets shattered the windows on the front. Linc returned fire and Allie rolled to her feet to go after Daria, who'd raced toward the back of the house. "Daria! Stop! Why are you running?"

"Because you're a traitor! Leave me alone!"

Then she was at the French doors leading out of the media room. With a quick twist, she had the dead bolt released and the doors open. Where did she think she was going? The doors led to the deck that had no stairs. But knowing Daria, she had a way down. Allie followed.

Traitor? Why would she think that?

Daria had tossed a rope over the side and was going down faster than a monkey. Allie almost yelled at the girl, but she wasn't listening and Allie didn't know who else was in the vicinity. "Linc, she went over the side of the deck." Daria no doubt planned to disappear into the wooded area at the bottom. "I'm going after her."

"Coming around the side of the house behind the shooter."

When Daria dropped to the ground, she disappeared into the trees two feet behind her.

Allie gripped the rope and swung over the railing just in time to see the shooter hot on the trail of Daria. "Hey! Up here!"

He never paused. She let herself down using her feet against the wooden post to control her descent just like Daria had done. No doubt Gerard had set that up for her. At the bottom, Allie darted into the woods and ducked behind a large tree. Listening.

Footsteps behind her. Linc. She went after Daria and the determined killer, with Linc right behind her.

Fear for Daria spurred her faster. She could hear footsteps up ahead of her. *Please let me be in time. Don't let him kill her.*

Allie heard the sirens in the distance, but knew they'd never catch up to them in time—even if they could find them.

"I'm going to see if I can cut him off," Linc said. "Try to get between him and Daria." He swerved to the right and stumbled through the undergrowth. Trying to run on the downward-sloping hill while dodging trees and limbs in the moonlight was actually a painful exercise.

Allie ducked under the next large limb and caught a glimpse of the two figures ahead. The trees had become less dense in this area, which allowed more of the moon's light to penetrate. That was great for her visual, but it also put a big bull's-eye on Daria's back.

Her attacker paused, lifted his weapon, and took aim.

Linc burst through the tree line to see the man stop and lift his weapon. "FBI! Put your gun down!" Linc held his weapon on the man, who hesitated but didn't move to drop his gun. "Put it down! Now!"

And then the man was on the ground.

Still gripping his gun.

Allie had tackled him from a full-speed run, slamming into his back and taking him down.

He lay there stunned, and Linc, holding his weapon on him,

raced forward, his intent to stomp on the man's wrist and get the gun. But before he reached him, the guy bucked, dislodging the knee Allie had against his back. She tumbled to her side with a yell.

Like a cat, the guy bolted to both feet in one smooth ninja move and spun his weapon toward Allie. Linc fired. The guy grunted, whirled, and disappeared into the trees.

"Go after Daria," she said. "I'm going after him."

Linc was already moving to apprehend the shooter, but Allie bolted past him. "Allie!" He thought he'd hit the guy, but if he had a bullet in him, it wasn't slowing him down. With a low growl, Linc spun and darted in the direction Daria had disappeared. His heart thundered and he wished he'd been quicker to go after the shooter, because while Allie could handle herself, she was still at a distinct disadvantage. Then again, maybe Linc had evened the odds a bit if he'd hit the guy. But what if he hadn't?

Linc searched for Daria for the next ten minutes, doing his best to stay focused, but he was worried about Allie, not sure whether to hope she had caught up with the gunman or that he had slipped away without hurting anyone else. "Allie? You there?"

Silence.

She'd gotten too far out of range for the COMMS to work.

Guilt slammed him as he slowed to try to figure out which way Daria had run. Of course, he wanted to find Daria and get her somewhere safe, but Allie . . .

Linc listened. Heard nothing. Either Daria was so far ahead of him he couldn't hear her moving, or she had stopped and was hiding somewhere.

For several seconds he simply stood there. He'd completely lost her. If he wasn't so worried about Allie, he might spend a little more time looking for the teen. However, for now she was safe, out of the hands of the killer. Unfortunately, Allie might have just propelled herself right into them.

15

The hairs on her neck spiked. Allie stood next to the tree, hovering behind it, hoping it would be enough shelter if the shooter could see her and decided to take aim and fire.

Heart pounding, she tried to listen, to hear any sound that he might make to indicate his location. She'd caught a glimpse of him only a few seconds earlier when he passed under the light of the moon filtering through the branches just ahead.

And then he was gone. Like smoke in the wind.

For a brief moment, in their struggle, their eyes had met. She didn't think he'd recognized her, but she certainly knew him.

Gregori Radchenko.

Just the possibility that she'd finally found him spurred her on. Granted, it was completely by accident, but she was desperate not to lose him.

Allie tried to calm her pounding heart. Deep breath in, then out. And again. The smell of rotting wood and wildflowers registered even as her eyes probed the area. She walked the perimeter of the tree, keeping the trunk against her back.

She almost expected to feel the slam of a bullet into her chest, and when it didn't come, she moved forward, nerves tight, muscles bunched, ears tuned to the sounds around her. Which wasn't much.

Her shallow breaths, the crunch of the underbrush, the whisper of the wind through the trees. But the insects were quiet, as though they knew something was wrong. And then a flash of movement caught her eye just ahead. A branch falling from a tree? Or had he thrown it? Or was there a second person around?

She stayed put.

He wasn't such an amateur that he would allow himself the mistake of breaking the branch, and she figured he was trying to draw her out.

Instead of moving toward him, she slipped sideways, doing her best to stay behind the cover of the trees—until something hard pressed against the back of her head. She froze, her heart flipped. Somehow, he'd doubled back.

Her fingers twitched around the grip of her weapon, but she held every muscle frozen, grappling with the best way to handle this. "Hello, Gregori, long time no see." She hoped she kept the fear out of her voice.

For a moment, he stood still. If he hadn't had the gun against her head, she wouldn't have known he was there.

"How do you know who I am?" His voice had changed, deepened. But it was still the voice from her childhood.

Would he kill her if she told him who she was? No, he was going to kill her regardless. "Guess it's time for you to finish the job you started fifteen years ago, huh?"

His stillness multiplied exponentially. "Alina?" Her name—a name she hadn't heard since her mother's death—was barely a whisper on his lips. One filled with . . . shock? Maybe.

Silence.

"Just tell me why," she said.

"Why what? Why did I kill them?"

The shock was gone—if it had ever been there—replaced with a nonchalant coldness that chilled her to the core.

Allie curled the fingers of her left hand into a fist while her right

152

gripped her weapon. All kinds of defense moves ran through her brain at warp speed.

And yet, she couldn't move.

She had to know. "Of course, why did you kill them?"

"Because your father was a liar and he deserved to suffer the consequences of his choices."

He'd been hanging out with Daria too long. "Can you not speak in riddles?" She gritted her teeth against the need to hurl. She'd dreamed of this moment. And now that it was here, she almost couldn't think, couldn't breathe, couldn't stand. Couldn't shoot.

"How would you feel if you had been lied to your entire life?" he asked.

"What did he lie about?"

"Everything. And she went along with it."

"Mom?"

"Yes, *Mom*." The sneer made her blink. "A liar and a cheat," he said. "She cheated her family and she cheated on her husband. She deserved to die."

Allie was horribly confused, but she continued to scramble for a plan while keeping him talking.

"And Misha? Eight-year-old Misha? What about her? Was she a liar and a cheat too? What's your excuse for killing her?" She went to her knees on the last word and kicked back with her right foot. She caught him with a glancing blow to the thigh that he ignored. His right hand shot out and he caught her shoulder, giving it a hard push.

Allie landed on the ground with a harsh grunt, rolled, and brought her weapon up. Quicker than anyone should be able to move, he kicked her in the wrist. Pain radiated up her arm and she lost her grip on the gun. He pointed his gun at her forehead while blood dripped from the wound in his biceps.

She glared up at him. Familiar gray eyes glittered down at her. "You'd better kill me now," she ground between clenched teeth. "Otherwise I will hunt you down and kill you myself."

His brow rose and he actually smiled. "Hunt me down? Really? Do you even realize what I do for a living?"

Of course she did. Now. "Do you even realize what I do?"

"No, but I'm interested now."

"FBI! Put it down!" Linc's shout came from her left. "Drop it now."

"Don't shoot him!" The words left her mouth before she could stop them.

Linc didn't shoot.

Radchenko stepped behind the nearest tree without taking his eyes off her, effectively preventing Linc from having a clear shot at him. He gave her a slow smile and it left her colder than she thought possible. "And so, the hunter becomes the prey?" he asked. "We shall see."

Then once again, he was gone, fading into the trees as though he belonged there.

Linc started to go after him and she grabbed his arm. "Don't," she said. "You won't find him."

He spun. "What?"

"He's gone."

"I'm calling it in anyway." He did, then came to her side and helped her up. "Are you okay?"

"I've been better," she muttered.

He studied her. "You know him."

"Yes."

"I recognize him. He was on your wall in your apartment. He's the guy who killed your family, isn't he?"

She locked her eyes on his. "He is. He was also in one of those surveillance pictures Henry showed us of Nevsky before I went undercover. I knew he worked for Nevsky, but he'd been dark for so long that I was starting to think he was dead. And then when I saw that picture—"

"You decided to go after him."

She shrugged. "We were going after Nevsky. Radchenko is one of his assassins. It was only a matter of time before he showed up." She paused. "Although I'll admit, I didn't expect him to show up the way he did."

Linc shook his head. "Let's get out of here, then we're going to have a talk."

"Where are we going?"

"Back to the cabin."

"It's a crime scene. CSU will be all over it."

"Maybe so, but Daria went there for a reason. You'll just have to keep a low profile."

The sirens were finally approaching along with the helicopter overhead. Radchenko would be on the run but hopefully wouldn't get far. Linc's phone buzzed and he glanced at the screen. "Henry."

"Don't answer," she said. "There's no way I want to explain all this to him right now."

"I feel that. Henry can wait a bit."

Once they were back at the cabin, Allie pulled her hoodie up and kept her glasses on. Linc led her inside and flashed his badge. "She's with me," he said, signing the crime scene log, then pulling on gloves.

No one questioned him.

"Anything in particular we're looking for?" One of the investigators glanced up, then returned to dig the slugs out of the door.

"See if you can find Radchenko's vehicle or evidence of where one was parked. Look for tire tracks as well as slugs and casings outside and in the front room," Linc said.

"You got it."

Allie kept her head down, refusing to make eye contact with anyone. Linc tugged on her sleeve. The conversation she knew was waiting to happen between them made her want to drag her feet. Only the fact that Daria was still out there kept her moving with quick efficiency.

Out of sight and hearing range of any of the CSU members, she caught Linc's arm. "How did he know to come here?" she asked.

"He had to have followed Daria. Her father must have installed some kind of tracker or something on her."

It made sense. Allie grimaced. "And he's going to keep her on the run until he finally catches up with her." She shook her head. "It has to be on her laptop or backpack."

Linc's head snapped up. "Can we track her laptop?"

"I wouldn't know how to do that. Ask Annie."

While his fingers worked the screen, Allie walked down the hall to the attic. The stairs were just as she'd left them. One of the CSU members was already up there going through everything. She'd have to see if Henry could do something about any DNA that turned up matching hers. He'd have to make up some story, like Daria was wearing one of Allie's hoodies. She climbed the stairs and her head popped through the opening. This time the area was lit up and she could see from one end to the other. She stepped onto the wood flooring and did a one-eighty. "Anything?"

The woman at the far end looked up. "Nothing significant, sorry."

"It's okay. I didn't really expect you to find anything anyway."

The words Daria had flung at her before running now echoed in her mind. *You're a traitor!*

Allie slipped back downstairs and out to Linc's SUV before dropping her head into her hands. *God, are you there? I think we need to talk.*

Silence.

Okay, so I'll talk. Daria's innocent in this whole mess. I don't know what I've done to make her think I'm a traitor, but you do. Can you please just watch out for her? Keep her safe? Let us catch up to her before her father or one of his hired killers does? As far as Gregori's concerned, I . . . I don't know what to say there. He deserves to die and you and I both know it.

She paused to see if she could discern anything in her spirit. Or mind.

But again, she got nothing but silence. "Yeah," she whispered into the empty vehicle. "I don't blame you for not wanting to talk to me. I guess I shouldn't talk to you when I've got murder on my mind, huh? I think there's a commandment about that somewhere, isn't there?"

The door opened and Linc slid into the passenger's seat. "Who are you talking to?"

"No one who appears to be interested in listening."

———

Okay. That was a strange answer. "God hears you, Allie."

"Hmm."

Fine. He'd let it drop for now. They both needed sleep, not to mention that they had a mess of legal issues to wade through. Linc had fired his weapon. Allie had fired hers. They'd have to give them up to Henry once again.

Hopefully, he would be able to pull some strings with those, and the powers that be would work out everything necessary to keep Linc from having to abandon Allie to talk to Internal Affairs. Henry. He glanced at his phone. The man had called nonstop for the past hour.

Allie climbed into the driver's seat and waited for Linc to buckle his seat belt before pulling away from the curb.

"I'm beat," he said.

"Yep. I'm familiar with that one."

"Where are we going?" he asked.

"I still don't have a place to stay, do I?"

"Nope."

"I don't suppose you want to go to Henry's?"

He paused as though considering it. "You think he'd let us sleep before yelling at us?"

"I doubt it."

"Then my place it is."

"Linc, I can't go there. Someone will see me or one of your siblings will drop by."

"By the time we get there, it will be three o'clock in the morning, but our arrival might stir some neighbor interest. Although they're pretty used to my crazy hours at this point." He paused. "Okay, a nearby hotel, then. At least for tonight in a town where no one knows us and until we figure out something more permanent."

"Where do you think Daria's sleeping tonight?" she asked softly.

"I don't know. I wish we could figure out what set her against you." He held his phone up. "Annie texted. No luck tracking the laptop or Daria's phone. Which brings us to you."

She groaned.

"You've got some explaining to do."

"You're not going to let that drop, huh?"

"Only for the next ten minutes."

"What's the nearest decent-sized city that has a hotel we can blend in with?" she asked.

Linc looked it up on his phone and punched in the navigation.

"Better call Henry," she said.

"First things first."

Thirty minutes later, she pulled into the parking lot of the hotel and he entered the lobby to check them in under his name. "It's a two-bedroom suite," he said when he returned. "We'll leave the doors open for safety reasons, but still be able to have a bit of privacy." He handed her a key and she tucked it into the back pocket of her jeans.

"At least I have a box with a few changes of clothes and some toiletries," she said. "What are you going to do?"

"I always have a go-bag in my vehicle."

"Right. So, no shopping tonight?"

"I never took you for a coward."

Allie snapped her lips shut and glared at him. He kept the satisfied smile from curving his lips. Good. He needed her mad so he could get answers. If she cried, he'd be putty in her hands. Once inside the suite, Linc waved her to the couch.

"You're not even going to let me wash my face before we do this, are you?" she asked.

"Nope."

"What about calling Henry? How many times has he called?"

"Twelve."

She winced. "We need to check in with him."

"I texted him and said I'd call him as soon as I could. After we talk will be the soonest I can call."

He wasn't going to budge on this. She set her box just inside the door, then slumped onto the couch and dropped her face into her hands while Linc paced in front of her.

"I heard your statement about hunting him down and killing him," Linc said. "Allie, that's . . . that's . . . we don't do that. Well, we hunt them down, yes. But we try to avoid killing them, remember? I mean, that's a last resort because we're the good guys."

His concern pierced her, and for some reason, that made her mad. She sprang to her feet. "Don't you think I know that?"

"Well, why'd you say it? Did you mean it?"

"I . . ." Her anger faded as fast as it had bubbled up, only to be replaced with a cold resolve. She settled back onto the couch and looked away from him. "Yes."

For a moment, he didn't speak, just continued his scrutiny. Long enough to make her want to squirm. She refused to give in to the urge.

"Allie?"

"What?" Her eyes met his again.

"You said before that you knew the killer before he slaughtered your family."

She blinked. "Yes."

"How did you know him? What was he to you? A friend? A boyfriend?"

"No." She studied him a moment longer. "My brother."

16

Linc went still. "What?"

"My brother. My older brother, who was supposed to protect me and my little sister no matter what. Instead, he killed my dad and my sister, and essentially my mother, who wound up committing suicide four weeks after I came home from the hospital because she couldn't live with what had happened. And, of course, he tried to kill me." Tears shimmered for a brief moment before they were gone. "I went into the foster care system and actually had a fairly good experience. My foster dad was a cop, the mom a special education teacher. I was there for two years. We exchange Christmas cards, but that's about it."

He had no words. The silence stretched. She rose to pace.

"And you don't know why he did this," he finally said, forcing the words through his tight throat.

Allie shook her head. "I've thought about it. Endlessly. I wondered if he'd suffered something like a psychotic break or had some kind of brain issue. Like an aneurysm or something. Anything but that he *chose* to do what he did. But, after tonight, I think he did. He made the choice to kill his family and apparently holds no regrets for doing so."

"I'm sorry, Allie."

"So am I, but he said some things that make me think I'm a little closer to figuring out his motives."

"How so?"

"Gregori said my father was a liar, but . . ." Frustration tightened her jaw.

"But what?"

"I already knew that and so did Gregori."

"So you need to know which lie it was he told your brother that would send him over the edge into such a rage that he wanted to wipe out his entire family."

Her breath hitched and her eyes flashed, but she nodded. "Yes."

"What was your brother's relationship with your father?"

She grimaced. "They were never very close, but it's not like they hated each other." She paused. "My father wasn't around much and he wasn't affectionate. He did seem to favor me and my sister over our brother—at least when he wasn't yelling at us or slapping us around."

He winced. "Was it obvious?"

She sighed. "I don't know. Does it matter?"

"It might. Come on, Allie, you're going to have to look at this objectively. Put your personal feelings aside and try to focus on this as just another case."

She blinked. "That's what I've been doing ever since I graduated from the academy and was handed my badge. And believe it or not, for the most part, I was actually able to do it. To compartmentalize, so to speak. And then I saw his picture with Nevsky and it brought everything back. Tenfold. Part of me really thought he was dead and I had almost come to accept that. But . . ." She blew out a breath.

"That picture changed things."

"Changed everything. Now my emotions are all over the place." She swallowed. "I . . ."

"Talk to me. Please, trust me." He raked a hand through his hair. "You owe me that at least."

Her jaw dropped. "I owe you?"

"Okay, maybe *owe* is a bad choice of words, but you . . . we . . . you . . . argh!" He paced with her. From one end of the small area to the other. "You let me fall in love with you and you had no intention of reciprocating those feelings."

It hurt. He'd admit it. He had only himself to blame for not acknowledging her signals. Okay, for ignoring them.

She spun and faced him, hands on her hips. "How dare you!"

He stopped and glared down at her. "How dare I?" He frowned. "How dare I what?"

"How dare you blame me? I'm the one who tried to keep distance between us, remember? I'm the one who said I didn't need to meet your family. I'm the one who insisted that being romantically involved was about as stupid a move as any two partners could make. Remember that? Remember those conversations?" She jabbed him in the chest and he didn't even flinch. Just continued to stare at her.

He did remember. But she'd seemed so lost, so lonely, he'd done his best to convince her to let her guard down. And she had. At least partially. Enough for it to hurt when she felt she had no choice but to put the walls back up.

"Don't love me, Linc. As much as I may want you to, you can't love me."

And just like that, her words gave him hope and shattered his heart all at the same time. "Why not?"

"Because I don't know where my future is going to be," she whispered. "I don't know where I'm going to wind up. My entire existence has been wrapped up in finding my brother and getting justice for my parents and my sister. I have nothing left for anything else."

"What about after?"

"After what?"

"After it's all over and Nevsky and Gregori are behind bars?"

She bit her lip and let her gaze run over him. His nerves stretched at the long silence. "Why don't we wait and see if I even survive?"

He winced and reached for her.

She backed away. "Don't."

Linc let his hands drop while his heart beat a frantic rhythm. "I don't want to lose you."

"You can't lose what you don't have," she said softly. "Good night, Linc." She turned to walk toward her room.

"Allie?" he said.

She stopped, but didn't turn.

"Look at me, please."

She hesitated for so long, he wondered if she would, but finally, she faced him, her eyes meeting his. Shuttered and cold. At first he couldn't speak. But the longer they stared at one another, she seemed to struggle to maintain her expression, and he thought he saw something seep into her gaze. Something that said she was hurting just as much as he.

She blinked and the look was gone. "What is it, Linc?"

"Just remember. Justice and revenge are two very different things."

Allie tore her eyes away from Linc's and shoved the hovering tears aside. She didn't have time to cry. Crying accomplished nothing except to stuff up her nose and make her head hurt. Her father's hand had connected with her head more than once because of tears, and she'd learned at an early age to hide them. Linc's words continued to echo, rolling around in her head, and she decided he was right. She did owe him. She owed him her honesty. It almost killed her to realize she couldn't give it to him. Not all of it anyway.

Justice. Revenge. He was right about that too. They were definitely two very different things.

She drew in a deep breath and returned to the couch in the shared living area. "I know, Linc."

"Could have fooled me." When she didn't offer to discuss it anymore, he shook his head, but his granite features betrayed his inner turmoil.

She'd hurt him terribly, which had never been her intent. "Linc—"

"Okay, on to something else," he said.

"What?"

"Henry sent the security footage of Daria leaving the day of the raid."

Allie perked up. As tired as she knew they both were, she wanted to see it. "Was he furious?"

"To put it mildly. He said for us to watch the footage and call him when we're done."

"I'm ready."

He hooked his laptop up to the large screen television in the corner and brought the footage up.

"He started it at the point where Daria runs out of the building." He ran the video. Daria darted out of the building, only to be stopped by one of the SWAT team members and Henry, who pointed them to the van. Then Henry reentered the building. "It's kind of jerky," Linc muttered.

Allie didn't take her eyes from the screen. "Might be an older camera."

Minutes later, Daria popped out of the back of the van with Smythe escorting her to a bathroom in a nearby building. Before entering, she turned, her attention obviously caught on something, then she swung away and stepped inside.

"What was she looking at?" Allie asked.

"I don't know, but Henry's right. This doesn't give us much."

"Play it again, will you?"

He did.

"Stop it right there," she said. "Just before going inside the building with the bathroom, she's looking mighty hard at something—or someone."

He played it a third time. "You're right."

When it ended, she leaned back. "I want to know what she was looking at so intently. What—or who—did she see that made her sneak out of the window?"

The video played for the fourth time. "There aren't any more angles?" Allie asked. "No other cameras?"

"Henry said two were broken. This one was the best of the two that were working."

She rose and paced from one end of the small area to the other. She snapped her fingers. "The news cameras. The media was there. They had to be filming it."

"Good idea. I'll get Annie to take care of that while we talk to Henry."

Tired of pacing but needing to move to stay awake, Allie slipped into the kitchen area and pulled a Coke from the small refrigerator.

"What in the blazes do you two think you're doing!"

Allie winced at Henry's outrage. Linc had the phone on speaker and had set it in the middle of the coffee table.

She walked back into the living area. "Hi, Henry."

"Are you out of your minds? How am I supposed to deal with your crazy stunts? I can pull a lot of strings, but I'm not a miracle worker! And why aren't you answering my calls? Can you count? Have you seen the number of times I've called? This is inexcusable!"

Allie met Linc's gaze and held a finger to her lips. He nodded. They'd let the man rant, then come up with another plan.

Henry finally fell silent.

The pause lasted longer than was comfortable. Allie cleared her throat. "Henry? You're . . . um . . . right. We're sorry. We should have definitely looped you in on everything. It's just things were going really, really fast and you were dealing with Killian—"

"Killian's dead."

Allie flinched. "What?"

"He died at the hospital. They were going to set his jaw, and

166

whatever pain meds they gave him caused him to have an allergic reaction and he died."

Linc dropped his head into his hands. "Were you able to get anything out of him about Nevsky before he died?"

"No. The man had a broken jaw. I was waiting for them to set it, then I was going to hand him my iPad and have him answer questions. Unfortunately, we didn't get to that point."

Linc pinched the bridge of his nose. "All right. Just out of curiosity, what's the status on the stolen equipment from the military bases? Did you get the people behind it?"

"Most of them. We're still rounding up the equipment, although it looks like a lot of it landed overseas. Terrorism is our first thought, of course, which is why we've got CTU, the JTTF, and our international branches all involved. I've been directed to stay on Nevsky for now."

"So," Allie said, "we have a problem."

"We have a lot of problems," Henry said. "Care to elaborate?"

"Gregori Radchenko knows I'm alive."

Henry swore and Allie grimaced.

"How?" he demanded.

She explained. "We feel sure Radchenko was sent to kill Daria. What we don't know is how he found her. We figure he's got some kind of tracker on her. Could be her laptop or phone. Annie can't access either device, so it's got to be something other than her GPS leading them to her."

Henry sighed. "Any other ideas on how to find her before Nevsky and Radchenko do?"

"No." Allie pursed her lips. "I think we should stop looking for Daria."

Linc raised a brow.

"If we can find Nevsky or Radchenko, then we'll find Daria," she said.

Henry fell silent, then finally said, "I'll work on it from that angle then and get back to you when I know something. In the meantime, stay out of sight. Nevsky probably knows you're alive at this point."

"Then I can come out of hiding."

"No! Are you nuts? There's always the chance that Radchenko hasn't said anything to him."

Allie frowned. "I doubt that."

"Let's wait until we know for sure."

"How are we going to know that?"

"We'll know."

Anger stirred and the man slammed a fist onto the dash as he stared up at the window. The dark seemed to mock him. They were in there. Both of them. Alive and scheming and who knew what else?

Six months of planning had gone down the drain because of . . . what?

He didn't know.

That was the problem. If he had even an inkling of what he'd missed, he wouldn't be so agitated. Okay, he would be, but whatever. But after so much careful planning, to have the plan fail left him reeling.

The drone had been a genius idea, and so no matter how many times he ran the plan around and around in his mind, he couldn't figure out what had gone wrong.

Because nothing had gone wrong. It should have worked perfectly. Everything . . . everyone had been in place. Death by drone had been a sure thing.

Except his target was still alive. Like a cat with nine lives.

He gave a growl of disgust and fought the rage that bubbled up, threatening to consume him.

No.

He drew in a deep breath and let it out slowly.

Control, remember? He had to stay in control or everything would be ruined.

He slipped out of his truck to pace and shoot glances at the still-dark window. Cars passed, people walked the sidewalk, with no idea that he had murder on his agenda.

While his plans fell apart, the city bustled on in ignorance. He ran a hand down a cheek that needed a shave.

Maybe his original plan couldn't be salvaged—or even the second one—but in the end, he could make it all come together.

He'd already started over and, so far, seemed to be on track.

This time he couldn't fail. He *wouldn't* fail.

His target would die and all would be right for the first time in a very long while.

Although, he couldn't help thinking, it should have been right by now. And would have been had Daria not interfered. Tonight, he'd almost had her, but she'd slipped through his fingers like the slippery little eel she was. She could ruin everything. More so than anyone else on the planet right now. More so even than Allie. If only she'd kept her nose out of things that weren't her business.

His fingers curled into a fist and he pictured himself smashing it into Daria's face. So much more satisfying than using a gun. He wanted to hear her scream before he killed her. He scoffed.

Never would he have imagined that a seventeen-year-old brat could ruin him. Fortunately, he didn't think she knew exactly how much power she held or she would have used it by now. Which meant he had to move quickly to make sure he kept it that way.

So . . . he had to get rid of Daria.

Permanently.

Then he'd deal with Allie.

17

Linc woke heavy-headed and feeling like he'd been drugged. After the caffeine crash, he hadn't been able to stay awake another minute. Allie had declared herself fit to keep watch and he'd had to let her. The bedside clock said he'd slept the sleep of the dead for five hours. He rolled out of the bed, automatically palmed his weapon from the bedside table, and padded into the living area to find the lights off and the room empty. He crossed the room to Allie's open bedroom door. The bathroom light was on and the door cracked. Nothing that set his worry meter off.

"Allie?" His hushed whisper echoed in the small area.

"Over here."

He whirled back to the common area to find her sitting on the floor under the window. Dressed all in black, she blended into the wall. "What are you doing in the dark?"

"Watching the door. The dark gives me the advantage."

If someone came in the window, she would be right there with the element of surprise. If someone came in the door, their silhouette would make an easy target. If someone came in shooting, Allie was already on the floor. She was smart. She was a good agent. And he had a feeling she could be even more deadly than he might have imagined.

"Hello?" She plugged in a small night-light and a soft glow filled the room.

"Sorry." He'd been admiring her as she'd been talking. "What?"

"Why are you awake? Or at least appear to be awake, but aren't answering questions coherently. Are you sleepwalking?"

He grunted a laugh. "No. I'm here because it's my turn to take a shift. Go to bed."

She rose to her feet in one smooth move away from the window and tucked her weapon into her shoulder holster. "I think I know our next move."

"What's that?"

"My family was going into the WITSEC program shortly before everyone was killed."

Linc stilled. "You just keep coming at me with the surprises, don't you?"

"I'm sorry. Truly. I . . . you . . ." She sighed. "You made me want more, Linc."

Her soft words seared something deep within him. "Same here."

"No, you don't understand. I never allowed myself to even hope that I could have a 'normal' life. I have way too much baggage to bring into a relationship. And then we became partners and you introduced me to your family." She gave a small smile. "You were all so normal. I thought you were all perfect too." He scoffed and she wrinkled her nose. "But then I got to know you all and realized you were people just like everyone else. People who'd suffered tragedy and hard times."

"It comes with being in law enforcement, I guess."

"It comes from simply being alive."

"Maybe so. At least I still have them, though."

"Yes, of course. But it gave me hope."

"Hope for what?"

"A future. A family. A life. When I started to believe that Gregori was dead, I wanted to believe that maybe 'normal' was possible for me."

"But?" he asked.

"But then I saw his face and I knew that I'd never have a future until he could no longer hurt anyone else." She locked her eyes on his. "He's out there killing, Linc. He's Nevsky's killing machine."

"One of them, I know."

"And it won't end until he's stopped."

"I know that too."

"So, here's what I'm thinking. Back to the WITSEC. As I've told you before, I had perfected the art of eavesdropping."

"You have quite a bit in common with Daria, don't you?"

"Why do you think I like her so much?" She quirked him a lop-sided smile that faded quickly. "Anyway, my dad came home the night before the shooting. He had new IDs and we were supposed to pack everything up and be ready to leave when the marshals came for us. I always had a go-bag ready, so I wasn't too concerned about it. Gregori had been preoccupied and sullen for weeks, but honestly, I didn't pay him much attention. When he was home, he was arguing with our father—" She broke off and stilled. Then paced to her room and back.

"What?"

"He said '*your* father.'"

Linc blinked. "You lost me."

"In the woods earlier, he said 'your father,' not 'our father.'"

"You said he called him a liar." Linc settled on the couch and looked up at her. "Maybe he doesn't claim him anymore? Maybe he disassociates himself from everyone he kills as his way of justifying what he does."

"Maybe." She frowned. "Anyway, my point to all of this is that I couldn't remember Gregori's new name. No matter how long and hard I thought about it, I couldn't remember it."

"And?"

"Tonight I did. I don't know if just seeing him sparked it, but I remembered it. Grayson Radcliffe. Of course, I knew the Radcliffe part, but not the Grayson. I searched every record I could find on Gregori Radchenko. His name only popped up in the police reports, never associated with any other crimes. Naturally, Gregori Radcliffe came up with nothing."

"What about the MO?"

"Several murders—victims found on their stomachs shot in the base of the skull—have been attributed to assassins in Nevsky's organization, but no doubt carried out by Gregori. No one's been able to prove it, though. He's like a ghost. I can't believe he let himself get caught on that one camera shot."

Linc rubbed his eyes. "I'll do some research while you sleep. Go."

"If I can. If not, I'll come back out here and work with you."

"Allie—"

She frowned at his abrupt halt. "What?"

"What's your real name?"

"Alina Radchenko."

"Allie?"

"Short for Alina and also works for Allison. My little sister called me Nina."

Nina. The name she'd told him to call her when they were crashing Nevsky's party. "Why was your family going into witness protection?"

"I don't know. I questioned my mother about it, but at first, she wouldn't say anything. She just kind of withdrew into her own little world after I got out of the hospital—and then she was dead." She shook her head. "It was the weirdest thing. While I was recovering, she held my hand and did everything a mom was supposed to do, but the day I got home, it was like a light switched off. She was never the same after that." She rubbed her eyes. "I finally pushed her one day, screaming at her that it was all her fault, that I'd overheard the conversation between her and my dad, and

I wanted to know who Nevsky was. I told her she owed me some kind of explanation." Allie looked away.

Linc went to her and pulled her into an easy embrace, not wanting to hold her too tight if she didn't want the hug. However, she leaned into it and he settled her against him. "Did she give you one?"

"A small one. She said that except for the day she went to see him to ask for money, she hadn't seen Nevsky in years and neither had my father. Apparently, Nevsky went to my father and told him my mother had come to him and he'd given her the money. If my father would work for him, he'd forgive the debt. Father was furious. He said there was no such thing as forgiving a debt and they'd never get out from under Nevsky's thumb now. I heard the conversation about the WITSEC thing and then Gregori shot us."

She fell silent and he continued to hold her, wishing he could take her pain away even while admiring her strength and resilience. Her breathing evened out and her body slumped heavy against him. He sank to the floor, carefully pulling her with him until his back rested against the wall and his gun lay next to his right knee. Allie shifted, then snuggled against him and fell deeper into sleep.

In the early morning, the parking lot was mostly empty. In fact, the sun was just coming up. Next to an old, beat-up Bronco, he waited until the woman had finished loading her groceries into the back of her car and shut the hatch before he approached.

"Hello."

She spun and pressed a hand to her chest. "Oh, goodness, you scared me to death, but hi. Fancy running into you here."

"I'm in town visiting friends and tying up some loose ends. I stopped to get a bottle of wine for dinner, thinking that would be an appropriate gift. What do you think?" He held up the bag and used the smile that said he could poke fun at himself.

She smiled. "I think that's the perfect gift."

"I'm not very educated on wine. If I tell you the brand, do you think you could confirm that I made a good choice?"

"I'm probably more in the same category as you are. I don't know much about wines." She glanced at her phone. "My husband's texting me, I'm sorry. I really need to go. He's keeping the kids so I could get some shopping done before I have to take them to school."

"Of course. Nice seeing you again."

"You too." She climbed into her car and he turned as though to head to his own vehicle.

The clicking sound from her engine pivoted him back around. He strode over to her and she opened the door.

"Everything all right?"

"Obviously not." She sighed. "I'll have to tell my husband to come get me. It might be the battery."

"Want me to take a look?"

"Sure."

"Pop the hood and I'll see what I can do."

"Thanks. You're a lifesaver. If Tom had to come, he would, but it'll be nice not to have to bother him if you can take care of it."

She settled back into the driver's seat and he leaned in, squeezing his hand around the paper bag. A stream of liquid caught her in the side of the face and she gasped, jerked her head up to look at him, then closed her eyes and slumped over the console.

From his pocket, he took the latex gloves and slid his hands into them, then pushed his victim over the console. Her head hit the floor, the rest of her body sprawled on the passenger seat. Once he had the battery hooked back up, he settled himself behind the wheel and picked up her phone. A quick text to her husband explaining she'd run into Nancy from work and would be delayed a bit longer took two seconds, then he backed out of the space and drove away.

175

Allie woke with a start. Sweat ran down her back and she pulled away from the heat source. She looked up to find Linc staring down at her. "I fell asleep," she said.

"Standing up. I've never seen anyone do that before."

"I was really tired."

"I think that's a given."

"And I'm hungry." Her stomach growled on cue and his lips turned up. A dart of longing swept through her. Longing to be normal. A longing to have him at her side without worrying if he would die because of her. "How long did I sleep?"

"A few hours. It's around lunchtime, I think."

"What? Seriously? Oh, good grief. I'm sorry."

"I'm not. I snagged a couple more hours myself."

"I'm going to get ready to face the day—or what's left of it." She pulled away from him and stood, then reached back to scratch at her stitches. "I'll be glad when these heal up. They're driving me crazy."

He rubbed the area lightly and frowned. "Let me see that."

"Why?"

"It feels swollen. You might need to have those looked at."

"It's fine. They filled me up with antibiotics at the . . . place."

"Place?"

"The rehab place I mentioned earlier."

"Yeah, you never did explain that."

"It wasn't a hospital, but it sure looked like one from inside the room. Catherine, one of the nurses, said Henry had brought agents there before who needed extra special care without media interference."

"Huh. Interesting."

She held her hair up and he lowered the neckline of her T-shirt over her left shoulder. With gentle fingers, he probed and she flinched. "It's tender."

"That doesn't look right. I think it's getting infected."

She waved a hand in dismissal. "Whatever. I'll have to deal with it later. I'm going to take that shower now."

"Let the warm water beat down on it. It might help. Go. I'll keep watch, although it's been blessedly quiet."

"How long do you think that's going to last?"

He grimaced. "Not long."

"I'll hurry."

Ten minutes later, she returned to the living area to find Linc with his head resting against the back of the couch. His eyes opened. "Ready?"

"I suppose."

"So . . . we go to Henry's to regroup?"

"Why? He's just going to yell at us."

"Are you whining?"

"Yes."

He grinned and her heart flipped once again. "My turn to get ready," he said. "We can walk out the door in less than fifteen minutes."

True to his word, they were climbing into the SUV in twelve. Allie kept the hoodie and the dark glasses on, not wanting to take a chance on being recognized.

When Linc pulled into Henry's drive, Allie couldn't help but admire her boss's home. She'd only been there a handful of times, but each time she saw it, her muscles seemed to relax a fraction.

The house wasn't large, but it was neat and well kept, with trees on either side of the property and lush vegetation surrounding the perimeter. All in all, Allie found it welcoming. And since it sat on two acres of land, his neighbors were a respectful distance away.

Linc followed Henry's directions and pulled around to the back. Their boss met them at the garage and motioned for Linc to drive in.

When he turned the SUV off, Allie climbed out and Linc followed her and Henry into the house. Still, having not spoken a word, the man gestured them to the kitchen table. He dropped his keys onto it and took a seat.

Allie's mouth watered at the sight of the food in front of her. Henry had laid out sandwich meats, bread, and fixings as well as two bags of chips and a pitcher of sweet tea. Linc and Allie silently fixed their plates, then Allie cleared her throat. "When do you have time to do all the yard work?"

"I don't. I have someone who comes once a week. But we're not talking about my yard. We're talking about you two."

"Are you going to yell again?" Linc asked.

Henry closed his eyes. "No. I'm going to beg the Almighty for some patience. And wisdom."

"Whatever it takes to make you a believer, Henry," Linc said in all seriousness.

"I'm starting to think some divine help might not be a bad thing to have." He practically growled the words, and Allie could tell he was about at his wit's end with them.

Allie stayed silent, sending up a quick prayer that Henry would one day come to know the God she'd found, because even if she was kind of frustrated with him, she still believed and knew she'd be with him if she died. Not that she was in a hurry for that to happen.

Linc seemed to think her silence was wise and followed her example, clamping his lips shut while linking his fingers on the table in front of him.

Henry drew in a deep breath. "All right. Here's the deal. We got nothing about Nevsky from Killian before he died, so right now we're regrouping. Linc, you have to go fill out paperwork and talk to SIRG about the shooting. I've managed to hold them off to this point, but they're ready to come after you. SIRT's finished their review and all looks fine, but SIRG still has to talk to you. Again, it all looks like a clean shoot and you'll be cleared in no time, but—"

"It's policy. I know. I'll go now while Allie has you to watch her back."

"That would be best."

"Coward," she whispered as he stood and headed for the door with a quick wave. She noted he didn't even bother to deny her accusation.

Linc left and Allie leaned forward to rest her arms on the table. "What now, Henry? How did Radchenko know to find us at the cabin? He had to track us, because even Annie can't get a read on Daria."

"Unless there's something on her clothes or shoes."

"Maybe, but I don't think so. I think it has to be us. Somehow." He frowned. "Then I don't know. We swept Linc's vehicle—"

"And he's been sweeping it every time we get in it."

"So no trackers there."

"Wait a minute. Daria texted me to leave her alone. If someone was monitoring her phone and she had it on longer than it took to answer my texts—"

"He could have gotten the coordinates and tracked her down."

"But straight to the cabin?"

"What if she has something on her phone that's not connected to her phone GPS?"

Allie blinked. "You think someone got ahold of it and put an actual tracker in it?"

"It's possible, right?"

"Or her laptop. Which would explain why Annie can't pick it up according to location services on it, but someone knew where to find her." She frowned. "But Daria's smart. She'd know better than to leave a trail like that."

"She's a seventeen-year-old kid. You might be giving her too much credit."

He could be right. She raised a brow and sighed. "Well, I wish we could figure out how they're tracking her so we could beat them to her. In the meantime, do you have a couch I can crash on for a while? My head is pounding and I feel sick."

Henry stood. "Of course. I'm sorry. You're still healing and here I am, making you rehash everything. We'll work more on Nevsky when you feel like it. Come on, you can use the guest bedroom."

His suddenly solicitous demeanor took her a little by surprise, but she decided to simply be grateful for it. She was asleep the minute her head hit the pillow.

18

Linc's phone rang two hours into his meeting with SIRG. They were just about finished, so he requested to take the call and they dismissed him with kudos on taking an assassin off the street. Linc didn't bother to tell them any more than he had to, but he'd wanted to tell them everything. Henry was really putting him and Allie in a tight spot, and the more he went along with it, the less he liked it.

In the hall, he answered the phone. "Linc St. John."

"Allie's friend?"

The voice was familiar. "Yes. Who's this?"

"Roland Carter. One of Allie's neighbors. We met the day you cleaned some stuff out of her apartment."

"Oh, right. Yes, sir, Mr. Carter, what can I do for you?" And how had he gotten Linc's number?

"Allie's got a squatter, I believe. You want to check it out or you want me to call the cops?"

"Someone broke into her apartment?"

"I don't know about broke into. I don't see any sign of forced entry. But yeah, someone's there and they're not answering my knocks."

"I'll check it out. Thanks for letting me know. You didn't happen to get a plate on the car the person drove, did you?"

"Nope. Would have if she'd been driving one, but the girl just walked up."

"Girl? How old?"

"Heck if I know. These days twelve-year-olds look like they're nineteen. But if I had to guess, I'd say around that. Eighteen or nineteen."

"No sign of forced entry, so how'd she get in when I know I locked that place up tight when I left?"

"Had a key, it looked like."

Immediately, Linc flashed back to the conversation between Daria and Allie when she'd made the sarcastic comment about how it would have been easier to get a key to Nevsky's office if he had just kept one in the plant by the door like she did.

If that was Daria in Allie's apartment, she'd obviously remembered that—and the address Allie had shared with her. "Thanks, man. I'll be right there."

Linc texted Allie as he headed to his SUV. When he got no response, he called her.

Voice mail.

"Call me when you get this, will you? Looks like Daria's at your place." He hung up and focused on the drive. Twenty minutes later, he pulled in to Allie's apartment complex and wove around to the back.

Roland Carter sat on his second-floor balcony in clear view of Allie's first-floor walkway and door. Linc approached with a wave. "Thanks for calling."

"Sure thing."

"How'd you get my number?"

The old man laughed. "I still have my connections." He sobered. "She went in a little over an hour ago. Haven't heard a peep from her since."

"She could have gone out the back."

"She didn't."

"How do you know?"

Carter shrugged. "I've been keeping a watch. Trust me, she's still in there."

The girl had him curious. Somehow she managed to travel pretty much wherever she wanted to go without trouble. Not only that, she'd dodged a trained assassin who worked for her father, along with several FBI agents who shouldn't have had any trouble locating a teenager with no experience in eluding the law.

Or had Gerard trained her to do that very thing? It wouldn't surprise him.

Linc nodded to Carter. "You got my back?"

A gleam entered the man's eyes and he stood. "You know it."

While he waited for Roland to come down, Linc scoped the apartment with a quick glance. Would Daria be watching? Knowing her, she'd probably have some kind of booby trap set up in case someone opened the door.

He made his way around the back, with Roland following at a respectable distance. Linc slipped up the stairs that led to Allie's screened-in porch and found it unlocked. However, the back door was secure. He peered around the sheer curtain and got a good view of the kitchen and the half bath straight past that, but nothing beyond or on either side. Allie's bedroom was to the right of the kitchen, her second bedroom to the left.

Linc reached into his pocket and pulled out the key he'd kept since he and Allie had been there after her "death." It didn't take long to ascertain that there was nothing blocking the door that would set off any alarms for Daria. If it was indeed her. Linc opened the door and slipped inside.

He was going to scare the daylights out of whoever was in the apartment, but if it was Daria, he wasn't about to warn her of his presence and send her running again. He needed to talk to her and get some answers. On silent feet, he made his way through the kitchen and peered around the corner into the small living area with sliding glass doors.

He blinked. Daria lay stretched out on the couch, one hand tucked under her left cheek, the other resting on a wicked-looking revolver. He returned to the window and found Carter watching, a hand resting at his back. He met the man's eyes and gave him a thumbs-up. Carter grinned and returned the gesture before walking back toward the front of the building.

Linc retraced his steps to the living area to look down at Daria once more. He raked a hand through his hair and sat down to text Allie and plot out his next move.

Allie woke with a gasp, the nightmare fading too slow to suit her. Drones with bombs, cold water that stole her breath, gunshots, her little sister missing the base of her skull.

With a groan, she sat up and looked around, trying to shove the images from her mind and get her bearings.

Oh, right. Henry's house.

A glance at the clock said she'd been asleep a little over two and a half hours. She swung her legs over the side of the bed, and the action pulled at her back, once again setting off a wave of pain and itching in her stitches.

She rose and padded into the bathroom to pull off her shirt. She turned her back to the mirror and got a good look at the area for the first time and winced. "Ouch. No wonder." The area was swollen, red, and inflamed. "Great."

Allie rummaged through the cabinets until she found a bottle of alcohol. Splashing some on a wad of toilet paper, she held it to the area. It stung, but probably wasn't doing much good. The infection was deep and she figured it might need some professional attention.

As soon as she was able to, she'd get it.

Ignoring it for now, she dressed and grabbed her phone from the nightstand to find a text from Linc. And a voice mail. Both with the same message.

"Call me when you get this."

She frowned and did so.

The call cut off immediately. And a text came through.

Linc

Can't talk. Daria is in your place. Letting her
sleep for a bit before I wake her.

Allie's heart jumped into a double-time rhythm. She texted him back.

I'm on the way.

She had no vehicle.

Somehow

She bolted out of the room, down the hall, and into the den. "Henry! Henry!"

He leaped from the couch, weapon in his hand faster than she could blink. "What is it?"

"Sorry. You don't need that. Daria's at my place. I need to get over there ASAP."

He frowned and tucked his weapon into his shoulder holster. "How do you know that?"

"Linc texted. This is our chance to get what we need on Nevsky. Now will you please come on?"

"Allie, you're still not a hundred percent. Let Linc handle it."

She stared at him. "Do I have to call an Uber?"

He rolled his eyes. "Of course not, but it'll take us twenty minutes to get there. Linc will probably have it all under control at that point and can contact us with what he finds."

"He's got it under control now, but I'm going. With or without you." She knew she was pushing it. Technically, he could order her to stay put.

"Not going without," he finally said, with narrowed eyes and a chill in his tone.

"Thank you, Henry."

"Right."

"So, let's move!" Only the fact that she was mindful that he was her boss had her tacking a "Please!" on the end.

"Get in the car," he said. "I'm coming. Going to grab a couple of vests. Which you will wear."

"Gladly. I'll be in the car." Allie darted past him. She was in the passenger seat waiting impatiently with her seat belt on when he finally threw a vest in her lap and climbed in.

Once they were on the way, Allie slipped into the vest and started texting Linc.

> On the way. Is she okay?

> Yes. She's still asleep.

> We'll be there in about twenty minutes.

Linc's phone had blown up with text messages from his family, and he had to start answering them or they were going to put a BOLO out on him. One by one, he sent his responses, then set his phone aside and watched the young girl sleep.

Dark shadows were visible under her pale lashes and she looked too thin under the baggy shirt and jeans. She had to be absolutely exhausted.

His heart pounded in sympathy with her situation. It hadn't been of her making and she didn't deserve the hand she'd been dealt—or the family she'd been born into. He sent up a silent prayer of thanks for his own large, loud, loving family.

He started to send another text to Allie when a spray of bullets hit the sliding glass doors. Daria jumped up from her dead sleep and Linc tackled her in front of the sofa. A scream escaped her, and his hand clamped around her weapon, taking it from her easily.

"I'm not here to hurt you!" He dragged her across the floor and shoved her behind the love seat as more bullets pelted the sofa.

Daria let out another squeal, squirmed, and landed a solid punch to his right cheekbone.

"Daria! Stop it! I'm trying to keep you alive!"

Another hail of bullets seemed to convince her to be still. Linc kept his body over hers, not only to protect her, but to keep her from landing any more well-placed blows. "I only took the gun to keep you from shooting me." The fact that they'd both moved so fast was all that had kept them from getting hit by the second round of bullets. He wondered how she'd learned to do that. Gerard?

"Well, who's shooting at us?"

"Not sure. If you'll stay still for a second, I'll try to figure that out." When she complied, he rolled off her and pointed to the floor, keeping his weapon—and hers—away from her reach. "Stay here. My name is Linc St. John and I'm an FBI agent. I'm also a friend of Allie's. Now, no running off this time, got it?"

She nodded, terror in her pretty blue eyes.

"I promise, I'm not the bad guy," he said. Bullets peppered the windows. "The guy shooting is!" From where the bullets landed this time, it was obvious the shooter had changed position. Trying to make sure he covered the whole place so anyone in the living area wouldn't be able to walk out. And he'd been aiming for the sofa. If the bullets had been two inches lower, Daria would have been Swiss cheese.

Linc called for backup, then crept to the shattered sliding glass doors to look out. Stillness. No one moved. Doors stayed shut.

The cops would be arriving shortly. And so would Allie and Henry. He dialed Allie's number.

"What do we do?" Daria asked from her position behind the couch.

"Help's on the way."

Allie answered before the first ring stopped. "Hey, what—"

"Got a shooter here! He was in front. Don't come in unarmed." He wanted to tell her not to come in at all, but didn't bother. She was his partner and only circumstances beyond her control would keep her from helping him. "How far away are you?"

"Three minutes out." All business, she relayed the information to Henry.

He could hear the sirens.

"Give me the phone." Henry's order reached Linc. Henry spoke again. "Allie's not entering this gunfight. We need her to stay out of sight if we can do that without you getting killed. I'll back you up."

"We're okay right now." He dared a peek out the nearest window. "The cavalry will be arriving soon."

"We'll be right there with them, but I'm the one coming in."

"Be careful." Linc hung up. The shooting had stopped. Linc dialed Roland's number. Voice mail. He tried again. And again with the same results. What if the man had been hit? He hesitated, then looked at Daria. "Do you promise not to leave if I go check on someone?"

"You're leaving me?"

For the first time since he'd started listening in on her conversations, she sounded like a scared teenager who needed a protector.

"I'm just going to step out the door and see if I can spot my friend. Cops are almost here and I'm guessing the shooter may have taken off. He isn't going to wait around to get caught." He hoped. "If you stay hidden right where you are, you should be fine."

"I won't move, I promise."

He believed her. Linc bolted to the front door. Weapon held ready, he opened it and darted a quick look to the right before jerking back behind cover of the wall. Nothing. He made the same move once again, this time looking to the left.

Again, nothing. He stepped out and let the door close behind him and hurried to the end of the short walkway that took him into the parking lot. Empty.

As was Roland's small porch on the second floor.

Linc dialed the man's number one more time as he hurried back to Allie's apartment. If Daria hadn't been there, he'd go searching for Roland, but he couldn't leave the teen. Once inside, he checked to see Daria exactly where he'd left her. Roland's phone rang three times, then went straight to voice mail. "Come on, Roland. Let me know you're okay." He hung up and moved to the shattered sliding glass door. A man dressed in jeans and a short-sleeved black T-shirt walked toward him. He lifted his weapon. Linc dove backward. The bullet whizzed past him to dig into the wall of Allie's kitchen.

Daria squealed.

"Stay put!" Linc swung out, weapon up, ready to fire.

At nothing.

Where had he gone? Wherever he was, Linc had no doubt he planned to show up again.

Sirens screamed into the complex, growing louder with each passing second. He turned to Daria. "Get ready to run when I give the word, okay?"

She nodded.

19

Allie kept her hoodie and sunglasses in place, but the truth was, she was more concerned about Linc and Daria than keeping her identity hidden. Linc had stopped answering his phone two calls ago and Daria had yet to answer hers.

"Stay low," Henry ordered. He flipped on his lights and siren and rolled into the parking lot at the same time as the local police. One cruiser stopped at the entrance and Allie knew that officer would set up a barricade. No one except law enforcement would be allowed in or out from this point forward.

"I'm going to pull around," Henry said.

"Just get as close to my apartment as possible, then let me out. I can cover the back."

"SWAT will be surrounding the place, Allie, I don't think—"

"SWAT's not here yet. At least, they're not in position. Linc and Daria could be hurt. Let me get in there and help if they need it. I've got a full first-aid kit in there and I know how to use it. Just do this, okay? Please?" She shot him an unwavering stare.

He stopped the car and she slipped out of the vehicle to race around the side of her building. Linc and Daria were darting down the steps of her screened-in porch.

"Linc! Daria! You're okay."

They ran for the cover of the trees and Linc pulled to a stop, scanning the area. She reached him and Linc nodded to the teen. "Take her and find a motel. For now, the shooting's stopped, but the shooter's not in custody. Where's Henry?"

"He dropped me off. I'm not sure."

Allie looked over his shoulder and flinched, turning. "Roland's headed this way," she murmured. "See if you can stall him so we can get out of here. There's a hotel three blocks from here. I'll text you the room number." She grabbed the girl's hand and led the way through the trees, taking the path residents often used to get to the service station behind the complex. The same one where Linc had met her after packing up her family's crime wall.

She and Daria pounded down the path.

Until a soft pop reached her ears. Something hard slammed into her back and Allie dropped to the undergrowth, her lungs paralyzed, her gun flying from her hand as she fell. Daria screamed and ducked behind the nearest tree. *Run!* She mentally screamed the order at Daria while she flailed on the ground like a fish trying to breathe. She managed to roll to her side, caught the teen's eye, and mouthed, *Run!*

Finally, her lungs jumped back into action and she was able to drag in a wheezing breath and fill them. "Go," she rasped. "Go!"

"But—" Daria's eyes flitted from one spot to the next, sheer terror on her face, then her gaze hardened. "I'll get help. I promise, Allie, I'll get help." She darted through the trees. Allie watched her go while she struggled for another breath. Footsteps crunched, drawing nearer.

When she tried to roll to her knees, lightning bolts of pain shafted through her back and she gasped, collapsing back onto the ground.

Black shoes filled her line of sight. She reached out, grasped the ankle, then dropped her hand. Breathing was becoming easier, but she didn't let on. The person wearing the black shoes leaned over and placed the muzzle of the weapon on her forehead.

"So, we meet again," Gregori said.

"I'm going to kill you," she whispered. "If it's the last thing I do, Gregori Radchenko, I'm going to end you."

He laughed and fury bubbled through her. "You never did know when to quit, did you?" he said.

She dragged in another lungful of air.

He reached out, clamped an iron hand around her upper arm, and yanked her to her feet. Her legs wouldn't hold her.

Tsking like she was a disobedient child, he tossed her over his shoulder. Her phone tumbled from her pocket and she grabbed for it. And missed.

"I can see we have a lot to catch up on," he said.

The pain in her back flared blowtorch hot, and she cried out, even as she fought against the darkness that threatened to pull her under.

Gregori tossed her into a car he'd hidden behind the service station. "Got you in the vest, did I?"

"Yeah. Were you aiming at Daria?" She winced as she shifted, trying to find a comfortable position.

"A moving target's harder to hit," he said. "Fortunately for me, you had the foresight to wear the vest."

"I guess when you have your victims on their face, the base of the skull isn't nearly as hard to find, huh?"

His fist shot out and she ducked, just not quite fast enough. His knuckles grazed her jaw and pain shot through her skull. She let her head fall sideways and kept her eyes shut. He grasped her throat and squeezed. Her eyes flew open and she jabbed out with the knuckle of her right index finger. The punch landed in his right eye. He screamed, jerking his head away from her. She scrambled for the door handle. His fingers caught her hoodie and yanked her back around.

Their eyes collided and she shuddered at the pure rage behind his gaze.

"What happened to you, Gregori?" she whispered. "What happened to my big brother that I loved?" Tears gathered and she choked them back.

Gregori flinched and drew back, dropping his hand. "That boy is gone forever."

"Why?"

"Because I was never really your brother."

"What?"

"You haven't figured it out."

She wasn't sure what to do with his amusement. "No, Gregori, I haven't figured it out. Could you just spell it out for me?"

"Of course. How's this? I am not your brother because I am Vladislav Nevsky's son."

Henry rubbed a hand over his head. "Go check on Allie and Daria and let me know where you land," he told Linc. His gaze flicked over the organized chaos that came with a full-blown manhunt. Helicopters circled above. "I'll keep you updated on this end." He turned abruptly and headed for the officer in charge.

Roland Carter stepped up next to Linc. He was glad to see the guy unharmed. "Thanks for your help," Linc told him.

"Anytime."

"Linc!"

He spun to find Daria racing toward him.

"He took her!"

Linc grabbed her arm. "What?"

"We were running," she gasped, "and he shot her. She told me to run."

"Shot her!"

Daria nodded, tears dripping onto her cheeks.

"Show me."

"Need some help?" Roland asked.

"Can you find Henry, the guy I was just talking to, and let him know we're going after the shooter? He has a hostage." Thankfully, Daria hadn't mentioned Allie's name.

"Of course." He trotted off, and Linc fell in behind Daria as she turned and took off toward the back of the complex. "Is she hurt bad?"

"I don't know."

"What happened?"

"We were running and then she fell."

"Did you hear the shot?" Because he hadn't.

"Yeah, kind of. Like a muffled pop. He must have used a suppressor." She led him into the wooded area, and when she came to a small path, she stopped and pointed. "There."

Examining the area turned up nothing other than signs of a struggle—and Allie's phone . . . and her gun. "There's no blood."

"He got her in the back. It seemed to knock the wind out of her because she couldn't talk. She mouthed for me to run, so I did."

He dialed Annie and focused on slowing his heart rate. Without revealing he was looking for Allie, he filled Annie in on as much as he could. "There's been a kidnapping at the apartment complex on Billings. I need any security footage in this area and the convenience store on Hampstead. See if it picked up anything and can give us a direction."

"On it," Annie said.

If the footage showed Allie's face, so be it. Getting her back was far more important than keeping her "dead."

Daria swiped another tear. "I'm sorry I ran. I should have stayed, but she told me to go and I thought it would be best if I let someone know. I . . . I couldn't help her, I'm sorry."

"It's not your fault," Linc said. "You did exactly right. If you hadn't run, he would have killed you or taken you too."

She swiped a stray tear. "I didn't know you were trying to help me. I thought you two were working for my father like the man you were with."

Linc stilled. "What man?"

"The day you and Allie found me being held in the office, my father had ordered his men to take me there and said he would be there soon to get the information from me. I'm guessing he meant the security footage I have."

"How did he know you had it?"

"I don't know that either. I figured Allie or you had told him."

Linc's lips tightened and he led the way to the convenience store. "Wasn't us."

"I'm starting to see that now."

"Who was the man you saw us with?"

"I don't know. He had on tactical gear like everyone else. I saw him once at my father's house, maybe like six months ago, and I only recognized him because he stared at me for a minute. I didn't like the look in his eyes and ran."

Which might have been the best thing she could have done in that particular situation. Only now Linc wondered exactly who she could have seen. His blood chilled. There had been people from all branches of law enforcement that day. SWAT, FBI, CPD, and more. And all had worn tactical gear.

The footage Henry had managed to get from Annie hadn't revealed who she'd been looking at, so he would have to approach things differently. "I want to show you some pictures and footage at some point, but right now my focus has to be getting Allie back, okay?"

"Of course."

"What?" Gregori glanced over at her. "No response?"

Allie hadn't spoken since he'd stated he was Nevsky's son. She was still reeling, trying to gather her scattered thoughts and settle her racing pulse—and ignore the pulsing pain in her back. She absently ran her hands over the seat's fine leather grain and noted the many high-tech features of the expensive automobile. "You like nice things."

"I do."

"Material things can't make up for what you're doing," she said softly.

He gave a choked laugh. "They have their comforts."

She raised a brow. "Not to your soul."

He laughed. "Shut up." She fell silent again and he sighed. "That's all you have to say to my announcement?"

"It can't be true."

"Why not?"

"Because . . . because it's . . ." She rubbed her eyes. "Okay, suppose it's true, how'd you find out?"

"Nevsky came to me and told me."

She scoffed. "And you believed him?"

"Not at first, but then he brought me proof."

"What kind of proof?"

"He approached me one day as I walked off the football field. He said he was an old family friend and he had something that he thought I'd be interested in. He told me he had a job for me and I could make a lot of money. I started doing some deliveries for him. He helped me open a bank account, and I was putting more money into it than I'd ever seen."

Allie swallowed. While they'd lived in a large house and looked to all the world like they had money to burn, their parents had provided the basic necessities and spent lavishly on themselves. Neither she nor Gregori had ever had much money except when their mother decided to go all out and spend on them. Looking back, Allie remembered her mother's manic episodes and figured she'd been an undiagnosed bipolar.

"About two weeks later, Nevsky asked me to take a medical test.

He refused to tell me what kind, but I didn't care at that point, I would have done anything to keep the money coming. Later, he came to me and hugged me and called me his son."

Allie shook her head, but her tight throat wouldn't allow any words to escape.

"I was still confused, but he promised me I'd understand later that day. He came to the house when Maxim was out, brought me in, and confronted our mother about the DNA test results that proved I was his son." He referred to the man who'd raised him for the first seventeen years of his life as Maxim. "She fell to the floor, crying, saying she hadn't wanted me to know. I demanded answers and she said she'd kept me from my father because she hadn't wanted me growing up in the organization. Apparently, while Maxim was my father's best friend, he was also in love with our mother." Although she'd be the first to admit the man hadn't been much of a father. "So, she married Maxim, and together, they betrayed my real father. And me."

Allie reeled. Shocked and hurting. "And that was the reason you killed them?" she finally asked, noting that he seemed to be driving aimlessly, with no purpose. Which was fine with her. As long as he was behind the wheel, he wasn't killing. Her or anyone else.

"Yes."

"Mom lived for a while, you know. Then killed herself."

His fingers tightened briefly around the wheel and he shot her a short glance. "I didn't know. I assumed she was dead."

"Might as well have been." And that was that, apparently. Allie's heart thundered in her ears. He'd become a monster. Grief shuddered through her.

Trees lined the two-lane road and his directionless driving suddenly seemed to have purpose. He was driving them into a deserted area. Why? To get rid of her, no doubt.

"What did Misha and I do to deserve that? Misha, especially."

He slammed a hand on the steering wheel and she jumped. "Because you were the most loved by *him*," he shouted.

Him?

Their father. Or rather, her father. Maxim.

"He never gave me the time of day," Gregori said. "I didn't understand it, and when I asked Mom, she refused to give me a straight answer. I just wanted you gone. Both of you. All of you. And my father said that it would be best, that I would be able to start over with a new family. I agreed and made it happen."

"Daria calls you her brother, but you never saw her or built any kind of relationship with her. How is that starting a new family?"

"She's not a part of the new family."

"Why not?"

He shrugged. "She was never important. She was only two when everything happened and Father ignored her for the most part." A hard smile tilted his lips. "He told me now that he had his son, he had no use for her and that our family was the organization."

"So Nevsky made her feel like my father made you feel. Ignored and worthless."

He stiffened. His jaw tightened and he clamped his fingers around the wheel.

Throat tight, she drew in a deep breath. "And so you started killing for Nevsky. It's really that simple?"

"Not quite so simple as that." He paused. "But, yes."

He braked and turned off on one of the side roads. For some reason, the area was familiar, but she couldn't think why. She decided to get answers while she could—and pay attention for any opportunity that would allow her the upper hand. She needed a weapon. Needed to distract Gregori so she could act when she had the element of surprise. "So, let me get this straight. Our mother had an affair with Nevsky when they were younger—sometime during college. She got pregnant and Dad married her."

"Maxim, yes."

"That's why Nevsky wanted to cut all ties with the man, right?"

"Yes. My father was very hurt. He couldn't understand why his two good friends would betray him in such a way."

She wasn't addressing that one.

Allie still saw no way to escape. The doors were locked and she had a seat belt on. She slid her elbow back on the center console until her thumb rested on the seat belt latch. *Talk. Keep him talking.* "So what was his side of the story?"

"He asked her why he should help—he had no obligation and she had made her choice clear. She blurted out the truth and asked him how he would feel about his son winding up living on the streets."

It had been *that* bad? Allie didn't remember it that way.

"After the blood test," Gregori said, "he gave her the money."

"And then he told you everything."

"Everything. He was furious with them. He paced and raged over our lost years together. And I finally saw what I had been missing. My father's love."

"You *were* loved, Gregori. I loved you. Misha loved you!"

"It wasn't enough!" He snapped his lips shut and made another turn. Allie was desperately trying to note the twists and turns but was getting mixed up.

"It could have been. Our parents may have been wrong. They may have lied and fought and treated us like we were nothing upon occasion, but they didn't deserve to die. Not like that. Not by your hand," she whispered. "And Misha certainly didn't."

He said nothing, although a vein pulsed in his forehead. "What's done is done. My father took me in, gave me everything. I would do anything for him."

"Including kill."

"Of course."

She swallowed. "Does he know I'm alive?"

"No."

Did she believe him?

He chuckled. "You think I'm lying?"

Was she that transparent? "Why wouldn't you?"

"I would if I needed to, but no, he doesn't know."

"Why not?"

"Because I have my own agenda right now."

She stared and his lips quirked in a way she remembered from when they were teens. It sent a shaft of pain through her so strong she gasped. "Your own agenda?"

"To make as much money as I can."

"You have to be extremely wealthy at this point."

"One can never have too much money. Did Mother teach you nothing?"

Wow. "And Gerard?" she asked. "Why did Nevsky want him dead?"

"Because he was too close to Daria. Treated her like a daughter. That made his loyalty questionable."

"She loved him like a father because she desperately wanted one."

He shrugged.

Allie pressed her palms to her eyes. She was so confused, but something Daria had said rang through her mind. "You helped him kill someone she loved before too, didn't you?"

He shot her a sharp glance. "What are you talking about?"

"She said her father was a murderer. I asked her who he'd killed and she refused to say, but I'm sure you know."

"I do. It was one of her former bodyguards. He fell in love with her. Father killed him."

Gregori was slowing for an old pickup in front of him. Allie leaned forward slightly, letting out a moan and reaching for her back to rub it. She didn't have to feign the back pain—it was still real. With her left hand still near the seat belt latch, she slid her right hand down the door's armrest closer to the lock. When he braked for the pickup to make a left-hand turn, she released the belt, unlocked and threw open the door, and dove out of the vehicle. Gregori's shout echoed behind her as she hit the asphalt rolling. Pain arced through her, stealing her breath once more, but the vest helped protect her.

Tires squealed and Allie continued her rolling momentum until she hit the side of the road. Ignoring the dizziness and pain, she managed to get to her feet and stumble into the wooded area, lurching and scrambling to find cover.

Linc had scanned all of Daria's belongings looking for a bug or anything that could tell him how she was being tracked—because this latest incident left no doubt that Radchenko had some way of following her.

Which left him no choice but to stash her in a hotel room and ask if the local police would be willing to have two officers guard her room. They'd agreed and he'd darted out to hop on the chopper that had landed approximately ten minutes after Daria let him know Allie had been taken.

Henry was still out of sight, so Linc had simply texted him the situation. All Henry had said was, "Use every resource available and find her."

Linc settled the headphones over his ears and gave the pilot, Diego Sanchez, a thumbs-up. Annie was connected to the Bluetooth speaker that went directly into his and the pilot's headset.

"Annie?"

"Here."

"What have you got?"

"The footage from the convenience store shows a woman being forced into a black sedan. It's a Mercedes-Maybach S650. That's a two-hundred-thousand-dollar vehicle, people."

Linc let out a low whistle. "Which way?"

"North out of the parking lot. And since I have the plate number, I can attach it to the vehicle's info . . ." Keyboard keys clacked in the background. She finally gave a grunt of satisfaction. "Here's the good news. It's very high-tech and super hackable."

"How long until you're in?"

"Um . . . one second . . . and . . . now. Okay, I'm sending you the coordinates where the Wi-Fi signal is coming from."

Linc's phone pinged and he called them out to Diego. The chopper banked and Linc prayed his latest meal would stay put—and that Allie would be alive when they arrived.

"I'm going to need a place to set her down, Annie," the pilot said.

"Got that coming. Just a sec." A pause. More keyboard clicks. "Okay," she said, "the vehicle seems to be stopped at the moment. Here are the coordinates. There's a landing area about half a mile away. It's a soccer field and is currently clear to land on. I've got backup on the way as well, but you're going to get there ahead of them and it will be several minutes before the backup arrives."

"Several minutes that this woman might not have. I'll take my chances on going in alone."

"Who is she?"

"Someone very important to a case."

"Must be."

"Thanks, Annie."

"You got it."

"Got the coordinates programmed," Diego said. "Heading there now." He glanced back at Linc. "You okay?"

"Wish I'd had time to down a Dramamine, but yeah, for now." He hated flying in helicopters. Didn't much care for planes either, but at least on an airplane, he didn't feel like his stomach was constantly trying to catch up with the rest of his body. He closed his eyes and decided that made it worse. *Hang on, Allie, help's coming.*

20

Allie stayed still. Listening. Barely breathing. She had no phone, she had no weapon, she had no idea where she was, and her brother wanted her dead. Not exactly ideal circumstances. But she'd work with what she had. Which was two good feet and a brain.

Scrambling for a plan, she thought about the fancy GPS unit on the vehicle. Gregori was looking for her. She'd heard him cursing as he threw open the car door.

Could she somehow circle around and get back to the vehicle before he gave up searching for her in the wooded area? It was very possible he had a weapon somewhere in the car. In fact, she was almost willing to stake her life on that.

For now, she heard nothing. Was he far enough away that he wouldn't hear if she moved? Or was he like her and staying put until she made some noise? Indecision warred within her.

Did she dare pray?

God, please . . .

She had no words. The prayer wouldn't come.

Allie slipped from behind the tree and crept back the way she came. Her pulse pounded, but she made it back to the road without seeing any sign of Gregori. Vaguely, she noted the thumping of chopper blades somewhere above and wished it was coming for her. However, with no way to track her, she wasn't going to hold out hope. The car sat where Gregori had left it with the driver's door open. She approached with caution, the painful bruise on her back a reminder that getting shot hurt. Not that she needed the reminder. The scars in her back from the bullet and multiple surgeries were reminder enough.

Still . . . she had no wish to experience it again.

And this time, he'd probably be aiming for her head in spite of the mysterious "agenda" he'd mentioned.

While the driver's door was open, she slid into the passenger seat and opened the glove compartment. Just like she figured, the weapon was there. Without hesitation, she removed the Ruger, checked it, and found it loaded. Of course, it would be.

A light footfall behind her sent her diving into the seat and slamming the door behind her. No bullets hit the vehicle and she raised her head with caution. Gregori walked toward her, his venomous expression chilling. She scooted into the driver's seat and started to shut the door, then decided she didn't want to be trapped and slipped out onto the asphalt.

A car's engine caught her attention. "No, don't come this way," she whispered. It drew closer and stopped.

A young man in his early twenties stepped out. "Do you need—"

"Get out of here and call the cops!"

Her yell startled him back into the driver's seat.

Gregori's bullet punctured the side of his black Charger, and Allie couldn't get a good shot at Gregori from her awkward position behind the car.

With a squeal of tires, the would-be Samaritan backed up and peeled away.

Allie stepped sideways, keeping the car between her and Gregori. "Give it up, Alina, you can't beat me at this."

"You might be surprised." She paused. "Why didn't you kill

me when you had the chance? You said you had your own agenda. What is it? Where were you taking me?"

"It doesn't matter. Drop the gun and get in the car or the next person who approaches will die."

She was going to have to chance that. "This ends here, Gregori."

A chopper flew overhead, drawing her attention, along with Gregori's. Elation filled her. They'd found her. Gregori turned to bolt behind the nearest tree.

And was tackled to the ground.

Linc!

Gregori's weapon tumbled from his hand—but was still within reaching distance if he moved just right.

While the two men grappled for the upper hand, Allie shot from behind the protection of the vehicle and raced toward them. Gregori's fingers grazed hers as she snatched the gun. She stumbled back, lost her footing, and landed hard on her backside. Pain shot through her. She ignored it and lurched to her feet, Gregori's weapon in her left hand, hers in her right. "Gregori! Don't move!"

Her shout distracted him for a split second. Just long enough for Linc to land a solid punch to the man's gut. The air whooshed from his lungs and he went still.

Allie stepped up and held the gun on his head. "Don't. Move."

He stayed frozen in between his gasps for breath.

His eyes locked on hers while Linc rolled to his feet, breathing hard, weapon pointed at the man.

Allie stared. Gregori stared back.

She could pull the trigger and it would be done. She'd have justice for her family. Her baby sister. This is what she'd been living for so long.

Her finger twitched.

Just remember, justice and revenge are two very different things.

Linc's voice echoed, but she never took her gaze from the man on the ground. He seemed to sense her inner conflict. "Are you going to do it?" he asked, his voice soft, almost mocking.

"I've wanted to. For a very long time. It's why I became an FBI agent. So I would have every resource at my disposal to hunt you down and kill you like the animal you are."

"So what are you waiting for?"

Justice and revenge are two very different things.

"Allie?" Linc's voice was just as soft. "You don't want to do this. I mean, you might want to right now, but is it worth it in the end?"

Justice and revenge are two very different things.

"It is mine to avenge; I will repay," says the Lord.

Allie backed away with slow, measured steps, her gun never leaving Gregori's face.

"Allie, don't do it," Linc whispered.

She never flicked her gaze away from her brother, but a rush of . . . something filled her. She could shoot him in self-defense, but not cold blood. Linc's weapon didn't move from the man. With an agonized groan, she lowered the gun to point it at the ground but stayed ready in case she needed to lift it again. "I'm not, I won't."

"Coward," Gregori hissed.

"No. Someone once told me justice and revenge are two very different things. I didn't realize it until just now, but I want justice, not revenge. Besides, killing you lets you off the hook. I want you in prison for the rest of your life." She gestured to the expensive ride behind her. "It's clear how much you value your possessions and your money. You could have gotten rid of me a couple of times but didn't want to take a chance on hitting your car. That's just . . . wow." She scoffed. "Prison will hurt you so much more than death will."

Linc grabbed Gregori by the collar and hauled him to his feet. He looked at Allie. "Cuff him."

As Allie holstered her gun, the man lunged toward her. Linc dove forward, grasping his collar again and yanking him back as a crack sounded. Linc pulled Gregori down with him, then let go and rolled.

"Linc!" Allie went to her knees and spun her weapon toward the source of the bullet.

Another loud crack. Gregori, rising to a crouch in midflight, jerked and fell, and his eyes went blank.

"Linc! Are you hit?" Allie grabbed his arm.

"Not hit," he said, scrambling to his feet and pulling her behind a tree.

"I thought for sure he'd gotten you," she said on a gasp.

"If Radchenko hadn't moved to go at you when he did, I'd have a bullet in my head." Linc shuddered at the close call and pulled his phone from his pocket to speed-dial Henry.

"Where are you?" the man asked.

"Dodging bullets." Although the shooter hadn't sent any more flying their way. "Where are you?"

"On the way. What's going on?"

Linc gave him the condensed version.

"But you're okay?" he asked. "And Allie?"

"We're fine. Radchenko is dead. Sniper is still in the wind."

"I'm having the chopper come get me. Backup should be there any second."

He could hear the sirens. "See you when you get here."

"Keep Allie under wraps. Radchenko may be dead, but we've still got Nevsky to nail. And Radchenkos are a dime a dozen. When Nevsky finds out he's dead, he'll just send someone else."

Linc wasn't so sure about that.

By the time Henry arrived, the medical examiner was already working on Radchenko. Allie stood out of sight near the tree line watching the man work, her face expressionless.

Linc slipped over to her. "You okay?"

"Before I answer that, how's Daria? Is she okay?"

"She's fine. At a hotel and waiting for us to join her. She's the only one on the whole floor with guards strategically placed."

"Good."

"So, are you okay?"

"Yes. No. I . . . I . . . don't know. I thought I would feel different."

"Different how?"

"Glad. Victorious. Justified. Anything, but—" She clamped her lips shut and tears filled her eyes. She blinked them away.

"But what, Allie?"

"I don't feel any of those things," she said softly. "Instead, I just feel . . . sad. Just so . . . very . . . sad." She leaned her head against the trunk of the tree and continued to stare at the ME who was now directing the transfer of the body into the black bag.

"I'd think that's normal," Linc said.

She glanced at him. "Is it? Ever since I was fourteen years old, my goal in life has been to find Gregori and kill him. That's why I joined the FBI. It's why I worked so hard to be one of the best agents in the field."

"You succeeded in that."

"I did." She paused. "You don't seem surprised that I'm feeling the way I do."

"I'm kind of surprised you're surprised. I'm not a shrink, but over the past year, while you left out a few pertinent details of your life, I believe I've gotten to see the real you—or at least the you that you want to be. If that makes sense."

She bit her lip and looked away with a short nod. "It does. And you could be right."

"You're not the kind of person who'd rejoice in someone else's death. No matter who he is or what he's done."

Her gaze shot back to his. "Don't make me out to be someone I'm not. I almost pulled that trigger," she said. "Don't think for one minute that I didn't want to."

"I'm not making you out to be anyone but you. You couldn't shoot him, could you?"

"No." A sigh slipped from her. "I couldn't. If he'd been armed and aiming a weapon at me, I wouldn't have hesitated, but . . . he wasn't."

"Do you regret it?"

"I regret a lot of things, Linc, but I don't regret finding out that I'm nothing like my brother. Or my parents."

"I'm glad."

She locked eyes with him once again. "If I'd killed him, I'd be no better than he. I would have chosen a path of no return. I would have been a murderer." She shook her head. "In my head I kept hearing you saying that justice and revenge were two very different things. And then that Bible verse popped into my head. The one about how vengeance is the Lord's. When we went to church that last time, the pastor preached on that passage, and I guess it stuck with me."

"God has a way of doing that. Of sticking with you and speaking to you when you need it. Or least expect it."

"You think that was him? Speaking to me when I was so very tempted to end Gregori's life?"

"Absolutely."

She nodded. "It's because of you and your family, you know. I think that if I hadn't met the St. John clan when I did that I might very well have pulled that trigger today."

"What?" He raised a brow, then frowned. "I don't think you would have, but how do you come to that conclusion that you didn't because of anything I, or my family, did?"

"Ever since my brother killed my family, I guess I just figured that with my genes, there was always the possibility that I'd turn out just like him. Or even my mother, who was a very sad woman with no backbone and an addictive love of money." She huffed a harsh laugh. "Guess that's where Gregori got it from. It's what he saw day in and day out."

"You didn't?"

She shrugged. "I guess I did, but it didn't influence me that much. We had a huge house, three boats, a private jet, and all the clothes and shopping I could ever want. Then I remember Dad selling the jet and thinking it was weird. I guess, in hindsight, that was when he started scrambling to stay ahead of the creditors." She sighed. "I still don't know where those large withdrawals were going."

"You may never know."

"True."

"We all have choices in life, Allie. I think it's clear that you've made yours. You want to make a difference and stop the bad guys no matter what it takes. I admire that."

She blinked and swiped a tear. "You take my breath away sometimes, St. John." She paused. "You know, I may not be giving my foster parents enough credit. They were hardworking, God-fearing people who did their best with an angry teenager. But one summer at a camp in the woods of North Carolina, the speaker encouraged us to give our lives to God. He didn't promise everything would be perfect, but he did promise we'd never be alone and God would never give up on us. I went forward that night and gave my life to God." She shook her head. "I don't think I fully understood what I'd done, but God did, didn't he?"

"Absolutely."

"Maybe that's why I couldn't pull the trigger."

"I don't think he physically kept you from pulling it—that choice was yours."

"True."

"But yeah, I think he was encouraging you not to make that choice."

"I do too."

"I'm glad you listened to him."

She huffed a short laugh. "Same here."

Henry headed their way and Allie dropped back slightly. Linc turned to face his boss. "Any word on Nevsky?"

"No. It's like he's dropped off the planet. But he's on the airlines' watch list. We've got eyes on all of his homes and so far he hasn't shown up."

"He'll show," Allie said. She drew in a deep breath. "It's time to come up with a new plan. He's going to be super careful about letting anyone in his house at this point."

"Yeah, I'd say your cooking days are over," Linc said.

"Just as well. I think I'm ready to go see Daria and get that evidence from her so we can take down Nevsky once and for all. I'm so over that man."

Linc took her hand. "I like that plan."

"I can give you a ride back to the hotel," Henry said. "Talk to the girl and find out what you can. Then call me. I'll be dealing with all of this while I wait to hear from you."

Allie kept her head down and slid into Henry's SUV. Linc climbed in beside her.

It didn't take long to reach the hotel. Henry let them out at the back and she and Linc took the stairs to the third floor.

"Stay here until I get rid of the guards," Linc said.

She nodded.

Linc stepped out of the stairwell and spotted the two men in front of the room next to Daria's. He'd gotten five rooms and had them guard one of the empty ones. A female officer was in the real room with Daria. Linc flashed his badge at the two men and they nodded. He code knocked on Daria's door and Ginny opened it. "Hi, Linc."

"Hi, Ginny. I'll take it from here. I appreciate your help."

"Anytime."

Once she and the other two guards were gone, he retrieved Allie from the stairwell and led her inside the two-bedroom suite, much like the one he and Allie had stayed in earlier.

Daria opened the door to her bedroom, anxiety pinching her young face. "Are you all right?"

"I'm alive, so I'm going to count that one as a win."

The girl darted across the room and wrapped her arms around Allie, who gaped at Linc. He motioned for her to hug the teen back.

Allie did and he thought he saw a tear slip down her cheek.

21

Allie paced the room, her mind spinning, emotions churning. She'd come to care for Daria way too much, but there was nothing she could do about it now.

Daria sat on the sofa flipping channels on the television while Linc studied his phone.

"What are you looking at?" Allie asked him.

"The video."

"What video?"

"The one Henry sent me of the security footage when Daria went all Houdini and did her disappearing act."

"Hey," the teen said. "I had good reasons for that."

"I know."

She stood and walked over to Linc. "May I see it?"

"Sure." He held the phone so she could watch while Allie continued to wear a hole in the carpet.

"Something's nagging at me," Allie finally said.

Linc looked up. "What?"

"Nevsky's office."

Daria snapped her gaze to Allie's. "What do you mean?"

"You said your father kept everything under lock and key. His

213

home, his office, his desk. You even described him as OCD about it, right?"

"Yes."

"Would he ever leave one of his desk drawers unlocked if it was able to be locked?"

"No. And all of his drawers have locks on them."

The absolute certainty in Daria's voice brought Allie to a stop. "One of the drawers in his desk wasn't locked."

Daria frowned. "Maybe he forgot."

"You just said it would be locked. You really think he would forget?"

"No. I mean, I suppose it could happen, but it would sure be out of character." She paused. "No, it couldn't. Not with his OCD issues."

"That's what I thought. And the hard drive I sent to Annie was basically blank. There wasn't even a password on the laptop."

"Now, *that* is weird. He has passwords on everything." She turned her gaze back to the footage on Linc's phone.

Allie raked a hand through her hair. "So why would that drawer be unlocked? Unless he wanted me to find that stuff," she muttered, her brain trying to piece it all together. Unfortunately, that was impossible to do without all the pieces.

She pulled her phone from her pocket. All of the pictures she'd taken in Nevsky's office had been sent from the phone that had been destroyed in the blast, but—

A name from the television snagged her attention and she glanced at the screen. "Stop!"

Daria froze.

"Sorry, I didn't mean to yell. Can you turn that up?" She pointed to the television. Daria, still holding the remote, complied.

". . . has been reported missing by her family. It's been almost thirty-six hours since her husband last heard from her. No one has seen her since."

214

"Allie?" Linc frowned at her and she held up her hand. He waited.

The reporter continued. "If you have any word of Catherine Hayworth's whereabouts, please call the number at the bottom of the screen."

The video flipped to the outside of a large two-story home on Hilton Head Island. "Hi, I'm Tom," the handsome, dark-headed man said. He stood on the front steps of the home, hands at his sides. Reporters were gathered around, their microphones stretched toward him. "I'm Catherine's husband. In spite of the line of questioning by the police, Cathy and I weren't having any marital issues and we didn't have a big fight or disagreement before she disappeared. She was grocery shopping and I was babysitting the kids. We were texting back and forth and she said she ran into a coworker and would be home shortly. But she never arrived." Tears welled in his eyes. He looked away for a moment, biting his lip. "I need to know what happened to her. The security cameras covering the grocery store parking lot had been tampered with, so there's no footage for the police to use to help find her. A witness saw her talking to a man wearing a baseball cap and sunglasses and is thought to be in his midforties. It's also suspected that she was taken by that man. If you have her, or if you have any information that would allow us to bring her home, please call. I need her, our children need her, to come home safe and in one piece. Please," he whispered, his voice trailing off. He swallowed and spun on his heel and disappeared into the house.

"Wow," Daria said, "that was intense."

Allie pressed a hand to her mouth. "I know."

"What is it?" Linc asked.

"She was one of the nurses at the rehab place where Henry took me after the explosion."

"Rehab place?" Daria asked. "That's kind of weird. Wouldn't you go to a hospital?"

"No, actually, it made sense for what he had in mind. With me being dead and all."

"I'm still not sure that helped anything," Linc muttered.

"Well, no one went after your family, did they?"

"I guess not, but something still feels hokey to me."

"I'll tell you what's hokey," Daria said, "is this footage. Where's the rest of it?"

Allie frowned. "What do you mean?"

"It's been changed."

"How do you figure?"

"Can you put it up on the big screen?"

"Sure." Linc grabbed his laptop from the bag. Once he had the cables attached, he pressed play.

"There," Daria pointed. "In the background. See the guy standing in the doorway of the office building? Then in the next frame, he's gone."

"So he walked off," Linc said.

"Then we should see him walking off. We don't."

Linc rewound it and Allie squinted at the screen when he played it again. "She's right," Allie said. "He's there one second and gone the next. No walking. Just gone." She stared at Daria. "How'd you catch that when neither one of us, nor Henry, did."

The teen narrowed her eyes. "It's very subtle, but part of it is, I should have seen the guy I recognized in it. Part of it could just be the artist in me."

Had to be.

"So, we've got some missing footage," Allie said slowly. "Who would have been able to do this?"

"I think we need to ask Annie." He dialed her number and Allie wanted to pace again. Things were just not adding up. She raked a hand through her hair, then pulled it into a short ponytail. She missed the four inches she'd had to cut off.

"I still think it was a setup," she murmured.

Linc glanced at her, then went back to listening to Annie. His frown deepened with each word. "Uh-huh. Okay, thanks." He turned his attention back to Allie. "What do you mean, a setup?"

"The whole thing. It has to be some kind of a setup." Her brain was finally starting to put it all together.

"Explain, please."

"I told you Nevsky had photos of us in his office. He'd had them for a week. Why didn't he kill me? Daria said he's OCD about his privacy. Why would he leave that particular drawer unlocked along with a laptop on his desk with no password?"

"Obviously, rhetorical questions. What's your conclusion?"

"Nevsky wanted me to see all of that stuff."

"But . . . why?"

"I don't know!" She pressed her fingers to her lips. "It's like I'm working a puzzle with missing pieces. Annie said nothing was on the hard drive. At least the part I managed to copy."

"Right.".

"That doesn't add up either."

"Unless you had to pull the plug too soon and anything relevant just wasn't on there."

"Maybe. I'll concede that one. However, somehow Nevsky sends Gregori after me to kill me, but instead Gregori takes me hostage and says Nevsky doesn't know I'm alive. That's not possible, so explain that one."

Linc narrowed his eyes. "I can't. Unless Gregori was lying."

"I think Gregori would have lied about anything that would further his agenda." She paused. "But I don't think he was lying about this."

"Then Nevsky didn't send Gregori to kill you."

"Although I suppose Gregori could have been wrong, but say he wasn't. If Nevsky didn't send Gregori after me, who did?"

Linc sighed and looked at Daria, whose gaze bounced back and forth between them. "I have no idea," Linc finally said.

"At first," Allie said, "I thought Gregori was just taking me somewhere secluded so he could kill me and dump my body in a hard-to-find spot, but when I said something about that, he said he had his own agenda. What could that have been?" At their blank looks, she groaned and slumped to the couch to put her head in her hands. "The pieces won't fit."

Linc's phone rang. "It's Brady," he said. "Let me take this, then I'll tell you what Annie said about the footage."

"What's up?" Linc said by way of greeting.

"Got a couple of questions for you."

"Shoot."

"Okay, so, I got permission to view the evidence pulled from the bottom of the river after the explosion."

"You didn't say anything about doing that."

"Because I wasn't sure anything would come of it and I didn't want to go digging into a wound while it's still so raw."

Linc closed his eyes and almost told Brady the truth. Only Henry's insistence that they continue the charade kept his lips shut on that topic. "All right, so what'd you find?"

"Might be nothing, but I got word from another fed that it wasn't just equipment going missing from the base, but other things too."

"Like?"

"C-4."

"Ohhhh."

"Yeah."

"RDX residue was found on some of the recovered boat pieces."

"Which would suggest that Nevsky was behind the explosion." C-4 was 91 percent made up of a substance called RDX—a highly explosive material found on military bases.

"Yes. It would definitely suggest that."

"One other thing. There was a syringe that was recovered. Forensics said it hadn't been down there long, maybe a day or two, which was how long it took them to find it after the explosion. Now, granted, it could have been tossed overboard by anyone sailing those waters, but forensics seems to think it came from the catamaran."

Linc frowned, trying to figure out what it might have been used for. He came up empty. "What was in it?"

"Not sure yet. The lab's still working on it. My contact there said she'd have an answer sometime later today, most likely."

"Let me know when you know."

"Of course. And Izzy had one more thing she wanted me to bring up with you."

"All right."

"Neither one of us could get past the fact that you mentioned the dead guy had been killed by someone with a signature."

Linc grimaced. "Yeah?"

"We did some digging."

He should have known. "And?"

"There was a family who was murdered about fifteen years ago. There was some connection to Russian organized crime, but the killer made his victims lie facedown, then he shot them in the base of the skull."

"Uh-huh."

"There've been a few other killings with the same MO. You wouldn't happen to know anything about all that, would you?"

"Yes. The killer's name is Gregori Radchenko. He was captured and killed earlier today."

His brother fell silent. "How was he connected to Allie and Vladislav Nevsky?"

"What makes you think he was?"

"Because that's who you're chasing and that led you to Gerard Lamb, who was killed by Radchenko. It's also well known that

Lamb was one of Nevsky's daughter's bodyguards. So it's not a long stretch to think there's some connection to Allie."

"Radchenko was her brother. He killed her family—the one Izzy discovered via her research. I knew about her family's assassinations, so when I saw Gerard, I knew exactly who'd done it."

"And you couldn't say anything?" If Brady was shocked at the revelation, Linc couldn't hear it in his voice.

"Not at the time."

"Okay. Anything Izzy and I can do on our end?"

"Don't think so. Right now Nevsky is still a loose cannon. Henry and I think we're getting real close to getting the evidence we need to put him away for good." Linc looked back at Daria. "Hey, Brady, can you do me a favor?"

"Sure."

"Can you check with the media? Channels 10 and 19 were the ones in the choppers that day. I need every bit of footage you can get me on the raid that went down at Nevsky's office building." He gave him the date and time.

"All right, but don't you have resources for this kind of thing?"

"Let's just say I'm branching out right now, willing to work with the locals, if that's all right."

"It's fine. I just want the full story when you can give it to me."

"Of course. And one more thing."

"This is turning into a lot of things."

"Can you and Izzy stand by in case I need some backup?"

"Backup? From us lowly detectives? What about all the feds you have at your fingertips? Still branching out?"

"Something like that. I might need them too. Just . . . stay close to your phone."

"Is this going to be like Nevsky's house?"

"I don't know, I just know I might need you guys."

"You got it." All traces of teasing and mockery were gone from his voice. "I'll let you know what the lab finds on the syringe."

"Thanks." He hung up and turned to find Allie and Daria watching him.

"What did Annie say about the footage?"

"She never got the request for it. It wasn't her that worked on it."

Allie blinked. "Then was it another tech?"

"It's possible. Annie's going to check."

"But Henry said he was sending it to her."

Linc shrugged. "He could have changed his mind."

"Right," Allie said. "Could have, I guess."

"Now, Daria," Linc said, focusing his gaze on her, "it's your turn."

"What?"

"Where's that evidence you have on your father? We need it, like, yesterday."

22

Allie waited until Daria slipped into the bedroom before turning back to Linc. "She hid it in one of her paintings? Of course."

"Clever. Hidden in plain sight."

"I should have known."

"I shudder that she doesn't have a backup copy on the cloud or somewhere, though," Linc said.

"It's actually pretty smart. It's a bargaining chip. And it may explain why she's still alive. She wouldn't give it up when Nevsky had her at his office, so he didn't kill her."

"She never said that," Linc said slowly. "Maybe we're making assumptions."

Allie gave a slow nod. "True." She went to the door and knocked. Daria opened it and blinked at her with a yawn. "Sorry, hon, but we need to know if your father knows you have that security footage on that flash drive."

She shrugged. "Obviously, I never told him."

"Who'd you tell?"

"You and Linc and Gerard."

"Gerard, huh?"

She frowned. "But he wouldn't tell my dad."

Allie wasn't so sure about that, but would go with it for now. "Why'd you tell Gerard?"

"In case something happened to me."

Allie closed her eyes for a moment. Something was there. So close, she just had to reach out and grab it, but it was like she was paralyzed. What was it her brain was trying to tell her? "Then why was your father sending one of his assassins after you?"

"I don't know. Unless"—she shrugged—"he knows I have the evidence."

"So, it's possible."

"Yes. It's a long shot, but I mean, I downloaded it from his server, so if he suspected someone had hacked into it, it would have led him—or someone he hired with the skills to find it—back to my laptop."

Made sense. "Why did he have you shackled in the office that day?"

"I don't know. He never got around to explaining it. He simply had Gerard bring me to the office, then sent Gerard on an errand. Later, my father came in and yelled at me for a bit. His usual stuff about how stupid I am and how I'm nothing but trouble." She frowned. "Although he did add the word 'traitor' to his diatribe, but other than that, he didn't try to hurt me. And he never mentioned the flash drive or security footage." She paused. "He did ask about you, though."

"Me? What'd he want to know?"

"What I thought about you. Were we close. That kind of thing."

"What did you tell him?"

"That he'd messed up the best thing to come into our lives in a long time."

Which was why Nevsky had used Daria to lure her to the office building. He knew Allie would come if she was somehow still alive. But had he known Linc was going to be there too? And that seemed kind of self-defeating to use his own building.

"Did you text me on your laptop or your phone?"

"My phone." A small smile curved her lips. "I have a cloned phone. My dad took the phone he bought me, but he doesn't know about the other one."

"And yet, he left you with your laptop."

She gave Allie a tight smile. "Why not? I didn't have access to the internet and he told me to entertain myself. I played solitaire when they were watching. When they weren't, I used my cloned phone as a hot spot and was able to tap into the security cameras and see what was going on. I couldn't hear anything though."

"So you knew we were coming."

"I saw you outside near where I was and was able to block the camera so it didn't show on the other monitors."

"How?" Allie held up a hand. "Never mind, I wouldn't understand it anyway. You and Annie *must* get together."

"Who?"

"I'll explain later." Allie pursed her lips. "Why do you think he called you a traitor if he didn't know about the flash drive?"

"Probably because I defended you. He knew I lied about the reason you were in the office."

But would that be enough for Nevsky to kill his own child? Probably. "Thanks, Daria. For now, you can head back to bed. One of us will be up and keeping watch."

"My father will just send someone else, won't he?"

"Probably. But we've got your back."

"Thanks."

"And once we get that other security footage from Brady, Linc's brother, we'll get you to look at it and point out the person who you've seen with your father."

"Okay."

Daria returned to her bed and Allie found Linc on the sofa. She sank down beside him.

"You okay?"

"No. My back is killing me."

He touched her cheek. "You're flushed. I think you have a low-grade fever."

"Figures. I've felt kind of icky all day."

224

"I've got some ibuprofen." He disappeared into his room and returned with four of the little orange pills. "Hospital dose according to Ruthie. It will help with all the other aches and pains you no doubt have."

"Thanks." She downed them without hesitation and closed her eyes. Aches and pains. Yes, she had those.

"You need to process, don't you?" Linc asked quietly.

"I will. At some point." Her phone pinged and she sighed. "It's Henry."

"What's he want now?"

"To come up."

"Why?"

She shrugged. "He said he had information on Nevsky he needed to share ASAP."

"He couldn't call?"

"You can ask him when he gets up here." Another text from him. "Make sure Daria's out of listening distance." She frowned and looked up. "I'll check to make sure she's sleeping."

Allie slipped into the room to see the teen snuggled under the covers, her breathing deep and even. She'd been out like a light. No doubt exhausted from all of her running. And terror. That could wipe a person out.

Back in the living area, she texted Henry that the coast was clear. He texted back.

Coming up. I had a meeting with a CI so I'm in disguise. Don't freak out when you see me.

She opened the door before he could knock and he stepped inside the room. He wore a long wig with a ball cap on top, scruffy clothes under a black trench coat, and sunglasses.

"You wear that well, Henry," Linc said.

Henry smirked and removed his glasses. "Scared everyone in the lobby. The cops may be knocking on the door, so I'm going to

225

make this quick. Rumor has it that Nevsky is coming out of hiding tomorrow to meet with some buyers of the military equipment he still has stashed somewhere. We want to catch him in the act."

"Are you planning a raid?" Linc asked.

"No. SWAT's going after him with a tranquilizer dart. They're mapping out the strategy as we speak."

"What?"

"We want him alive. I don't trust him not to kill himself in order to avoid capture."

"Good point," Allie said. "I want to be in on it."

"I don't think so. We don't need him catching sight of you just yet. He thinks you're dead. He feels safe and is coming out of hiding. Let us get him once and for all, then you can rejoin the land of the living."

Allie frowned and started to argue, but Henry's phone rang and he blew out a disgusted sigh. "I've got to take this." He glanced down at himself. "And I really don't want to do this in the hall." He nodded to the room where Daria slept. "You mind?"

"Use the other one," Linc said. He swept a hand to his room. "Help yourself."

"Thanks, I'll just be a minute." It was actually five minutes later before he returned. Allie had just finished opening two bottles of Coke. She handed one to Henry and he downed half in one guzzle. "Sorry, but I've been waiting on that phone call for the past two hours. Another CI had some information on another case."

"It's no problem," Linc said.

Allie passed him a sandwich. Someone had stocked the refrigerator well. "Henry, do you remember that nurse, Catherine Hayworth, from the place you took me after the explosion?"

"Of course. Nice lady." He took a bite and swallowed. "I've talked to her several times over the years. Why?"

"She's missing."

He stilled, and his gaze locked on hers. "What?"

"I saw it on the news earlier. Can you do something? Have a couple of agents investigate her disappearance?"

"The local cops are working the case, I'm sure."

"They are. I think the FBI has also been called in, but maybe you could pull some strings to make sure things are being handled in the best possible way. Not that it won't be." She sighed. "I'm not expressing this well. She was just really kind to me, and I want to make sure everything possible is being done to find her."

"Ah, I see. Yeah, sure, I'll do what I can."

"Thanks."

He finished off the sandwich, handed Allie the empty bottle, then stepped outside and shut the door behind him. "Well, that went . . . okay?" she said.

Linc shook his head. "I'm grabbing a shower while things are calm. You good for about fifteen minutes?"

"I'm good." Allie rubbed her eyes and plugged her phone in. Then yawned and turned off the lights before she remembered she hadn't mentioned the location of the flash drive to Henry. She glanced at her phone. She'd let it charge and text him later, bring him up to speed on her plan to go after the drive tomorrow. As soon as she filled Linc in on his part of the plan. Images from her childhood started blipping across her mind. Then the events of the day invaded.

Finally, a tear slipped out, then another. And another. Until she curled into a ball on the sofa and let the sobs take over.

And that's how Linc found her. When he stepped out of his room, at first he thought she'd fallen asleep, but her shoulders shook even though she made no sound. On silent feet, he went to her and knelt beside her. "Aw, Allie, I'm sorry."

The shaking stopped. For the next five minutes, there was an occasional sniffle. Then she sat up and sighed. "I was supposed to be done with that before you got out of the shower."

He stood, knees popping, and hobbled to the chair facing her. "I'm not meant to crouch that long."

She gave a weak laugh. "You're getting old, St. John."

"Yeah, I know. You okay?"

"Better, but I hate crying."

"I do too."

"You cry?"

"More than I'm comfortable confessing to."

"I'm okay with that."

"I don't sound like a wimp?"

"No, not to me. Not knowing what you see on a regular basis."

He nodded. "I think that's one of the reasons I like you so much."

His phone pinged the same time hers did. She frowned. "It's Henry."

"Good grief. What now?" His notification was for an email, not a text from Henry.

She read the text aloud.

Just got word. Nevsky's moving. So you still
want in? If so, meet me downstairs in ten.

She shot to her feet and swiped a hand across her face.

Linc tilted his head. "Wonder what made him change his mind."

"Probably figured I'd just follow him if I learned about it."

"True. You really want to do this?"

"I've lived for this moment for a very long time. I think once Nevsky's either behind bars or dead, I can face the future with some hope." She met his gaze. "And yes, I know where my hope comes from, but . . . ." A shrug. "I have to do this, Linc."

"I know. I'll stay with Daria, but you've got to check in with me on a regular basis."

"I will."

With her mussed dark hair and red-rimmed eyes, he still found her the most beautiful woman on the planet. He swiped another one of her tears. "I'm crazy about you, Allie. Come back to me, okay?"

She swallowed but didn't look away. "I don't think you know what you're asking for."

"You. That's all I'm asking for. Just you." He kissed her lightly, ready to pull back if she offered any resistance. When she wrapped her arms around his neck, he deepened the kiss, reassuring himself he was okay with her leaving to be a part of this operation. She was trained for the kind of work she was about to go do, and he had full confidence in her abilities. And then she hugged him, holding on tight like she didn't want to let go. He tightened his own hold.

"We'll talk when I get back," she said, her voice husky and raw with emotion. "You make me crazy, you know that, right?"

"Ditto."

With a small laugh and roll of her eyes, she disappeared into her room. Seven minutes later, she emerged while he was downloading the video Brady had sent him with "Media footage" in the title.

"Be careful, Allie."

"Always. And let me know what Daria tells you about that."

"You'll know as soon as I do."

With a conflicted heart, he watched her go, then pressed play.

23

Allie slid into the passenger seat of Henry's SUV. He was still in his undercover clothing. "Am I overdressed?" she asked.

"No, just didn't have time to change before I got the message."

She looked up at the room where she and Linc and Daria were staying. A faint glow came from it and she figured Linc was watching whatever Brady had sent. "We're going to get him this time, right?"

"That's the plan."

"That's always been the plan, but it's never worked out."

"Well, this time is going to be different, I can guarantee it."

Allie shot him a frown. "There are no guarantees." She paused and pressed a hand against her head. She was definitely running a fever and hoped the ibuprofen would kick in fast. "Henry, I think I've been played."

He started. "What? Been played how?"

"I keep going over it and over it in my head and there are just too many inconsistencies."

"Like?"

"Everything!" She sighed. "I'll explain on the way. Let's go."

"We've got a few minutes. I want to hear this."

She shrugged and winced at the ache in her upper back. She

knew she needed to see a doctor, but when? Catching Nevsky and keeping Daria safe were the top priorities right now. "I just . . . I don't know. Everything that's happened has been so odd. I was just talking about this with Linc. And I just don't know."

"Well, something's triggered that thought. Talk it out and let's see if we can figure out what."

"It's a combination of things."

"Like?"

"So, we're after Nevsky. I work my way into his home and my cover is blown a full week before I know about it, and yet Nevsky continues on like nothing's wrong. There are pictures of Linc and me and Linc's family in an unlocked drawer that should have been locked due to his OCD personality. There's no password on the computer— again, if he's so OCD about his privacy like Daria says he is—and I would agree with that after being in his home for four weeks—then that doesn't match up. Add that to the fact that there's nothing on the hard drive, according to Annie and—" Her phone rang and she snapped it to her ear, glad for the interruption. She'd already been over all that with Linc and Daria. If they didn't have any answers, Henry sure wouldn't. "Hey, what is it?"

"It's Henry."

"What's—"

"Henry's the one who scared off Daria."

"Oh. Okay. Well . . . there's probably a good explanation for that."

"Yeah, there is—he doctored the footage and edited himself out of it."

"Because?"

"He's working with Nevsky. And if Henry and Nevsky are working together, you're in danger."

She glanced at Henry and found him watching her with a glitter in his eyes she'd never noticed before. "I'd say that would be a correct assumption."

"He suspects?"

"I think so."

"Get away from him as soon as you can, but don't head back to the roo—"

The explosion rocked the hotel. The window to the room where they'd been staying blew out and flames greedily sucked every particle of oxygen in their path.

Allie couldn't even scream. She stared, her heart shattering. A sting in her left shoulder whipped her head around and she found Henry watching her, holding a syringe—and smiling. "For once, that went exactly as planned."

Her vision blurred and darkness pressed in.

He'd drugged her. It was Henry all along.

Unlike the last time she'd felt the same sensation of being too tired to hold her eyes open, she didn't bother to fight it.

This time Linc was really dead. And Daria too.

This time the darkness was welcome.

She sank into it with a sigh of heartbroken surrender.

The hotel shuddered with the second blast and Linc covered Daria's body with his own until the dust stopped falling. "Are you okay?" He choked, pulling his shirt up over his face.

"Yes, but what just happened?" She trembled against him, her fear thick enough to touch.

He helped her hold her own shirt over her nose and mouth. "Confirmation. Just a few minutes too late."

"What?"

"Henry, the guy you saw at the scene and in the security footage, is working with your father—and that bomb just proved it." In the stairwell at the end of the hall, they'd made it down one floor before the explosion hit.

While Linc hadn't known about the bomb, he'd gone with his

screaming gut to get out ASAP. He'd grabbed Daria and they'd raced out of the room and into the stairwell, where he'd called Allie to warn her about Henry.

He pulled Daria with him to the bottom of the stairs and snagged his phone from the debris. When the explosion hit, it had knocked him to the steps and his phone out of his hand. A quick check showed the call had been disconnected.

His finger hovered over the redial button.

"What is it?" Daria asked.

He met her gaze. "We're supposed to be dead."

She coughed into her shirt.

The stairwell quickly filled with people fleeing the hotel, and Linc shifted, pulling Daria into the corner. The third floor had been empty, as he'd reserved all of the rooms and had guests transferred to other hotels, citing a gas problem. Hopefully, no one had been hurt in the blast.

Daria blinked and rubbed her eyes. "And if you call Allie back, Henry will know his plan failed and he'll also know that he's a wanted man. That will send him into hiding and it'll be harder than ever to find Allie."

Linc stared at the teen. "If you don't become an agent, it will be a huge loss for the Bureau."

She lowered her shirt and flashed him a weak grin. "Thanks."

"All right, cover your face back up and let's get out of here. We're going to have to avoid the cameras, cops, ATF, EMS, and everyone else that's sure to be on scene when we walk out."

"Where are we going to go?"

"To my truck." Fortunately, he'd parked it behind the hotel when he brought Allie back from their showdown with Gregori.

"And then what?"

"If Henry and your father are working together, there may be something on that evidence that will tell us where Henry plans to meet your father and hand Allie over to him."

"So, we need to go to my house and get the flash drive. Then what?"

"I'm not that far into the plan, but it'll consist of doing whatever it takes to find your father, Henry, and Allie."

Daria studied him through red-rimmed eyes. "You're going to kill him—or them—aren't you?"

He swallowed his knee-jerk response and sighed. "That's not my goal, but if it comes down to a choice between them or Allie . . ."

"You'll pick Allie, of course."

"Every single time."

Tears spilled over onto her cheeks. "I wish I had someone to care about me the way you care about her."

Linc's heart shattered. He reached over to pull her into a hug, then looked into her eyes. "You do, Daria." She frowned. "Allie's been searching half her life for the person who murdered her family when she was fourteen years old. When you disappeared, she put all that on hold and made sure we understood that you were the priority."

Her jaw dropped, more tears spilled, and she waved to the stairs. "Let's just go."

Awareness came slowly. Allie blinked and stared at the smooth white ceiling, wondering where she was. Her eyes lowered to land on pale blue walls. Her hands shifted, feeling the soft bed beneath her, and she could hear the hum of the air conditioner.

Henry.

The explosion at the hotel.

"Linc!" The word came out on a whisper. "Daria." She wanted to jump out of the bed and go looking for them but was afraid to move too fast as nausea curled through her. She licked her lips and glanced at the water pitcher on the dresser opposite the bed, wishing she had the energy to get up and get it.

Henry had done this.

Why?

She tried to figure out what she was feeling. Shock. Definitely that. And anger. So much anger.

Allie closed her eyes, fighting the fear and confusion—and the overwhelming grief. She wasn't sure how long she lay there, letting the drug wear off, before she sensed the presence. The eyes watching her.

Blinking, she focused and Henry's face came into view. Without taking her eyes from him, she sat up, swallowing against the waves of sickness running through her.

"It'll pass in a bit. The bathroom is through there. You should find everything you need."

His words registered, the meaning not so much. "I . . . what?"

He gave a huff of impatience. "After much planning and scheming, we're finally where I've pictured us from the very beginning."

Okay, that sounded very weird. Instead of admitting her confusion, she drew in several cleansing breaths. "You drugged me."

"You were getting hysterical."

That's not how she remembered it. She closed her eyes. Saw the explosion happen again. Saw Henry with the syringe. And that smile—

She shuddered. "Linc and Daria didn't get out."

"Unfortunately for them, it doesn't look that way."

Unfortunately? For them?

She pulled in another breath, desperately trying to figure out how to play this. *Linc! Daria. Oh, God, please . . .* But what could she pray?

First things first. "Where am I? Where's Nevsky? You're going to hand me over to him, right?"

A smile curved his lips and his eyes softened. "Ah, Allie, no, I won't be handing you over to Nevsky. And this is my home away from home."

Which told her absolutely nothing. But, why take her if not to pass her on to the man who wanted her dead?

"I've been working on it for a while now. Built it myself and planted every tree on the property. One of the best features is that it's completely off the grid. Except when I need to be on it."

A low laugh tumbled from him, and Allie pressed palms to her eyes, praying for patience and wisdom. And trying to push aside visions of Linc and Daria being blown to bits. The need to scream and rant and wail left her shaking with the effort it took to hold it all in.

Finally, she was able to speak again. "What about Nevsky and the sting last night? You warned him, didn't you?"

Henry shoved his hands into his pockets. "Warned him?" He laughed. "No, Nevsky's out of the picture now. There was no sting."

There was no sting. He'd deliberately gotten her out of the room because he knew it was going to blow. And he'd wanted Linc and Daria dead. Daria, because she'd seen Henry and recognized him as someone who'd visited her father's home—and assumed they were working together somehow. But on what? "Henry, what's going on? If you're not handing me over to Nevsky, why drug me and bring me here? What are you doing?"

He sighed. "Well, let me put it this way. It's been a long time since I've felt a connection with someone like I feel with you. I tried my best to get you to notice me, to tune in to my feelings, but Linc St. John was the only person on your radar."

Allie stilled even while her heart picked up speed. What was he saying?

"So, I decided I needed to remove the competition, but I had to do it in a way that couldn't be traced back to me."

Hence the disguise. There'd been no informant. He'd worn that getup so no one would recognize him on the security footage when they investigated the explosion. Or in case Daria happened to come out of her room while he was there.

Allie didn't move, still unsure of the best plan of action. "Can you explain that a little more?"

He gave a short laugh. "You're going to make me just spell it out, aren't you? I'm in love with you, Allie. I have been since I interviewed you for the position."

"In love with me? In lo—" She gaped. How was it possible for her to be so blind? She'd never once had an inkling. No, that wasn't true. There'd been a few times she'd noticed he gave her preferential treatment over someone else or seemed to treat her with a bit more deference. Or looked at her in a certain way. But it hadn't been overt and she'd ignored it. Chalked it up to her imagination because the whole idea had made her uncomfortable.

And look where that had landed her.

"And so," she said, "because I don't return your affection—and am, in fact, in love with someone else, you feel that by eliminating said competition, I'll forget about him and be swayed over to your side. Henry, do you hear what that sounds like?"

"Of course I do. It sounds crazy. It sounds like people we've arrested and put behind bars, but . . ."

How could he sound so rational? Because it was clear that he was insane. "But?"

"I can understand how those people think. I now understand the desperation that drives them." At her stare, he sighed. "Until you experience it, it's very hard to comprehend—or explain."

Can I scream now, God? "You killed the man I love! Why do you think this will work out in whatever way you've envisioned?"

"Because I've covered every conceivable angle. The fact that everyone thinks you're dead helps. And you'll get over Linc eventually. Don't worry, I'll give you some time."

No, he wasn't insane. He knew exactly what he was doing and was making a choice to behave this way. Because he was completely confident that he could get away with it.

A coldness like she'd never experienced before encased her, freezing her, momentarily disrupting her thought processes. "You can't do this to me, Henry." She hated the shakiness in her voice. "I have a life!"

"What life? One bent on revenge? You were so focused on finding Nevsky and your brother that you all but isolated yourself."

"I have friends at the Bureau. I had Linc." She ended on a whisper. "I had Linc."

"And even then, you couldn't bring yourself to fully let go and love. This arrangement will allow you to do that. So, while you'll still have a life, the course of it has just changed. It'll be a bit different than the one you planned—but better, I feel sure."

"You feel sure it'll be—" Allie finally understood what he was telling her. She was his prisoner in every sense of the word. "You killed Linc and Daria! Two people I loved!" She pinned him with a laser glare. "You planted a bomb in the room when you went in to take that call and blew them up! I'll never forgive you. Ever."

He smiled again. A smile she would have said conveyed sympathy and compassion—if she hadn't known better—curved his lips. "You'll be fine, Allie." His eyes hardened, emptied. "Just don't cross me."

"Cross you? Don't cross you? Do you even know me at all?"

"I do. That's why I've arranged a small incentive for you to do as I ask."

She stilled. "What kind of incentive?"

He picked up the remote control from the dresser and aimed it at the television, turned it on, then tapped something on his phone. "She was one of the few people who knew you were alive, so I decided instead of killing her, I'd let her be useful."

The screen blinked, then lit up.

A woman lay curled on a twin bed in a room that looked almost identical to the one Allie was in, except there was no carpet, just concrete. Henry panned the camera to the right and she saw the bars on the windows. He tapped the screen on his phone and music blared into the room. The woman jerked to her feet screaming, hands over her ears.

Allie flinched and sucked in a harsh breath. "Henry, stop!"

He did. Immediately. Sobbing, the woman dropped to the floor and wrapped her arms around her knees.

Allie curled her fingers into fists, the desire to smash Henry's face nearly overwhelming. But that wouldn't help the woman in the room and it wouldn't help her. "You were the one who kidnapped Catherine Hayworth? The nurse from the rehab center?"

"That was me."

A picture flashed into the left-hand corner of the screen. Two little girls beamed at Allie. Catherine's daughters. "They miss their mother, poor kids."

"Why?" Allie whispered. "Why would you turn into this kind of monster?"

For a moment, she thought he would strike her. Instead, he looked at the television, then punched his phone and the music blared again. Water fell from the sprinklers in the ceiling and wind howled through the small room. The woman huddled tighter into herself, wrapping her arms around her head, shivering uncontrollably. Allie watched a digital readout on the TV as the temperature in the room dropped from seventy to sixty to fifty to forty.

"Stop!"

He did. "There's more, Allie. So much more."

"Warm it up, please. She's freezing!"

"Since you said 'please.'" Henry complied. Slowly the temperature rose to over a hundred, a hundred and ten, a hundred and twenty. The woman unwrapped herself and began to pant, gasping in between her sobs.

"Henry, stop! Don't hurt her anymore. Please!"

"Do we understand each other now?"

"Yes," she cried. "Yes."

Finally, after the temperature returned to a comfortable level for a soaking-wet woman, he tapped his phone once again and allowed her to see the array of ways he could torture his captive. Red ants, spiders, scorpions, bees, and more. Allie had seen evil. She'd faced it and beaten it many times over, but to be on the other end of it yet again brought back memories, and she closed her eyes, reliving the feelings from the night her brother had killed her family. The night that she'd become a helpless victim.

"So, every time you disobey me," Henry said, "displease me, or ever try to escape, I will punish her."

24

Linc pulled up to the area in front of Nevsky's home and parked. Daria slept in the passenger seat. The poor kid. Linc had had to be creative to get out of the hotel parking lot without being seen—including driving over a couple of curbs and through the back lot of a used car dealership—but as soon as he'd hit the highway, Daria had closed her eyes and zonked out.

He wished he could do the same, but Allie was in danger and he needed to figure out where Henry would have taken her. He hoped the house in the distance would offer up that information. Once on the road, he'd called in reinforcements—which consisted of everyone that he thought could help, including his siblings.

Brady had texted him an hour ago.

> Contents of the syringe were ketamine. Talked to
> one of the EMTs who worked on Allie in the boat.
> Said she kept fading in and out of consciousness,
> but he couldn't see what had knocked her out.
> The hit on her head would have hurt, but wasn't
> that bad. At least not that he could tell.

Linc remembered hearing her call his name. He'd caught a glimpse of her swimming with fairly strong strokes before Henry had caught up with her. If she'd been knocked in the head hard enough by something from the explosion to make her groggy, wouldn't that have happened immediately? Could she have not noticed the hit until later? He didn't think it worked that way.

He texted Brady.

She was drugged, wasn't she?

It was probably a stretch, but it made sense with the syringe.

Can't know that unless someone did a blood
test looking for it. Might be in her medical chart.

Linc didn't need a blood test or medical records to tell him what he knew. Henry had drugged her when they were in the water. It was the only thing that made sense.

Or someone else dropped that syringe shortly before the incident. But he really didn't think so.

With all the debris floating around, she wouldn't have even noticed a quick prick of the needle. And then Henry had simply dropped the evidence and taken charge of Allie, later reporting that she'd died while hiding her away in a rehab hospital.

Those last moments before the drone hit clicked through his mind. *"Allie, come here a sec,"* Henry had said. *"Linc, see if you can get any identifying marks off it."*

Henry had sent Linc to the very area the drone had struck. If Linc hadn't seen what was happening and spun to head back to Allie and Henry, he would have been killed. So, was it possible that Henry, working with Nevsky, had set up the whole thing?

Probably.

Allie had been in Nevsky's home, and Nevsky had known she was FBI and yet he'd done nothing about that. And then he'd conveniently come home while Allie had been in his office and caught her. And he'd entered the house from the back so neither

Linc nor Henry could see him. Because Henry had told him what was going down? Of course he had.

As for Linc, he'd had lots of close calls. Too many. But why? He couldn't figure out the motive. To get him out of the way so he wouldn't go after Allie once Henry turned her over to Nevsky?

The thought sickened him.

Back at the hotel, as soon as he'd seen Henry's face on that video, he'd known the man was in cahoots with Nevsky and things started falling into place. The final one being that Henry had come by when he could have made a phone call, which meant he'd come to get something—or leave something.

Turned out it was both. For some reason he'd come to get Allie— and leave the bomb somewhere in the room.

His phone rang. Izzy. "Hey."

"We're two minutes out."

"I'm waiting."

"Brady, Chloe, and Derek are closing in fast too." She paused. "You're sure Allie's alive?"

He hadn't had time for long explanations. "Trust me. I'm sure."

"And Henry's behind everything that's been going on with Nevsky?"

"Somehow, yeah." Once he'd started looking at Henry as part of the problem, everything had started making sense. "Think about it. Everyone who knew Allie was alive was a target. The only reason that theory even popped into my head is due to the missing nurse Allie said worked at that rehab place Henry took her to after the blast."

"Rehab place?"

"In Hilton Head. As near as I can figure out, the only people still breathing who know Allie's alive are me, Daria, the doc, and possibly Nevsky."

"Okay."

"Those who've been killed are James Killian, a bodyguard who recognized her the night we crashed the party, and her brother, who was one of Nevsky's assassins and was shot by a sniper—most likely Henry—once we had the guy subdued and were going to bring him in. And now the nurse is missing."

"What about the doc? Do we need to bring him in for protection?"

"No. I think he's in on it. Or could be. Regardless, Henry may have decided the man has served his purpose and try to get rid of him too, since he's probably the last remaining person breathing who knows Allie's alive. I don't want to tip him off. But I've been thinking. Allie's sick. She was running a fever when she left the hotel last night and her stitches are infected. She's going to need medical attention sooner or later." If he didn't plan to hand her immediately over to Nevsky.

"And if so," Izzy said, "Henry will call the doctor to provide it."

"Exactly. If he hasn't turned her over to Nevsky. In which case, I'm not sure how much time she has or if he'll bother with medical stuff, but I'm still thinking Henry will get rid of the doctor one way or another and we need to be there when he tries."

"Okay, I know people in Hilton Head. I'll see if we can get some eyes on him in case Henry decides to take her back to the rehab facility—or have the doc come to him."

For some reason Henry had wanted Allie to be dead to everyone. The biggest question racing around Linc's brain was why? What did Allie have that Henry wanted? Proof of his involvement with Nevsky? It was the only thing he could come up with. But Allie would have shared that with him if she'd had anything. Unless she didn't know she had it?

Daria still slept, but her breathing had changed and he figured she would wake shortly.

"Pulling up now," Izzy said and stopped behind him.

Linc reached over to shake Daria's shoulder, and she jerked awake, hands up in a self-defensive gesture. "Whoa," he said. "It's okay."

"Sorry." She dropped her hands to her lap. "We're here, I see." She sighed. "I hate this place."

"Come on, let's go get that evidence and you'll never have to come back again."

"He's not in there, is he?"

"No, we're not sure where he is, but he's not here. Which is why I'm letting you come inside with me."

Daria drew in a deep breath. "Okay, good." She paused. "What's with the crime scene tape?"

He explained about Killian's attempt to take him out. Killian, who'd called Linc's name. So Linc had, once again, been the target, not Allie. Because Killian had been told not to hurt the woman with Linc? But told by whom?

Henry hadn't known about their plan. No one had. But Nevsky had known not to be at the house—and he'd known to have Killian on hand to try and get rid of Linc.

Confusion set in. He and Allie hadn't filled Henry in on their every move, but someone had.

So . . . who?

As soon as Allie had calmed down after his announcement that her behavior would determine whether Catherine lived or died, Henry had backed toward the door. "I'll just leave you alone to think for a while. The bedroom door is open. You have the run of the house—except for the doors that are locked. If you try to enter one of those, Catherine will suffer. Do you understand?"

"Yes," she'd said through gritted teeth.

"Why don't you take a shower and relax. Then come into the kitchen and we'll have a bite to eat and chat."

"A shower? I don't think so."

"There aren't any cameras in there, Allie. I can respect your privacy." He'd shrugged. "There's no way for you to escape anyway. You might as well start adjusting to your new life now."

And he'd walked out.

Allie had sunk onto the bed and dropped her head into her hands. "Oh, Linc, I need you."

But he couldn't come. Because Henry had killed him and Daria. Swiping a hand across her eyes, she rose and went to the bathroom. And searched it from top to bottom. To her surprise, she came up empty.

Unless he'd figured out some extremely creative way to hide a camera, the bathroom was clean.

With an aching head, body, and heart, she stepped into the shower and turned the knob. Time passed. She wasn't sure how long she stood under the hot water and let her tears fall, grieving all the losses in her life. Most specifically, Linc and Daria. Was it possible they had somehow escaped? Her heart wanted to cry out yes, but her mind refused to play that game. She'd been on the phone with him when the explosion hit.

He was gone.

Daria was gone.

The sooner she came to terms with that, the better off she'd be.

When she finished the shower, she wrapped herself in the large bathrobe and regrouped. Grieving could come later. After she figured out how to get away from Henry.

She was a federal agent, she was smart—and she knew how her enemy thought. Or at least she thought she did. So she needed to come up with a plan. One that wouldn't cause Catherine more torture—or death.

In front of the mirror, she slipped the robe from her shoulder and turned to look at the stitches. Angry red skin surrounded them. Red welts spiderwebbed out from it and she grimaced. The area was truly infected and she needed to do something about it.

Or get Henry to.

The more she thought about it, the more she liked the idea. And figured it was worth a shot. The ibuprofen was wearing off and her fever was coming back up. Which would help.

Allie dressed and went to the door to twist the knob, surprised when she met no resistance. But Henry had said she had the run of the house. Apparently, he'd created an inescapable luxurious prison for her. He wouldn't use the word *prison*, of course.

First thing on the agenda was to find Catherine. Which was going to be tough, knowing that Henry could be watching her every move. At least he probably would in the beginning. The thought sent her appetite fleeing. The beginning of what? How long would she be trapped here? How long would it take to either build his trust, find a way to escape, or convince him to let her go?

Or discover a way to kill him?

Please don't let it come to that.

Once in the hallway, she stopped to get her bearings. To the right was a great room. To the left, a hallway led to a door at the end that she figured opened to the garage. No doubt, that was one of Henry's locked doors she was banned from looking behind. Beyond the great room, she could see a deck and a body of water. A lake?

Taking a deep breath, she walked into the kitchen and could see the front door to her right just off the great room. She turned to find Henry standing at the bar, reading something on his phone and sipping a cup of coffee. He looked up. "Enjoy your shower?"

"I did."

"Hungry?"

"Not really, but I probably should eat something."

He frowned and narrowed his eyes.

Allie frowned back at him. "What?"

"I didn't expect compliance this quickly."

She gave a low sardonic laugh. "Well, you kind of have me in a tough spot. Obviously, I don't want to do anything that will cause you to hurt Catherine." She sighed. "And truly, I simply don't have the energy to fight you right now." She rubbed her head.

He continued to eye her. "What's wrong?"

"What do you mean?"

"Your cheeks are flushed."

"I just got out of the shower."

"Thirty minutes ago. I left you alone because I know you're still processing everything."

Wow, what a gentleman. She bit her tongue, unsure if the sarcasm would set him off. Probably. "Yes. I'm definitely processing."

"And trying to figure out how to escape."

She met his gaze. To lie or not to lie? "Yes, but I don't think that surprises you."

"Of course not. I expected it. Just as long as you don't attempt anything. Otherwise . . ." He raised a brow.

"I get it, Henry."

"And the fact that you didn't lie lets me know you understand the gravity of the situation. Because the next time I have to punish Catherine due to your misbehavior, she'll die."

Allie frowned. "Wouldn't that defeat the purpose of her presence?"

Henry laughed, his eyes crinkling at the corners. "Allie, if there's one thing I know about you, you want to protect everyone. Today, I can use Catherine. But if she winds up dying, I can always find a replacement. Like one of her children, perhaps?"

Allie swayed, nausea gripped her throat. "Trash can," she whispered.

"What?"

"I'm going to—"

Henry grabbed her arm and hauled her to the sink. She lost what little she had in her stomach. When she was finished, he shoved a glass of water into her hand. She rinsed and spit, then cleaned the sink while he watched.

"I didn't realize you had such a weak stomach," he said.

"I don't. Usually." Although the thought of Henry getting his hands on one of Catherine's children was definitely enough to make her sick. "I think I've actually come down with a virus or something."

"Don't play with me."

"I'm not. Do you have any ibuprofen?"

He hesitated. "You're really sick?"

"Yes. And a thermometer might be a good idea too."

He turned to a cabinet next to the refrigerator and pulled out a thermometer. She popped it beneath her tongue and waited. At the beep, Henry removed it before she had a chance. "101.8."

"You sound surprised."

"How'd you manage that?"

She laughed. "What? Give myself a fever?" She rubbed her head, seriously not feeling well. "It could have something to do with my stitches. They've been bothering me and don't look right." Henry would know the stitches were aggravating her, as she'd complained about them before the whole kidnapping thing.

"Let me look."

She waved a hand. "It's fine. Probably nothing."

"Let. Me. Look."

Allie studied him a moment. "Fine." She turned and grimaced when she felt his hands on her shoulder pulling her shirt away.

He drew in a deep breath and a shot of relief rolled through her. They looked as bad to him as they did to her.

"They're infected," he said.

"Which would explain why they're bothering me so much."

"I'll take care of it." He slipped her neckline back into place, and his fingers lingered, brushing lightly across the top of her shoulder.

Allie swallowed another surge of nausea and turned, pretending his touch hadn't bothered her. "Take care of it? How?"

"I'll get an antibiotic called in for you." He paused. "Let me take a picture."

"Why?"

"Don't question me."

"Fine."

He snapped the picture of the stitches. "I'll see what I can do."

"Okay. Thanks." That wasn't the response she'd been hoping for, and while she wasn't willing to relinquish the original plan yet, he'd have to leave the house to pick it up, right?

"Sorry, Allie, but you're not going anywhere."

"Right. I have another question, if you don't mind."

"Ask." He pulled his keys from his pocket and spun them while he waited for her question.

"Did you kill Gregori?" she asked.

"I did." His fingers closed over the keys and he dropped them onto the counter. "What made you ask that?"

"Because it fit. He said he had another agenda. I've been thinking about that. The only reason he didn't kill me is because he was delivering me to you, right?"

His brow rose. "Did he say that?"

"No. He didn't have to." She paused. "How much did you agree to pay him?"

"One million to kill Daria Nevsky and one million to deliver you in one piece."

"I see."

He washed the thermometer in alcohol and returned it to the cabinet. Then handed her two little orange pills and snagged the keys from the counter. "Take these for now. I'll make the call."

Linc stared at the empty walls in the pool house. "Dumb question alert, but what do you mean it's gone?"

"It's gone," Daria said. "They're all gone. Every last one of my pieces of art that my mother and I hung together." She raced to the large stone outdoor fireplace.

"Daria—" Linc followed her.

She choked on a sob. "He burned them," she whispered. "He burned them all."

A blast of fury rocked Linc. The man probably hadn't had a clue about the flash drive being in the painting but had simply found a way to hurt his daughter. Linc wrapped an arm around her shoulders.

"Unbelievable." She reached for the remains of one and stopped, dropping her hand. "He's going to get away with everything, isn't he?" she asked, her voice barely above a whisper.

"No. He's not."

Her wise, grief-stricken eyes met his. "Right."

"You didn't save it any other place?"

"Yes. On all ten of those flash drives that were in the sunflower picture." She nodded to the fireplace. "It's probably in there, but I don't know if any of them survived."

"We'll get someone to sift through that and see."

"But it'll be too late to help Allie." She choked off a sob.

Linc squeezed her shoulders, her despair a tangible thing. "You didn't save it on Dropbox or the cloud or any place accessible from another computer."

"No. I was too afraid he'd be able to have someone hack into my laptop or cloud or whatever and delete it."

Smart, but not helpful all at the same time.

Brady and Derek stood to the side with Izzy and Chloe, waiting for Linc to tell them the next move. He caught Brady's eye. "Did you get an agent working on that warrant for Henry's and Nevsky's phone records?"

"I did. He said he'd text you as soon as he had it."

Linc rubbed his eyes. "Henry took a leave of absence for the next three weeks," he said, "citing personal issues." His gaze touched on each sibling. "I can't wait three weeks to find him. Annie's already said she can't track his phone and he's not answering when she calls."

"Then we'll have to draw him out," Izzy said.

"What are you thinking?"

"What do you think he would do if he discovered you were alive? Would he hurt Allie?"

Linc thought about it. "If he thought getting rid of her was the only way to stay out of prison, he would and . . ."

"And?"

"He'd probably send someone to finish Daria and me off, simply because we survived and wrecked his plans."

"What if we put a BOLO out on Allie, got her on national news with Henry's face as her kidnapper?" Chloe asked.

"He'd kill her and go underground."

Derek shook his head. "That won't work. However, he's probably watching the news, and when your and Daria's deaths aren't reported, he's going to get suspicious."

"Guys?" Daria said. "I have an idea."

Linc turned to the teen, who'd been listening intently, her gaze bouncing from one to the other. "What kind of idea?"

"What if I just hack into the security system with one of your laptops and redownload the footage?"

"You think you can do that?" Brady asked.

"As long as he hasn't erased it or changed the password."

Linc cleared his throat. Izzy and Chloe exchanged a glance. "Um, yeah," Linc said, "why don't you do that?"

"I mean, I had over a hundred hours of footage, so it took me a while to get it. I couldn't stay in for very long without the possibility of getting caught."

"It's still worth a try," Linc said. "We'll get a warrant for that as well, just in case there's any evidence recovered. We'd want it all at some point, but for now, all we'd need would be the time he met with Henry. I want to know what they talked about. What do you need to make that happen?"

She shrugged. "Just a laptop and internet access—and the warrant, of course."

"We can do that. And, Daria?"

"Yes?"

"I'm really sorry about your artwork."

"Yeah, me too."

25

Sitting in his SUV not too far from his home, Vladislav Nevsky curled his hands into fists and resisted smashing the screen in front of him. The agent was still alive. Along with Daria, the brat. Henry had called last night and said they'd died in the hotel blast. And yet, there they stood, in his pool house.

Gregori was dead and they were alive—and that was unacceptable. Henry had said Linc was the one responsible for Gregori's death. Only the news that Linc St. John was dead had eased his grief and appeased his need for revenge.

And now to learn he wasn't dead, but apparently still looking for him sent his rage soaring to new heights.

Henry Ogden had proved useful in the past. When the agent had first approached him, Vladislav weighed the risks of allowing the woman federal agent into his home, versus the idea of having another federal agent who would owe him a lifetime of loyalty and favors on his payroll.

He'd decided it was worth it. And it had been. For a while. Until he'd learned it was Alina Radchenko in his house, befriending his traitorous daughter.

Needless to say, he'd considered killing her where she stood when he found her in his office, but again, Henry's worth as an inside man had been too good to mess up. And besides, Henry's plan included getting her out of his hair. Forever. Unfortunately, Henry's worth had just taken a nosedive and it was time to part ways with the man. Permanently.

"He's on the move and has been on the phone since he walked out of the building," Special Agent Mills said. Federal agents in Hilton Head had eyes on Dr. Nathan Forsythe. They'd planted a tracker on his vehicle and would keep him under surveillance until Linc and his team could pick him up as he got closer to Columbia.

"Good. We're waiting for him," Linc said.

Still at Nevsky's house, Daria sat at the table in the pool house and worked. She'd managed to get back into the security system and was downloading the footage to the laptop he'd provided. He had about an hour before he would need to fall in behind the doctor and follow him to his final destination. Which he hoped and prayed led them to Allie.

Izzy approached. "We got the warrant. Nevsky's and Henry's phone records are being pulled as we speak. They'll be sent to your phone as soon as they're available."

"What convinced the DA to give us the warrant?"

"Daria's partial testimony that her father was working with Henry and she'd seen him at the house."

Linc was going to owe Daria his firstborn. The thought sent his heart into a panicked overdrive. The only woman he was interested in having a family with was Allie. *God, please, let me find her. Alive.*

Izzy shook her head. "Stop with those thoughts. We're so close, I can feel it."

His sister always could read him. "Maybe, but are we going to be in time?"

She scowled. "Yes, so shut off the negativity."

If only it were that easy. "I was actually praying."

"Oh, well . . . carry on, then."

His phone dinged. The phone records. He glanced at Daria, then back to Izzy. "You okay staying with her?"

"Of course."

"Thanks."

Fellow agent Mark King stood next to the mobile unit that had arrived about thirty minutes ago. Linc hurried over. "I need to use the printer."

"Go for it."

Linc sent the phone records to the printer and stepped inside.

On both sides of the unit were chairs and monitors. And the printer was at the end. Linc pulled the sheets off, settled himself at one of the stations to spread the records in front of him. It didn't take long to match up the numbers, days, and times. There were three. The first conversation, which had lasted less than a minute, was on the day the drone had bombed the boat. The second was when he and Allie had decided to crash Nevsky's party. And the third when Henry had contacted Nevsky to tell him that Linc and Daria were dead?

His blood ran cold. They'd never told Henry the plan until they'd called him in at the end when he'd choppered in to get Killian, so how did he know where they were and to warn Nevsky?

"Oh no. No, no, no. You've got to be kidding me." He bolted out of the mobile unit and found Brady and Derek. "I need you guys to help me search my SUV. There's a tracker or a listening device in there somewhere and we missed it." Or it had been planted after the agent had found the one under his license plate shortly after the raid on Nevsky's office and Daria's rescue.

Brady, Derek, and Linc searched until Brady shook his head. "There's nothing here."

"What are you guys looking for?"

Linc blinked at Daria. She didn't have any trackers on her and he didn't have any on him. That only left one option.

Allie did.

Allie stumbled to the couch and stretched out on it, wincing at the bruise on her back and the stitches that pulled. She was a mess and couldn't afford to be right now.

Henry was still in the kitchen on the phone with someone, and she had to get the room to stop spinning or she would be no good to anyone, much less Catherine.

With a glance at Henry, who continued to pace the hardwoods, phone pressed to his ear, she grabbed the remote and aimed it at the television.

Catherine's room came up. She stared at the woman, who'd returned to her bed. She lay still, her back to the camera, her sobs silent for the moment.

"You can't rescue her," Henry said from behind her.

Not at the moment anyway. A rush of fear swept through her and it took her a second to make sure Henry wouldn't hear it in her voice when she spoke. "Where are you keeping her?" she asked. There was no sign of fear, but her words sounded dull, thanks to the fever the ibuprofen wasn't touching this time.

"She has her space, you have yours."

She had to find some energy. "Do you have any soft drinks?"

Her change of subject seemed to throw him, then he nodded. "Sprite?"

"Sure."

He brought her one and reached out to touch her forehead. She flinched and his eyes went cold. Without removing his gaze from hers, he pulled out his phone. Allie grabbed his hand. "Don't."

"Then don't ever pull away from me."

"I won't. Not anymore." She swallowed. "I'm going to make mistakes," she said, forcing a softness into her tone. "Please, don't punish her while I'm . . . learning what to do and what not to do."

His eyes narrowed. "Don't think you can play me, Allie."

She shivered at the ominous timbre underlying the words. "Henry . . ." She sighed. "You know me. I'll admit, if I could get away without Catherine being hurt, I would, but you know I won't take a chance on that. And right now I feel absolutely horrid, so you have me at your mercy."

For now.

Silence dropped between them when she stopped speaking. She'd heal. And as long as she could play her part well, she could keep him from hurting Catherine any further.

"You get one warning," he finally said.

"Okay."

His eyes glittered dark and malevolent as his hand reached toward her head. Allie held still, jaw clenched, eyes on his. The back of his hand connected with her forehead and he frowned. "I think your fever is even higher."

"I think I'm going to lie down in the room." She paused. "If that's all right." It took effort, but she kept all trace of sarcasm from her words.

"Of course."

Feeling his eyes on her back, Allie slipped around the corner and into the bedroom she'd been assigned. Carefully, trying not to jar her back or the stitches, she stretched out on the bed. She'd rest for a few minutes, then figure out how to get to Catherine.

Unfortunately, as the time passed, she continued to feel worse instead of better. She drifted, only to awaken with chills and nausea.

Trembling, Allie rolled from the bed to her feet. Standing, she swayed, then staggered into the bathroom, where she was sick once again. "What in the world is going on with me?" she whispered, wishing someone was there to give her the answer. She thought it might have been the drug Henry had used to knock her out. Maybe it wasn't completely out of her system yet.

She chugged the Sprite, then filled the can with water and drank it.

When the worst of the sickness and dizziness faded, she stripped her shirt off and turned to look at her wound. It was puffy and miserable looking. "Oh, gross." The infection had taken hold and she needed to lance it.

The thought sent her stomach back into spasms and she closed her eyes to gather her strength. She could do this. If she could find something to do it with. Right now she was Catherine's only hope of escaping alive—and her own.

Once it was drained, if Henry came through with the antibiotic, she should feel better in a day or so. At least the wound was high enough that she could reach it to do what she needed to do if she could find some sort of knife. The fact that there was hydrogen peroxide and alcohol in the cabinet along with the thermometer told her Henry wasn't worried about her trying anything like throwing the liquid in his eyes. It would sting for a short time, but unless he had a door open and ready to bolt through, all that would do would be to anger him—and cause Catherine more pain and suffering—or death.

With effort, she pulled on her shirt and made her way into the kitchen. "Henry?"

No answer.

"Henry?"

She stood in the kitchen, holding on to the wall. Was this a test?

Allie went in search of a glass and filled it with ice water. As she slowly sipped it, her stomach settled and she felt slightly stronger. She started to explore under the guise of looking for her captor. "Henry?"

By the time she finished, she'd seen no sign of Catherine and had found no way out of the house. And while she was glad she now knew the layout of the single-story home, she was starting to see just how well Henry had thought all of this out.

Despair clawed its way into her throat and she swallowed hard, refusing to give in to the desire to scream. That would accomplish nothing.

She returned to the kitchen and noticed there was no butcher block of knives anywhere to be found. So, he wasn't quite that sure of her. In one of the drawers, she found a small paring knife.

It would have to do.

With a deep breath, she grabbed it and returned to her bathroom to snag two washcloths, dousing one with alcohol. Once she had the knife as sterile as she could get it with hot water and alcohol, she stuffed the other washcloth between her teeth, turned so she could see in the mirror, and placed the tip of the knife against the wound.

Then pressed through the stitches.

Lightning-sharp pain arced through her and she bit down hard on the washcloth, keeping the scream from escaping. Warm wetness ran down her back and she grimaced as the sharp pain dulled to a piercing throb. She pressed again, cutting through another stitch and releasing more of the infection.

The blade sank into her flesh and clinked against something hard. Shaking, nauseated, and fighting the need to simply pass out, she stopped and drew in a deep breath. For a moment, she wondered if she'd somehow hit a piece of bone. But there were no bones where she'd placed the knife.

The room spun. She lowered her arm and leaned her head against the mirror. The pain radiated. Gulping down the nausea, she turned back to the wound.

With gritted teeth, she probed again. Blood and infection ran freely. The room swam, but the knife touched something hard once again, and she slipped the tip of the blade under it and tilted. A small round object shot through the hole and landed on the counter.

Allie dropped the knife and grabbed the alcohol-soaked rag. She slipped off the counter and sank to the floor before pressing the cloth to the wound.

Fire shot through her back and darkness descended.

26

Linc watched the laptop screen and gave a grunt of satisfaction when the tracker showed the doctor turning into the long drive of a secluded house set on four acres of lakefront property. Thick trees surrounded the home, offering it extreme privacy—exactly like something Henry would purchase with his blood money if he'd been planning this for a while. If Linc had just been traveling the road, he never would have known the house was back there except for the privacy fence and gate.

"Did you get the code?" he asked Mark King.

"Got it."

CIRG was right there, waiting and ready to do their thing, and Linc took comfort from that. The Critical Incident Response Group consisted of SWAT, a hostage negotiator, tactical aviation, a behavioral analyst, and more. If Allie was in that house, they were going to get her out.

Brady, Izzy, Derek, and Chloe and her K-9, Hank, were also around with other CPD officers. Before they could move in, they needed the layout of the place, alarm system, booby traps, hidden rooms, number of people in the house, and so on. Including finding out if there was any way to contact Allie without Henry noticing it.

Now that they had the address, Annie could work on getting blueprints and hacking into the security system so they could get eyes inside.

Nerves on edge, Linc wanted to pace, chew his nails, pull his hair out. Mostly, he wanted to rescue Allie and take Henry down. Hard. *He* wanted to do it. But would let it happen however it needed to happen in order to make sure Allie survived.

"He's got a lot of firewalls up," Annie said. "This is going to take a while."

"We don't have a while. Forsythe is inside. There was no way to get a listening device on him before he bolted out of his office. We need eyes inside the house."

"Working on it."

He knew she was. "Thanks, Annie."

"Hold up, people," Mark said, his voice coming over the earpiece loud and clear. "We've got another visitor. Or three."

"Who is it?" Linc asked.

"If I'm not mistaken, that's Vladislav Nevsky and a couple of his goons."

Allie woke slowly, noting the fire in the back of her shoulder had faded to a dull throb. She was still on the bathroom floor, which meant Henry hadn't come looking for her. Which meant she hadn't been out very long.

When she'd passed out, she'd done so sitting up and leaning against the wall. Fortunately, the cloth was still pressing against the open wound.

Reaching back, she held the fabric in place and slowly stood, making sure her legs would hold her.

They did.

In the bedroom, she glanced at the bedside clock. Twenty minutes had passed since her self-inflicted surgery. She downed three more ibuprofen and noted that her fever didn't seem to be quite as high—if she could gauge it simply by how she felt.

She returned to the bathroom to glare at the tiny round device sitting innocently on the counter. A tracker. So that's how Henry had stayed one step ahead of them each and every time. She'd led him right to Daria, and of course, he'd want her taken out because she was one of the few who knew Allie was alive—and that he was corrupt.

Allie figured the device had been placed in her by the doctor at the rehab center. Forsythe. And Henry didn't want her to leave the room because he planned all along to keep her "dead" from that point on. Only she unwittingly ruined his plans when she stopped taking the meds that had kept her sedated and left the room in search of a laptop.

She supposed the kicker had been when she ran into Catherine Hayworth. She sealed that woman's fate the moment she'd become Allie's nurse. Allie's anger came in waves, bringing tears and the need to defeat Henry in whatever way necessary. *Give me a plan, God, please.*

Voices reached her. Loud voices. In the well-stocked medicine cabinet, she found several Band-Aids and pulled out three. By the time she got them on, pulling the raw skin together as tight as possible, she was sweating, but at least the worst of the dizziness and nausea had passed.

"Allie?"

Henry was back. She almost tried to move to sweep the evidence of her actions into the cabinet under the sink, then let the items sit there while she awkwardly pulled her shirt on.

"Allie? You in there?" He actually knocked.

"Come in," she said. Her fingers curled around the knife.

The door opened and his eyes widened at the mess on the floor next to her. She stared up at him. Only the fact that she would lose in a hand-to-hand fight with him at the moment kept her from using the last of her strength to launch herself at him and bury the knife in his throat. That . . . and she still didn't know where Catherine was. "I had to get rid of the infection."

"Unbelievable," he muttered. "Unbelievable! I told you I would take care of it!" He pulled his phone from his pocket and tapped the screen.

He was going to punish Catherine because she was trying to help herself? "Henry! No!"

His hard eyes met hers. "Too late."

He tapped the screen again. The television in the bedroom came to life.

At first nothing.

Then a sharp cry reached her. Then a full-blown scream. Then another. "Stop it! Make it stop!"

Allie lurched to her feet and staggered into the bedroom to see Catherine standing in the middle of the room, swiping the red ants from her. Welts appeared.

This time Allie did hurl herself at Henry, her good shoulder connecting with the middle of his chest. The breath whooshed from his lungs and he stumbled back against the bed. Another shove sent him to the floor. Before he could recover from his surprise at her attack, Allie grabbed the hand with the phone and slammed it against the carpet, then jammed her elbow into a pressure point on his biceps. Henry howled and the phone tumbled from his fingers.

Allie grabbed it and stumbled back into the bathroom, slammed the door and locked it, shocked she was able to actually lock it. She glanced at the still-open screen and tapped the icon for water, praying that it was one that started the sprinklers so Catherine could use the water to help wash the ants away.

Then she popped the phone out of the case, dialed Linc's number, then stopped. He was dead. Grief nearly sent her to her knees, but she bit off a sob, hung up, and dialed 911. The operator picked up. "911. What's your—"

A hard slam on the bathroom door sent her adrenaline rushing faster. "My name's Allie Radcliffe. Catherine Hayworth and I are being held hostage by FBI Special Agent Henry Ogden. I just need someone to know I'm not dead and to find him—"

Another hard hit. "Don't make me break this door down, Allie!"

"Ma'am?" The operator's voice sharpened. "I can hear him. Where are you?"

"I have no idea." And she wouldn't have enough time to leave the phone on long enough for someone to try and trace it. If they could even do so. Which she doubted.

"Who are you calling, Allie? Who's going to believe you? You're dead, remember? Any calls you make will be looked at as some kind of bad joke. 911 can't even trace the call. Now open the door!"

She hung up and with a sob, dropped the device into the toilet, praying the water would ruin it before Henry could get it out. He probably had another way to control his torture room, but at least he'd have to work to do it.

"Dr. Forsythe is here to help you," he said.

She stayed quiet, thinking. Desperately thinking and trying to summon her strength for the showdown that was sure to come. *Oh, Linc, I wish you were here.* Well, not in a hostage situation, but—

"Let me in, Allie. All I have to do is find a drill and I can take the hinges off in seconds." The calm in his voice was almost more terrifying than his shouts. "If you open the door, I'll have Dr. Forsythe take a look at Catherine and make sure she's all right."

"I don't believe you." The words were out before she could stop them.

A heavy thud slammed against the door, then silence. She could almost picture him trying to control his rage. "It'll go better for you if you just open the door," he finally said. "The longer you make me wait, the worse it's going to go for you. And Catherine."

266

"Got a 911 call from someone claiming to be Allie Radcliffe," Izzy said, her voice coming over Linc's earpiece.

He sat in the back of the command center, doing his best to keep his heart rate steady. He'd had Izzy put the 911 center on alert for any calls coming in about Allie or Henry and to let him know ASAP.

"Did she say where she was?" Linc asked. "Is she okay?"

He couldn't describe the relief that flowed through him. The fact that Allie had made a call meant she was still alive. Now to keep her that way.

"Said she and a woman by the name of Catherine Hayworth were being held hostage by FBI Special Agent Henry Ogden, but she didn't know where they were. And then she hung up."

Linc stood and pulled on his tactical gear. "I'm going to approach."

Mark frowned at him. "You want to get her killed? And maybe you too?"

"The longer we sit out here, the more danger she's in. Will you back me up?"

"I will." Brady's voice came over the COMMS.

"Count me in," Derek said.

"Me too," Izzy said.

"We don't know what's in there," Mark said. "We need to wait until we have eyes in the place."

Linc narrowed his eyes. "Normally, I'd agree. But not this time. I know Henry. Once he knows we're out here, he's going to kill everyone that's a threat to him, cut his losses, and find a way out." His eyes met the other agent's. "And he will have another way out. One that we're not aware of and isn't on any blueprints."

Mark hesitated, then shrugged. "All right, then. Let's do it."

Allie shut the lid to the toilet and sat on it, gathering her strength and trying to think. Quickly. On the other side of the door, a low buzz reached her, then something dropped to the floor.

A screw. "You don't have to take the door down, Henry. I'm coming out." Delaying the inevitable was stupid.

The drill stopped.

She stood and opened the door.

Henry stared at her, and if his look could have killed, she would be dead. For real this time.

"You killed her, you know," he said, sullen and . . . pouting?

"No, Henry, *you* did." *I'm sorry, Catherine, so very sorry.* Pictures of the woman's two little girls flashed into her mind and she stiffened. Henry would not hurt them as long as she had breath in her body. "I didn't know trying to lance a wound would cause you to go off like that."

"Lance a wound? It looked like you were—"

"What?" Trying to dig a tracker out? Yeah, she'd bite her lip on those words.

"Nothing," he said. "Nothing."

He didn't need to know she'd found it. As long as she kept it in her pocket, he would still get the location on her. Her head pounded and she pressed her hands against hot cheeks.

Henry motioned with a sharp wave. "Get out here. Where's my phone?"

"I flushed it." She braced herself for the next wave of fury.

His eyes darkened and his cheeks flushed. Then he laughed.

Allie blinked.

Henry laughed harder, but she took no relief in the sound, as it wasn't an amused one. When he finally stopped the demented cackle, he sobered so suddenly, she took a step backward. "You think that will stop me? I thought you were smarter than that. Come on," he said. "Now."

Allie swallowed and followed him into the bedroom. She glanced at the television and saw Catherine on the wet floor covered in welts, but couldn't tell if she was breathing or not. Tears pushed against her eyes. That poor woman. *God, please! Do something!*

"Henry?" a voice called from beyond the bedroom.

"Be out there in a minute, Nate, just make yourself at home."

Allie flinched and swayed. "Forsythe is in this with you?"

"In this? No. He's a trusted friend, but if you say anything . . . well, that you shouldn't say . . . it could cost him his life, you understand? You've already killed Catherine, you want him on your conscience too?"

"At least I have one," she muttered.

His fingers tightened on her biceps. "I'm not playing, Allie. You understand me?"

"Yes." But that didn't mean she couldn't try to slip the man a note. Then again, Forsythe could be working for him, and Henry could be testing her to see if she would try anything.

She stepped into the hall and made her way into the den, where the kind doctor from the rehab center stood with his back to her in front of one of the large windows overlooking the lake. "Hello."

He turned. "Allie, good to see you again." A frown tipped his lips downward. "I hear you're feeling under the weather."

"I am. Was. I think Henry probably called you out here for nothing."

"I was coming out later this afternoon anyway. Henry simply urged me to come quicker because he thought you needed immediate attention." He shot the man a questioning glance.

"She has a fever," Henry said. "And her stitches are infected. Or at least they were."

"The Motrin finally seems to be doing the trick," Allie said, "but mostly, I think I need an antibiotic for the wound. I lanced it and think I got most of the infection out, but . . ." She shrugged with her good shoulder.

"Lanced it?" Nonplussed, he stared. "You mean you opened it up?"

"Yes."

"By yourself? With no painkillers?"

"Well, it hurt enough that I wouldn't have minded a few if they'd been available, but I managed."

"Let me take a look."

"I didn't have to undo all of the stitches and I've got it all bandaged up at this point, so I think we're good."

"Allie, let the man look at it." Henry gave her a steely-eyed glare.

She met him glare for glare until a strange certainty washed over her. He was going to kill the doctor as soon as the man finished with her. The fact that Forsythe had been coming to the house that afternoon anyway convinced her.

"All right. Do you mind if I lie down on the bed in my room while you look?"

"Of course not."

She led the way back down the hall and Henry followed them. The doctor was one of the few people who knew she was alive— other than the 911 dispatch officer now, but Henry didn't know about her. Yet. He knew she'd called someone, though, and the 911 call would stand out. With his connections, he'd probably be able to get the name of the person who took the call. At that moment, the burden of escaping and stopping Henry couldn't weigh any heavier.

The doorbell rang. Allie stopped in the doorway of the bedroom and turned to see Henry place a hand on his weapon. Her heart thudded an extra beat. He wasn't expecting anyone if his reaction to the bell was any indication. Hope sent her head spinning once again.

"Go ahead and check her out, Nate," Henry said, "while I deal with this."

Forsythe lifted a brow. "Sure."

Henry's gaze met her once again for a split second and she had no trouble reading the message there. *Keep your mouth shut.*

Convinced Forsythe was relatively clueless about Henry's criminal activities, she gave Henry a short nod, then led the doctor into the bedroom.

"What are you doing here?" Henry's shout rang out, followed by two gunshots.

Linc and Mark joined Izzy, Derek, and Brady and made their way to the edge of the property, staying out of range of the cameras. At the sound of the two pops, they froze.

"I'm in," Annie said, excitement tinting her words. "That was a challenge."

"Perfect timing. Just heard two gunshots," Linc said. "Can you see anything?"

Several clicks on the keyboard, then a gasp. "I think there's a body on the floor in the entryway."

"Male or female?"

"Male."

Not Allie. A pang of guilt hit him at his relief.

"Adjusting the camera and . . . there's a male suspect standing just inside the front door flanked by two mean-looking dudes. The guy in the middle is holding a weapon on the man on the floor."

"Is the guy on the floor moving?"

"Yes. Think there's a bullet in his shoulder. At least he's got his right hand over it. Wait a minute. That's Henry!"

Nevsky had to be the guy in the middle of his two bodyguards. He'd shot Henry? "What else?"

"Oh man. Female down in a bedroom. This woman's got her back to the camera, but I can see some welts on her hands and arms and she's not moving. Water is raining down on her and there are . . . wow."

"What?"

"It's hard to see details through the falling water, but it looks like some kind of insect zoo in there. Bees, ants, spiders, scorpions."

"Sounds like Henry," Linc said. "Where's the room?"

"I can't tell. Looking at the blueprints, it could be any room in the house."

Most likely, it wasn't on the blueprints. "Thanks, Annie. You've got every door in the place under surveillance, right?"

"Right. If one opens or anyone tries to leave, I've got eyes on them."

"Any sign of Allie?" he asked, not expecting a positive answer. If she'd seen her, she would have said.

"No. According to the blueprints, there's another room around the corner from the kitchen. If there's a camera in there, it's not turned on."

Linc frowned. "Okay, keep eyes on that door especially. Let me know if anyone comes out or goes in."

"Will do."

And now to figure out if the place was booby-trapped. Nevsky had seemed to simply drive right up and approach with no problem.

Then again, he'd probably been there before and knew the layout and if there were any areas he should avoid. Or Henry had simply assumed he wouldn't need to set any traps because no one would be able to find him.

Either way, Linc was about to find out.

Allie had heard the shots and turned to a stupefied Nate Forsythe. "Do not leave this room, do you understand?"

"But—"

"Do you want to die?"

He flinched. "Of course not."

"Then stay here." Without waiting to see if he would obey, Allie darted out of the room and around the corner. The great room was empty, but Nevsky was yelling from the foyer, a mixture of English and Russian. "He's alive, you incompetent idiot. I look at the cameras and what do I see? That FBI agent and my daughter standing in the pool house." Allie's heart soared, her blood flowed faster and adrenaline spiked. Linc and Daria were alive?

"You are no good to me now. Today, you die."

"No, wait!" Henry's fear rang in his plea. "I can still benefit you. I can."

Allie trod on silent feet to the end of the wall and peered around the corner to catch a glance of Nevsky standing over a groaning Henry, who begged for his life. Part of Allie wanted to intervene, but what could she do in her weakened state with no weapon, except get herself killed? That wouldn't do Catherine or Dr. Forsythe any good. The shakes hit her and she raced back to the bedroom.

"What is it?" Forsythe asked. "Who was shooting? Where's Henry?"

Allie grabbed the remote and turned on the television.

"Catherine needs your help more than Henry does at the moment. Look."

"Cath—" His horrified expression as he caught sight of the screen solidified her belief that he'd not been part of Henry's sick plans—he'd been a pawn.

Although he had put a tracker in her back. But she'd deal with that later.

"Give me your phone."

"What?"

"Your phone," she whisper-yelled. "Give it to me."

He handed it to her and she punched in Linc's number. While it rang, she turned back to Forsythe. "You've been here before." She pointed to the television. "Where's that room?" Allie moved back to the door.

"Linc St. John."

"Linc? Is it really you?" Never had she been so glad to hear a voice.

"Allie!"

Tears flooded her eyes and she blinked them back. "I'm at Henry's house. His other house. It's—I don't know where—"

"We know where it is. We're right outside."

"Then get in here. Nevsky shot Henry, but he's not dead." At least she didn't think so. He'd been breathing and talking, the last she'd heard, and no more shots had been fired. "Nevsky doesn't know Forsythe and I are in here." Yet.

"Is Forsythe a part of this?"

"I don't think so."

"Do you know of any booby traps? Trip wires? Anything like that?"

"I don't know. Nevsky didn't have any problem getting all the way to the door, but I have an idea he's been here a few times."

"We're on our way."

"Be careful." Allie left the phone on and tucked it into her pocket.

She turned her attention back to the doctor. The poor man looked shell-shocked. "The room," she said. "Where is it?"

"I . . . I don't know. I think it's the one at the end of the hallway to the left of this room," Forsythe said. "He showed it to me when he had it almost finished. Said it was going to be some kind of lab." He scrubbed a hand down the side of his face. "Who was that at the door? Do you know?"

"Yeah, I do. Tell me about the room."

"Um . . . he said it was his special project for research, that he was still studying insects. In fact, I think I remember those enclosures that the insects are in."

"I saw that door at the end of the hall and just figured it led to the garage," Allie said.

"It does, but then there's a small hallway to the right and that room is just off of it."

She had to get Forsythe to Catherine. It was very possible the woman was dead, but if she wasn't and had any chance at all of surviving, Allie had to get her help. But how was she supposed to do that when Nevsky was here with what was obviously his own agenda? Would he shoot her on sight? Could they sneak out of the bedroom and get to the room that held Catherine without Nevsky or Henry seeing them?

Her eyes landed on Henry's keys on the counter. No doubt, one of those keys fit the door that would lead them to Catherine.

She stood still. Listening. Heart and head pounding together. *You can do this, Allie. You don't have a choice. Catherine's family needs you to do it.*

A hand landed on her shoulder and she barely stifled the sharp cry. She spun. "What?"

"You can't go out there. Wait until help gets here."

"Right now they're making sure they're not going to get blown up on entering. We can't wait on them." She darted out, grabbed the keys, and returned to the room to sort through them. "Car, house, office," she muttered as she eliminated the ones she recognized.

That left about five she would need to try with no one seeing her.

"You can't do this," Forsythe said.

"So we should just leave Catherine to die?"

He swallowed. "No. Of course not." A pause. "Tell me what to do."

"FBI may breach. If they do, you stay in here and stay low. Keep your hands where they can see them when they come in. They know who you are." Had probably followed him here. She loved the brilliant people she worked with.

"But I need to help."

"You can help when I know for sure that Catherine's in that room." For a moment the room spun and she shut her eyes to let the sensation pass.

"What if they see you?"

"Just be ready."

He raked a hand through his hair and narrowed his eyes. "I'm ready. I can't believe what a schmuck I've been."

"Not a schmuck. A friend to someone who took advantage of you."

His eyes widened. "I put a tracker in you. He said he needed to do that because you were being threatened and if someone managed to get you, then he had to be able to find you."

Glad to have the explanation, but impatient to get to Catherine, she pointed. "You ready?"

He nodded and Allie slipped out the door to hear Henry say, ". . . and . . . and . . . I can give you Linc St. John."

"The man who killed my son?"

"Yes."

The lie infuriated her. But . . . first things first. She stood in front of the door and twisted the knob. Locked, of course. She tried the first key. Nothing. She shot a glance over her shoulder and could see someone's shoulder. Hurrying, she tried the second key. Wonder of wonders, it worked and she opened the door to a room-sized hallway. She registered that he'd probably converted part of the garage, resulting in the weird layout. The door on the left had a dead-bolt lock on the outside, but no key required. She turned it and shoved the door open.

And there was Catherine on the wet floor. The ants were mostly gone, drowned and washed away into the drains in the concrete floor. Allie hated to imagine what else Henry had in mind when he installed those.

She darted back to "her" room and motioned to Forsythe, who grabbed his bag and followed her to kneel beside Catherine. He placed two fingers against her neck and frowned. "I've got a slight pulse, but she's got a lot of poison in her. If she were allergic, she'd be dead already."

Insects buzzed behind their screens and Allie shivered. "What do you need?"

"To get her to a hospital."

"Well, well, what have we here?"

Allie spun. Nevsky stood in the door, his weapon aimed at her.

28

Linc wanted to kick the door in, but he didn't have to. Nevsky had kindly left it unlocked—and unguarded, now that the two bodyguards were down. He stopped just before entry. "Everyone a go?"

The chopper, with its thermal imaging capabilities, roared in closer. "FLIR shows several heat sources. Three at the back of the house, five or six . . . under it? No, wait. Three. Nope, there's another one." A pause. "Something's not right. The number keeps changing."

"Just be prepared for anything," Linc said.

"Let's do this," Mark's voice came over the COMMS.

Linc lifted the phone to his ear. "Allie? We're coming in now in a dynamic entry." Meaning fast and furious. "Be ready."

"Put the gun down, Nevsky." Her rock-steady voice laced with steel came over the phone. "It's over."

"Hold up. We have a hostage situation." Fury slammed him. He knew they should have gone in earlier. "Mark, Izzy, Derek, Brady, follow me. We're going slow and steady. Keep an eye out for Henry." He had no illusions that the man wouldn't shoot one of them on sight.

Linc stepped over the threshold, gripping his M4 carbine in one hand and the phone in his other. Blood on the wood floor greeted him. Henry's? He stepped around it and turned the corner into the great room. The kitchen was straight ahead. He moved quickly. Through the door that led to the garage. Saw Nevsky standing there with a gun aimed into the room. "FBI! Show me your hands! Show me your hands!"

When Linc's yell reverberated through the house, Allie took advantage of Nevsky's split-second distraction and dove at him. She clipped him around the knees and he went down with a hard thud. His weapon discharged and the bullet whizzed past her cheek, then his gun fell to the floor next to him.

"He shot the bees!" Forsythe's cry came from behind her.

Nevsky hefted his massive bulk into a sitting position. Allie swept out a hand and knocked the weapon across the floor. He lunged for it, and for a man of his size, he moved faster than she'd anticipated.

"Linc!"

She grabbed Nevsky's hand as he closed his fingers around the grip of the weapon and tried to slam his hand against the floor. Unfortunately, he was strong—and she wasn't at her strongest. He pushed against her hold and Allie's grip slipped.

In the background, she heard Linc yelling but couldn't allow her concentration to waver. With her left hand latched on to Nevsky's wrist, she hefted her body and managed to scramble on top of the man and jam an elbow into his throat. His struggles intensified and she held on, feeling like she was back in college trying to ride the mechanical bull at the local hangout.

"Linc!"

"I can't get a good shot! You're in the way!"

Finally, Nevsky released the gun just as her grip slipped. He growled and swung a fist at her face. She launched herself backward and he missed.

Only now Nevsky was unarmed.

"On your stomach!" Linc charged forward. "On your face! Let me see your hands."

Bees swarmed from the room and Nevsky noticed. He screamed and threw his hands up. Forsythe had Catherine in his arms and was ducking against the onslaught of the angry insects as he ran down the hall to the front door.

Breathing hard, Nevsky tried to scramble to his feet, screaming and swatting at the air around him. "Get them away! Get them away! They're stinging me!" One hand dropped to slap his pocket, and Allie sat frozen, hoping none of the bees would aim for her. With all of Nevsky's frantic movements, they were going after him.

"Be still!" she said. "Stop moving!"

He was too far gone to even comprehend her orders.

From the corner of her eye, she saw Forsythe helped out of the house by Izzy and Brady. Catherine was getting help. Nevsky was weaponless and helpless against his biggest fear.

She reached into the mess of bees, grabbed his arm, and pulled. Linc snagged his other arm and together they got him out of the house, where he fell to the ground, rolling and crying, screaming for help.

"Get the hose!" Linc ordered.

Seconds later, a hard stream of water covered the three of them, spraying for a good five minutes until all the bees were gone or dead.

Nevsky went still. His eyes caught hers and the absolute darkness there sent chills skating up her spine. "This is your fault."

Allie swept up the EpiPen that had fallen out of Nevsky's pocket during his battle with the bees. She popped the safety cap off and planned to offer it to him in case he needed it.

Linc still held his weapon on the man. Water dripped from his brow, but his focus never wavered.

"My fault?" she asked. "Why don't you put the blame where it belongs?"

"What do you mean?"

"This started fifteen years ago when you convinced my brother to kill my family."

"Your brother," he gasped. "He wasn't your brother. He was my son. Your mother kept him from me for the first seventeen years of his life, and your father"—he spit the word—"was going to take him away, so I took him first." His dark gaze turned to Linc. "And you killed him."

"It wasn't him, it was Henry," Allie said.

Nevsky stilled. "He would not."

"But he did, because Henry was killing everyone who knew I was alive. And Gregori was one of those people."

Nevsky seemed to have forgotten about the bees. "He said you were hunting Gregori and that it was only a matter of time before you found him with all of the resources available to you, that you wanted to kill him and that he was going to take you away forever if I would just help him."

"And it didn't hurt that he would be forever in your debt, did it?"

"Indeed. And you ruined all of that."

"It was my pleasure. Enjoy prison."

Nevsky rolled in a sudden heave of his bulk. Linc hollered at him to stop moving. A sharp pain shot through her calf. She cried out, turned to see a knife in Nevsky's hand coming back at her. She ducked, felt the blade swish past her face. She swung out with the EpiPen and caught the man in the ear at the same time Linc fired. Nevsky's body jerked, his eyes held hers, then closed.

Forever.

Brady swept the weapons away from Nevsky and cuffed him before turning to her. Linc dropped beside her and clamped a hand around her bleeding leg.

"It's nothing," she said, unable to take her eyes from him. "I can't believe you're alive."

"Daria and I are harder to take out than we look."

"Apparently." A thousand needles shot up her hands and arms, and she realized she'd been stung a number of times. "Getting hard to breathe, Linc."

"Are you allergic?"

"Not that I know of, but I've got a lot of stings and my throat feels a bit tight and—" She wheezed.

"Need a paramedic over here!"

Allie crawled to Nevsky and reached into his pocket—and pulled out the second EpiPen he was never without. She released the cap and jabbed herself in the thigh. Looking up, she caught Linc's startled gaze. "Better safe than sorry."

Then promptly passed out.

Linc awakened slowly with a crick in his neck. He turned his head to see Allie still sleeping in the hospital bed. His mother stood just inside the door, whispering his name. Linc drew in a deep breath and stood, then joined her outside the room.

"I decided to stop by on my way to the station," she said. "How is she doing?" She touched the welts on his hands. "How are *you* doing?"

"We're fine. Now. They gave me an antihistamine just in case and a topical cream for the itching. As for Allie, she's been sleeping a lot. When she wakes from the nightmares, I think it helps that I'm here to talk her through them."

"I'm sure it does." Her lips tightened. "It was Henry all along?"

He nodded. "Working with Nevsky. Allie came to and explained a lot in the ambulance before the paramedics gave her something to sedate her. It was obvious she was in a lot of pain. Anyway, apparently Henry had some kind of obsession with Allie that started when she first interviewed with him a year ago. It grew until he decided to fake her death, then spirit her away to his well-secured house on the lake where she was to live out the rest of her days with him. When he saw that Allie and I were getting close, he decided he had to get rid of me in order to have any chance at all of winning Allie's affections."

His mother shuddered. "What a sick man."

Linc rubbed his eyes. "Thank God that Allie is Allie. If he'd gone after anyone else, he probably would have gotten away with it."

"Yes. Thank God. I think that's what we should all be doing."

"I agree."

"What was Nevsky's role in everything?"

"He agreed to help Henry pull everything off, only he didn't count on his daughter helping Allie and us bring him down."

"Daria." His mother smiled. "I like that girl."

"Thanks for letting her stay with you until we can figure out what to do with her."

"She should be in custody of CPS."

"She'll be eighteen in three weeks, Mom. And besides that, she needs police protection. Henry's still out there. I wouldn't put it past him to snatch Daria to use as bait."

She frowned. "True. Then again, he could be gone, never to be heard from again."

"I'm not willing to take that chance."

"I don't think I would be either. Daria's fine where she is."

"I know Allie would take her in, but she's got a few days before she'll be back on her feet. She's got some powerful antibiotics running through her, and her fever spiked last night."

His mother nodded. "How did Henry manage to escape? I'm still flabbergasted at that."

Linc sighed. "He's a brilliant man, Mom. He had everything planned down to the last detail. Including an underground escape route. He built a tunnel with thermal imaging in mind."

"Meaning?"

"Meaning, he had dummies with heated coils in his tunnel. They were on some kind of timer. When they were on, it looked like a person was there. The timer turned them on and off, making it confusing enough that he got the response delay he was after. He was gone before they knew what to do."

She shook her head. "I'll request to be Daria's guardian until she turns eighteen. I'm pretty sure I'll pass the background check."

Linc hugged her. "You're amazing."

She gave him a tight squeeze and he held her for just a moment longer. When she pulled away, a sheen of tears stood in her eyes. "I hate what you've just gone through, but I'm so glad that darkness that was hanging over you is gone."

"Darkness?"

"You know what I'm talking about."

He did. "Thanks. For everything."

"How are you feeling about having to shoot Nevsky?"

He rubbed his chin and sighed. "There's always that heaviness for taking a life, but it was either him or Allie. There aren't any regrets."

"Good."

Ruthie appeared around the corner and headed straight for them. "Hi, Mom, you checking up on the troublemaker?"

Linc put on an affronted frown. "Hey now. Seems to me you've had your own share of being the troublemaker. Better be careful throwing those words around."

She laughed. "I guess you've got me there." Turning serious, she nodded to the room. "How's she doing?"

"She's sedated for now," Linc said. "She's got a lot of healing to do." Ruthie had been tied up in surgery when they arrived almost twenty-four hours ago. She'd been by twice since.

"Does she know Henry's still out there?" his mother asked.

"No."

"Then where are the guards for her room?"

"We're not putting them on it."

Ruthie raised a brow. "You're drawing him here, aren't you?"

"Every person on this floor is an agent. Including the doctor and two nurses. The patients in the other beds are also agents—ones Henry's never met before. If he sets foot on this floor, he's done."

"And if he doesn't?"

Linc sighed. "Then we go looking for him."

29

Allie didn't feel back to a hundred percent, but it was still one of the best days of her life. She lay in the hospital bed reliving everything, feeling her muscles bunch, flashing on the fear, but able to push it aside with the knowledge that her family had justice.

It wouldn't bring them back, but now maybe Allie could really and truly let it go. The fact that she'd started to do so even before Nevsky and Gregori had been caught gave her comfort, and hope, that in time, the past would truly be in the past.

Nevsky was dead and so was Gregori. She almost wished she felt more . . . *something* . . . knowing her brother was dead, but while she grieved the child she'd known, the man he'd become was a complete stranger.

So, yes. Justice had been served.

Now they just had to find Henry.

Her muscles tightened once again at the thought. Would he run? She had no doubt he had numerous false documents and hidden bank accounts, even though the ones they'd found had been frozen. And as good as he was with disguises, he could stay hidden forever—or he could pop up any time to continue his twisted plan to keep her locked up in some escape-proof fortress.

Which meant Allie would constantly be looking over her shoulder.

The thought nauseated her.

The door opened and Linc stepped inside, followed by his mother and Ruthie, Izzy, and Chloe. Then Daria, Derek, and Brady.

Allie pushed herself into a sitting position, wincing at the tug on her back. Apparently, she'd undergone minor surgery to clean out the wound and restitch it—minus the tracker this time.

Daria slipped over to the bed, leaned over, and hugged Allie. Allie held the girl and fought tears of relief. "I'm so glad you're okay," she whispered.

"Me? I'm fine. It was you we were worried about."

Allie swallowed and gave Daria one more tight squeeze. How this sweet girl ever came from someone as awful as Nevsky, she'd never comprehend. Maybe the fact that her father had ignored her was actually a blessing in disguise. "I'll be good as new in a few days." She pushed stray strands behind the girl's ear. "I'm so sorry about Gerard."

Tears hovered on Daria's lashes. "I know he wasn't a good man, but . . . he was when I needed him to be." She sniffed and sighed. "He said he regretted his choices, and if he had it to do all over again, he would've made different ones."

Choices. Allie nodded, so glad she'd made the choice not to shoot Gregori. She realized now she'd never regret it.

Daria stepped back and Allie's gaze found Linc's. "How's Catherine?"

"Recovering. She's surrounded by her family, and her husband has publicly expressed his gratitude to the Bureau and the CPD. Everyone's happy with that outcome."

"Good." She licked her lips and Linc handed her a cup of ice water. After she finished taking a few swallows, one by one Linc's siblings hugged her and Allie's emotions threatened to break free, leaving her blubbering all over these wonderful people.

When the hugging session ended, they all stood around her bed, and her gaze landed on each one before she bit her lip and sighed. "I'm sorry for everything."

Tabitha St. John frowned at her. "Sorry for what?"

"For putting you all in danger."

"Henry and his obsession—and Nevsky—are the ones responsible for any danger we might have been in," Izzy said. "Not you."

"And besides," Linc said, "I don't think anyone was ever actually in danger. I think it was all a setup to make you think they were. Henry knew you'd do anything to protect me—*us*. He gave those pictures to Nevsky, who planted them in the unlocked drawer. It was just all part of his plan to convince you to stay dead."

"But I wasn't even 'dead' at that point."

"I think he planned to fake your death somehow, using Nevsky to do it. I'm pretty sure it was supposed to happen in the house and then Henry was supposed to come to the rescue. The pictures were to convince you that I and my family were in danger, and I was supposed to believe you were dead just like it played out after the drone explosion." He slid her a sidelong glance. "Because, if you remember, he did actually convince you to go along with it."

"Only because I thought you and your family were truly in danger," she shot back. Then sighed. "So, yes, it worked. I was so stupid, wasn't I?"

"No, not at all," Linc's mother said. "You wanted to protect those you care about. Just like we all do."

Allie rubbed her head. "That's true." She'd always been that way. And after she'd failed to protect her sister—

She put the mental brakes on, refusing to go there. "Who knows what he was thinking?" She paused, then shook her head. "I wasn't supposed to get into the locked drawer, was I?"

"Probably not," Linc said. "But Henry and Nevsky worked it out to make it look like Henry had a big bust in Charleston to add to his stellar record. He really did put away a lot of the little people, but they were the ones who had no knowledge of Nevsky or Henry or anything."

"So, they were expendable."

"Yes, and couldn't offer any pertinent information that could do any harm to the organization or Henry. It really was a brilliant plan. Because he was right there, Henry knew exactly when to tell Nevsky to walk into the office and 'catch' you. Daria wasn't supposed to be there." He shot an apologetic look at the teen.

Daria narrowed her eyes. "I'm glad I was."

Brady tucked his phone into his pocket and patted Daria's shoulder. "Hey, my wife, Emily, just texted. She's down in the cafeteria and wants to meet you."

Linc nodded to Derek, who straightened from his casual stance against the wall. "I'll go too."

"If you want to talk privately, just say so," Daria said. "I don't need an escort."

Allie caught her hand. "Henry's still alive, Daria. He was after me the whole time. Not your father."

"And you think he may come back for you."

"Maybe."

"And so I get bodyguards because he may decide to use me to get to you."

Izzy and Chloe exchanged startled glances, and Allie huffed a small laugh. "Yeah." The more this family was around Daria, the more they'd realize how special she was.

Daria nodded. "Okay then. Bodyguards it is. I think I could use some ice cream."

Once she, Brady, and Izzy were gone, Linc's mother squeezed her hand. "I'm going to get out of here and let you get some rest."

"Thank you."

"No, hon, thank *you*." She shot Linc a knowing look, and to Allie's amusement, red tinted his cheeks.

"If you need anything," Chloe said, "let us know."

"I will. I appreciate it."

And finally, she was alone with Linc.

"I'm glad you're okay," he said, his voice low.

"I wouldn't have been without you and the others." The fear she'd kept so under control threatened to consume her.

"I'm here, Allie."

"I know."

"You're not alone anymore. Never again."

She wanted to believe him, wanted to grasp that promise with everything in her.

A tear slipped down her cheek, and he frowned as he brushed it away with a slightly swollen, cream-soaked hand. "What is it?"

"I once apologized to you for trying to live a life I was never meant to live."

"I remember."

"The truth is, I may not have been meant to live it, but I want it."

He sat on the bed next to her and pulled her into a hug. She rested her head against his chest, relishing the feel of being in his arms.

"I love you, Allie," he said, his voice husky with suppressed emotion.

"I love you too, Linc."

He tilted her chin up and she met his gaze. "My first inclination is to kiss you, but I need to know why you sound so sad when you say that."

A kiss would be lovely, but . . . "Because Henry's still out there, and as long as he's still a free man, you're a target—and it's because of me."

"You? You're not the cause of this. You're the victim."

She froze. "Oh no. No, no, no, no, no."

He sat back and frowned. "What? What is it?"

"I won't be a victim. I swore I'd never be a victim again and I'm

290

not starting now." Allie pulled into herself, drawing on the coping mechanisms she'd learned as a teen and then kept as a protective mantle whenever the memories threatened to be too much. She met Linc's gaze. "I'm not his target, Linc. You are. And I will do everything in my power to make sure that no one I love is hurt if I can do anything to stop it."

"Allie, that's not—"

"What? Reasonable?"

"Well . . ." He sighed. "Look, every single person on this floor is an agent and you better believe that every single one of them wants to be the one to bring Henry down. He's responsible for this. He betrayed us all."

She shook her head. "I appreciate the protection, but you know as well as I do that Henry's not going to come here. He knows the procedure. As long as we're here, we're safe, that's true. But the minute we walk out of this hospital, we're not. I really think he'll go with what he originally thought."

"Which is?"

"He has to get rid of you, because as long as you're alive, there's no way I'll ever be his."

Not that she would be anyway, but she was trying to think like Henry would. Because no matter what everyone else thought, she knew he was coming back for her. And this time she'd be ready.

Linc stood in the hospital cafeteria line and decided if he never had to set foot in a medical facility again, it would be too soon. But Allie had asked for a milk shake and he was determined to get it for her.

Quelling his impatience, he spent the time studying the people around him. Those at the tables. Those in the line. The doctors and nurses, worried parents, patients well enough to leave their rooms to eat but too sick to go home. And others. Fortunately, he didn't see anyone that he thought might present a threat to Allie or him or anyone else in the cafeteria.

When his phone buzzed, he grabbed it almost desperately. Mark King. "Yeah, what's up, Mark?"

"How's Allie?"

"Recovering. She should be able to get out of here tomorrow."

"Good."

"What have you got?"

"Someone who may have been Henry Ogden was seen sitting outside your home in a cable van."

"Was it him?"

"When the agents watching your house went to confront him, he left. They followed and found the van abandoned and the driver gone. There's no security footage that can tell us the man's identity."

Linc's blood chilled. "So, Allie was right on in her assessment."

"How's that?"

"She said he'd come after me."

"I've asked the interim SSA if we could work with the locals to keep an eye on your place and Allie's. He told me to arrange it. I figured since you're related to everyone on the CPD, you could take care of it."

"Not quite everyone, but yeah, I'll handle it as soon as I hang up and take Allie her milk shake."

"No sign of him at the hospital?"

"No. Allie doesn't think he'll come here."

"She may be right. He might be crazy, but he's smart."

Linc stepped up to the counter. "Hold on a sec, Mark." To the woman not so patiently waiting, he said, "I need an Oreo shake, please." His stomach rumbled. "Better make it a large." She turned to make it and he tuned back in to Mark. "Allie doesn't need to know he's been spotted and especially not where, okay?"

"Your head's going to roll when she finds out."

"I know."

He hung up and paid for the shake, then sipped on it while he headed back to Allie's room. A plan to catch Henry started to percolate in the back of his mind, and eager to share it with Allie, he took the stairs instead of the elevator. At her room, he knocked. When she didn't answer, he pushed open the door slowly, not wanting to wake her if she was asleep.

Only she wasn't sleeping. She was sitting up, talking on the phone. "Right. Okay, thanks. Bye."

She waved him in and he handed her the Orco shake. "What was that all about?"

"Annie. They just got word that Henry chartered a private plane. He's on his way to Mexico."

Linc frowned. If Henry was on his way to Mexico, who'd been sitting outside his house?

A decoy.

Henry had planted someone on Linc's house, keeping attention there, while he slipped away.

Allie tucked her phone into her pocket as the convenience store came into view. It seemed like every muscle in her body was sore, but with her adrenaline pumping and her energy level fueled by sheer determination, she figured she'd manage. Because while she ached, the fever was gone, and she felt stronger than she had in a while.

After being released from the hospital, Allie debated the wisdom of the plan that was slowly taking shape in her mind. Henry might have managed to get out of the country, but that didn't mean he got to escape the consequences of his actions. She was going to have to go after him. For several reasons. The main one being that she was done.

Done with being a victim.

Done with being a pawn.

Done with looking over her shoulder.

The smell of freedom was an irresistible lure, and freedom would only come if Henry were behind bars—or dead.

The Uber driver pulled to a stop. "This is good, thanks," she said.

"Yes, ma'am."

She climbed out and stretched carefully. Yes, the last thirty-six hours of rest had definitely done her some good.

With a wave goodbye to the driver, Allie made her way to the back of the convenience store and to the path in the woods that would lead to the back of her apartment. When she came to the place where she'd been shot, she swallowed and kept going.

Finally, at the tree line, she paused. After a quick scan of the area, she darted across to the steps and took them up to the screened-in porch. Looking at the place from this side, she thought it didn't look too bad. Did she dare hope the key was in the plant? A quick search turned it up. Bless Daria's little heart. She'd used it to get in, then returned it to the hiding place. Not that she needed it. From what Linc had said, she could probably go around to the front and enter through the shot-out sliding glass doors.

But then she'd be taking a chance—more of a chance—on someone seeing her. And she wasn't quite ready to explain her resurrection from the dead to her neighbors. Especially Roland Carter. Although the man's eagle eye had her confident that no one was inside the apartment, or the local police—or Linc—would have heard about it.

Not that she wouldn't double-check.

Once inside, Allie stood still and took a moment to breathe, get her thoughts together, and take in the destruction. Destruction that looked like it had been cleaned up. Bless Roland's heart. It had to be him.

Allie reached into her pocket, pulled out the remains of the little silver tracker, and placed it on the counter in the kitchen. Then she grabbed the biggest knife from the butcher block and held it in front of her.

A few minutes later, after a thorough search of her home, she lowered the knife and drew a forearm across her forehead before the sweat could drip into her eyes.

Moving quickly, she slipped back into her bedroom, ignoring the plywood that had been nailed over her sliding glass doors, but noticing the glass had been cleaned up from the floor. No doubt she had Roland to thank for that as well.

She opened the closet. Her safe, bolted to the wall on the left, held two weapons. A Glock 17 and a SIG Sauer P226. She grabbed them both, checked to see they were loaded, and shoved one into the band of her jeans at the small of her back and simply held the other in her right hand.

Arming herself helped calm her racing heart.

He's gone. He's in Mexico and he probably will stay there for a while.

Linc texted her.

Are you all right?

She tapped back,

I'm fine.

I'll be over in a bit, I just have to finish up some paperwork.

No problem. I'm just going through my apartment, trying to figure out what needs to be done.

All right. See you soon.

After a second, the word "Thai?" came across her screen.

She laughed, already feeling her muscles relax a fraction.

Perfect.

Allie shoved her phone into her back pocket and planted her hands on her hips. Mentally, she ticked off the things that needed to be done, such as the phone calls to start the process of getting her apartment put back together.

Every so often, she'd check the window, glancing out the front, checking the back door. She couldn't help it.

She downed some ibuprofen and went back to cleaning. The sofa and most of her den furniture would have to be thrown out. Walls needed repairing and some of her dishes in the kitchen were broken, but overall, the damage wasn't anything that couldn't be fixed with some elbow grease.

An hour passed. Then another.

How was she supposed to just move on with life while he was still out there?

Her stomach had twisted into one big knot of tension.

"He's gone," she muttered. "It's time to get back to the land of the living and move on."

But Henry was in her head and he wasn't leaving anytime soon. She carried her weapon into the bathroom, locked the door, and took a shower, her mind spinning. "He's gone," she whispered.

Then again, what if she was wrong? What if he wasn't gone? Or, even worse, what if he was and she'd have to live the rest of her life looking over her shoulder, afraid he'd return to finish the job? Oh no. No way. She couldn't give him that much power. Not this time. She would *not* be a victim again.

She stepped out of the shower, dressed in comfortable sweats and a T-shirt. Her shoulder holster completed her outfit. Allie drew in a deep breath. She should just fix some tea and get ready for Linc to arrive with the food.

Snatching her phone from the counter, she headed for the kitchen when the device buzzed.

Linc

I'm going to be late. Sorry. Lots of paperwork and questions.

She could imagine. No doubt when she decided to rise from the dead, she'd face the same thing. She checked her alarm. The doors were armed, but honestly, that brought her very little comfort. She knew she had agents watching from afar, and that helped. If something were to happen, it would take them a bit of time to get to her, but that was the plan. She had to look like she was home alone. Henry would case the place before he made his move, and he'd spot any watchdogs in a heartbeat.

After pacing a hole in the hardwoods, Allie moved the recliner into the farthest corner of the room, where her back was literally against the wall. She settled into the chair and drew in a deep breath. Fatigue pulled at her, reminding her she wasn't at a hundred percent yet. Her lids drooped and with her fingers wrapped around the grip of the Glock, she finally gave in to the need for sleep.

inc finally walked out of the conference room at the Bureau
office. They all knew Allie was alive now and he was to pass
the word that she was to show up tomorrow morning at nine sharp.
As he headed to the Thai restaurant, he grappled with something
that was bothering him.

Henry Ogden had chartered a flight to Mexico.

Henry Ogden had.

Or had he?

And that's what bothered him. It was too easy. Too . . . pat.
Everything had been nicely tied up in a pretty little bow.

He pulled into the parking lot of the restaurant and snatched
his phone to dial Annie's number.

She answered, her voice husky with sleep. "Linc . . ." She groaned.
"Do you know how many hours I've been awake?"

"I do, but I think Allie could still be in danger. Can you help
me out?"

"She's got guards on her place as a precaution, doesn't she?"

"Of course."

"All right. Tell me what you need." All traces of sleep were gone.

"Can you get the security footage from Watson's Airstrip?" A
private company that chartered flights, the one Henry had suppos-

edly chartered for Mexico. "I want to see who actually got on the plane. If it was Henry, fine. If it wasn't, then Allie's still in danger."

"I'll need a warrant."

"I'm not worried about using this in court, I just need to make sure I'm wrong. Or right. Please."

She sighed. "Fine, but if this comes back to bite me, I'm blaming you."

"I'm okay with that."

While Annie got herself situated at her home computer, Linc texted Allie.

> Any sign of Henry?

His next text went to Mark King.

> Head to Allie's apartment. Not sure this is over yet.

He gave him the address.

"Okay, I've got it," Annie said. "What am I looking for?"

"Footage of everyone who walked into that office yesterday or this afternoon. Tell me if you see Henry. Oh, he may have a sling on his arm. Nevsky shot him in the shoulder."

"Ouch."

"Yeah." She fell silent and the seconds ticked into minutes. "Well?"

"This is a busy place, Linc, hold on."

He held. Barely. He put his Suburban into drive and backed out of the parking spot. "I'm heading to Allie's while you search. Call me when you know something."

"Will do."

"Thanks, Annie, I owe you."

"Yes, you do, but I'll be in touch." She hung up.

Linc pressed the gas harder and turned his blue lights on.

Allie woke to an all-encompassing, mind-numbing fear. Gasping, she shot out of the chair and aimed her weapon at the door.

Seconds passed.

Nothing.

The apartment was dark. She'd forgotten to turn some lights on before falling asleep.

"Just another nightmare," she whispered. "It's okay. Just a dream."

The wind ruffled her hair and she froze. Wind?

Turning to her right, she noted the piece of plywood that had covered the broken part of her sliding glass door was no longer there. Instead, she could see the complex lights through the gaping hole.

Someone had pulled the tape off and removed the piece while she slept. And she had a feeling she knew who. Sweat broke out across the base of her neck and her forehead, even as her fingers tightened around the grip of her weapon.

"I know you're here," she said. Her phone buzzed indicating a text, but she refused to look away from the open area. "Come on, Henry, I know it's you!"

And then he stepped inside her apartment, gun raised. "Yes, Allie, it's me."

"Thought you were in Mexico."

He laughed. "That's what you were supposed to think. If everyone thought I was still in the vicinity, there would have been so much protection around you, I wouldn't have been able to do this."

"So, what now? I'm not going with you."

"No, I realize that."

His tone sent another dart of fear through her. "Okay, so why are you here, then?"

He sighed. And looked almost sad. "I'm not meant for a life on the run."

"Oookay."

"But I can't imagine life without you. Even the afterlife."

"So, you're going to kill me and take me with you," she said.

"It's the only way."

"Allie!"

Linc's voice registered and Henry's lips tightened. "Well, I guess I'm going to have to speed things up a bit." He leveled his weapon at her, center mass.

She dove to the right as three shots rang out.

Allie hit the floor, surprised when the only pain she felt was from banging her elbow too hard when she rolled.

"Allie!"

"Henry's here! Stay back!"

Pounding footsteps reached her and she surged to her feet, weapon aimed. Only to pause when she saw the body on the floor. Henry lay gasping, his hands clutching at the hardwoods, opening and closing. He finally gave one last coughing gasp and stilled.

Running footsteps and her guards appeared, weapons drawn. She lifted a hand to let them know she was all right. They'd done what she'd asked. Stayed far enough away to ensure that Henry felt safe in approaching. It had been risky, but . . .

Allie looked back to see Roland Carter, gun still pointed at Henry, standing just outside. "He was going to shoot you," the former officer said.

"I know. Thank you." She paused. "How did you know to come to the rescue?"

He gave her a faint smile. "I have a camera that monitors the back of the complex. It beeps every time something passes in front of it. Saw you sneak in and continued to monitor it." He shrugged. "You never know who's going to cause trouble around here." He blew out a breath. "I knew you were alive, just not the reason you were pretending to be dead." He glanced at Henry. "Now, I guess I know part of the story."

"I'll tell you the rest sometime later."

He nodded. "I'd like that."

Linc and Mark, along with Brady, Izzy, Chloe, and Derek, stood watching them.

"Allie?" Linc looked down at Henry, then at Roland, who set the gun on the floor and lifted his hands.

"I got this," Brady said. "Go check on her."

Linc bolted to her side and wrapped his hands around hers. She blinked and realized she was still aiming her weapon at Henry. She let Linc remove it from her numb hand and set it aside.

"Allie?" he asked softly.

"I'm okay," she whispered.

"It's over."

"Yes. It's finally over."

He pulled her against his chest and she closed her eyes.

It was over.

And now it was time to start living the life she was created to live.

"I love you," he whispered against her ear.

"And I love you."

Epilogue

Allie sat at the table between Linc and Daria while Derek cut the cards, then began to deal. Ruthie and her husband, Isaac, sat to Derek's left. Izzy and Ryan on his right. Chloe, Blake, and their daughter, Rachel, had just arrived and taken their seats, while Brady and Emily whisper-argued in the kitchen.

"What's going on with them?" she asked Linc.

He shook his head, his bemusement with his family clear on his handsome features. "I'm clueless."

The front door opened and Marcus St. John stepped inside the foyer to hang his raincoat on the hook. He removed his hat and swiped a hand through his salt-and-pepper hair. "It's a soggy one out there." He took in the sight at his dining room table and let out a mock groan. "It's Phase 10 night?"

"Never mind that," Izzy said, popping up from her seat, "what took you so long?"

He frowned at his daughter. "I texted Brady and told him I'd be a little later. What's the rush?"

"The family's all here and Ryan and I have an announcement."

Tabitha St. John stepped out of the half bath off the hall and greeted her husband with a kiss. He smiled down at his wife, and

Allie sucked in a breath at the love she saw the two still shared after nearly forty years of marriage. She snuck a look at Linc and found him watching her. With the same look on his face for her that she'd just seen on his father's face. Her heart stuttered. Then sped up. She smiled and he gripped her hand, then leaned over to place a light, sweet kiss on her lips.

Blake cleared his throat. "So, Chloe and I have an announcement too, but Izzy, you go first."

Brady and Emily finally joined them. They were holding hands, so whatever they'd been arguing about in the kitchen must not have been too big of a deal.

"Well, that's interesting," Brady said. "Emily and I have something we want to share too."

The elder St. Johns exchanged baffled looks and raised brows. "All right," Tabitha said, "Izzy, you and Ryan first."

"We're pregnant!" She practically squealed the words, and the grin that spread across Ryan's face was priceless, in Allie's opinion. She couldn't help smiling too.

The whoops and hollers along with hugs and a few tears took a while to die down, but Ryan finally stepped up behind his wife and wrapped his arms around her. She leaned against him beaming.

Tabitha turned to Chloe. "And you, dear? What was it you wanted to share?"

"Um . . . well . . . I don't want to rain on Izzy's parade now. It can wait."

Izzy's brows shot up, then she narrowed her eyes at her sister. "You're pregnant too?"

Blake snorted. Chloe laughed. "Yeah. I hope you don't mind."

"Mind? Are you kidding me? That's fabulous!" Izzy bounded over to Chloe and wrapped her in a hug. "How many weeks are you?"

"Eleven."

"I'm fourteen!"

"Oh, my stars," their mother said, placing a hand over her heart. Tears streamed down her cheeks. "*Two* grandbabies? It's almost more than I can handle."

Brady cleared his throat and Emily giggled. Everyone stopped and stared.

"You too?" Marcus finally asked.

Emily nodded and Brady grinned. The same grin that Ryan still had on his face.

"How many weeks?" Allie blurted.

"Twelve."

"Unbelievable," Linc said. "Well, I guess this calls for some major celebrations."

"Um, not just yet," Ruthie said softly.

All eyes turned to her and Isaac, who flushed a deep red but couldn't seem to keep his lips from turning up. Ruthie lifted her hands, palms up. "Ten weeks."

Tabitha stumbled to the nearest chair and sank onto it. "*Four* grandbabies? I'm going to have to retire!" And she burst into tears.

Her husband's eyes were suspiciously wet as he gripped Tabitha's hand. "They're happy tears," he said. "And she's not really retiring."

"Yes I am!" the woman sobbed. "I get to take care of grand-babies!"

Allie's gaze bounced from one person to the next until her eyes finally locked on Linc's. He leaned forward. "Can we make our announcement now?"

She gaped. "*I'm* not pregnant!" The room went silent and Allie felt the heat sweep into her cheeks. "Er . . . well . . . I'm not."

Linc laughed. First a snort, then a full-on guffaw. Allie thought about punching him. Instead, she crossed her arms and glared at him while his family snickered.

When he got himself under control, he turned to his staring family. "Um, sorry. I need to talk to Allie outside. Congratulations, everyone."

His hand grasped hers and he pulled her out of the dining room, through the den, and out onto the porch, where he sat on the swing and directed Allie to the seat beside him. "I'm sorry," he said. "I didn't mean to embarrass you."

"It's okay."

"But . . ."

"But?"

He kissed her. Deeply, warmly, passionately. Allie's heart thundered in her ears and she sank against him, eagerly returning the kiss.

Finally, he lifted his head. "I love you. I think we've established that, right?"

Allie leaned her forehead against his chest and opened her mouth, but nothing came out.

He tilted her face back up to his. "Allie? Why so quiet?"

"I'm trying to catch my breath and reboot my brain," she finally said. "You can't kiss a girl like that and then expect coherent conversation seconds later."

Linc threw back his head and laughed. And laughed . . . and laughed some more.

"Get ahold of yourself, St. John. It wasn't that funny—and I'm a little miffed you don't have the same problem."

That set him off again. He finally got his chuckles under control and wiped his eyes. "Yeah, it kinda was that funny—and trust me, you take my breath away fifty-nine out of sixty minutes of every hour." She raised a brow and he cleared his throat. "But anyway, what I'm trying to say is, I love you and I want to marry you, but I know you're kind of leery about it, so I'll give you all the time you need, but I just had to tell you because I'm going crazy keeping it inside—"

Allie placed her finger against his lips. "I'd marry you tomorrow, Linc St. John."

"You would?"

"I would."

"I believe that's 'I do,'" a voice said behind them. Derek, the rat. "But if you're going to be a St. John," he said, "you have to learn to play Phase Ten, so get in here, you two."

He ducked back inside and Linc scowled, but stood and pulled Allie up beside him. "In all of our get-togethers, you've never had the pleasure of joining in on a Phase Ten game with us, have you?"

"Nope."

"Then you need to understand that Derek cheats. So, *you* have to learn to cheat so you can beat him at his own game."

"I don't cheat!" Derek called over his shoulder.

"He cheats," Linc muttered.

"That's okay," Allie whispered, "I know how to play and I cheat really well." She lifted a finger to her lips and winked.

Linc gaped, then grinned and slung an arm around her shoulders. "That's my girl."

And they went inside together, where Allie soaked in the love and acceptance of her new family. She sent up a prayer of thanksgiving to the One who'd made it happen.

Then promptly stomped them all in the first game.

Without cheating.

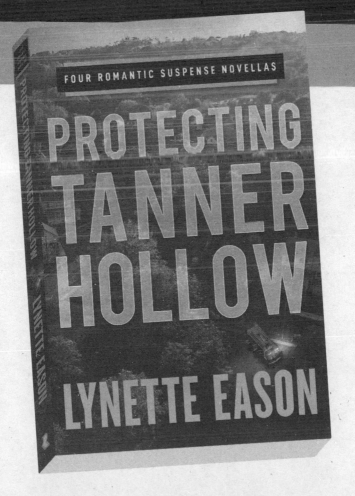

1

It had been a long day, and all Claire Montgomery wanted to do was crash on the couch with her microwave dinner and a cold glass of water—and try to forget the evil in the world. Just for a few minutes. Against her will, her to-do list started running like a ticker tape through her mind and she groaned.

Rest would have to take a backseat to packing. Since accepting the job as one of the supervisors for the forensics department in Asheville, North Carolina, three months ago, the commute was taking a huge toll on her, and she'd decided to start house hunting. In fact, if she hadn't been able to continue to work from home two days a week, she'd already be living in an apartment somewhere near her office. But she didn't want an apartment. She wanted a home.

Now her schedule was about to change and she really needed to be in the office five—or more—days a week. Moving was her only option if she wanted the opportunity to enjoy that home.

Claire parked in the drive, wishing she had a garage with a remote. "But you don't, so quit whining and get inside where it's warm." However, she moved that little item up on the priority list for what she wanted in her forever house. *Her* house. Not a rental, but a home where she belonged.

With a garage door that had a remote.

She had to admit her little rental house was the first place that had come close to feeling like a real home. She'd miss it—and her landlord. Mr. Abrams was the best.

She grabbed her bag with her laptop and other work notes from the passenger seat, climbed out of the Suburban, and slammed the door. Darkness had already fallen even though it was only a little after six o'clock, but night came early to the small town of Tanner Hollow during the winter months—and November was forecasted to be extra cold this year.

"I think the weatherman got it right this time," she muttered, shivering as a gust of wind found its way beneath the collar of her heavy coat. She really needed to stop talking out loud to herself. Someone was going to get the wrong idea and call the men with the white coats to come get her.

Claire darted up the porch steps only to jerk to a stop on the second step and hop back to the ground. She'd bypassed a muddy boot print on the first step.

Weird.

No packages indicating the print could belong to a delivery guy. She noticed the second footprint on the next step. Then more right up to her door.

With a gloved hand, Claire twisted the knob and found it locked. Okay, so someone had walked up on her porch and then left.

"Hi, Claire."

She spun to find Levi Harrison, her next-door neighbor, standing next to her car. Levi had autism—and a fascination with crime, which meant he had a fascination with her. In a totally non-creepy way. It was her job that was the draw.

"Hi, Levi. What are you doing out here?"

"Looking for you." He ducked his head. "I have been waiting for you to get home. I was hoping you would tell me some more stories about the bad guys and the good guys. And how the good

312

guys put the bad guys in prison because the bad guys always leave evidence behind. I want you to tell me about your new microscope again and maybe I can look at it?"

His stilted speech always made her smile. Whenever he actually used a contraction, it threw her. "The new microscope is at my office. And I can't tell any stories tonight, but maybe tomorrow?"

"No. Tonight. Please. And the old microscope is fine. The one in your home office. It's cool too." His eyes focused somewhere in the vicinity of her left ear.

"Sorry, Levi." She simply couldn't talk about her job. Not after today. "But what if you come over tomorrow around lunchtime. I'll take a break to tell you one story, let you look at a slide under the microscope, and might even have a dinosaur for you." The twenty-year-old also had a fascination with all things dinosaur.

"Okay. That's exciting. I can do that. Thank you." He turned to go, and her gaze dropped to his feet. Hiking boots. Her pulse slowed. He'd probably climbed her porch steps to look in the window and see if she was home in spite of the fact that her car hadn't been in the drive. Levi could be very persistent. Most of the time, she was okay with that. Tonight, she had no energy for the young man and was grateful that when she said no, he didn't press.

"Levi, you gotta quit leaving the house without telling me." The snapped words drew her gaze to the other man leaning against the wrought-iron fence that separated the two yards, his glare darting between her and Levi.

Bart Wells, Levi's cousin and guardian. She liked Levi, actually enjoyed his company—and the innocence he brought to their conversations delighted and refreshed her. But his cousin creeped her out a bit. He hadn't been inappropriate in any way, so she wasn't sure why he put her off. She waved anyway, and Bart returned the gesture without smiling. "You shouldn't encourage him," Bart said.

Claire raised a brow. "I'm sorry?"

"Telling him stories, making him think he can one day do a

job like yours. He's a good construction worker and he'll make a decent living under my supervision." Bart's construction van sat in the driveway, and she knew Levi helped him during the day. "But if you keep filling his head with things he'll never be able to do—" He broke off and curled a strong hand into a fist. "Well, just stop. It's cruel to encourage that, so just leave him alone." He grabbed Levi's hand and led him into the house while Claire gaped. Then sighed. Was it cruel?

"Absolutely not," she muttered. Levi had a lot of potential and remembered every single detail she told him. She could only wish to have a memory like his. "He'll probably surprise us all and be *my* boss one day."

Once Levi and Bart were out of sight, Claire pulled the edges of her coat tighter against her throat and hurried up the front porch steps to unlock the door. When she stepped inside, warmth washed over her, soothing her ragged nerves and barely leashed emotions.

Shucking her heavy coat and hanging it on the rack by the door took the last of her energy. She stumbled to the couch and crashed, facedown, while she tried to re-center herself. But it had been a tough day. Tougher than most. Blips from the crime scene flashed in her memory, and no matter how hard she tried to keep them at bay, they pushed through her well-formed barriers. A child had been murdered by his father because the system had failed to protect him. Bile rose in the back of her throat and she bolted to her feet, the past rushing back to her.

She needed to go for a run and pray she could rest when she got back home. A low thump from the back of the house froze her, the memories scattering for now.

Claire put a hand on the weapon at her side and took a step toward the noise. Paused. Snagged her cell phone and dialed 911. She might wind up looking the fool if it was just a mouse. Or . . . something.

Floorboards creaked.

Her heart thudded faster.

Okay, that wasn't a mouse.

"911. What's your emergency?"

"Someone's in my house," she said, her voice low as she backed toward the front door. "I'm leaving, I'll be in—"

A figure in a dark hoodie and a black ski mask stepped from her bedroom at the end of the hall. He darted toward her. She raised her weapon, fired. Missed.

He tackled her and she hit the floor with breath-stealing impact.

"Derek St. John. As I live and breathe, I can't believe you came to visit," Sheriff Nolan Tanner said from the driver's seat of the squad car.

"Yep. You've got me for two whole weeks." Derek grinned at him and shrugged. "Why not? You invited me and I needed some time away. Hopefully, you won't feel the need to renege on the invite." The grin faded quickly.

"Not a chance. So, who broke it off? All you said was that you and Elaine had decided to go your separate ways."

"It was mutual. I could tell she knew something was wrong, but she didn't want to address it. I finally brought it up in the form of a question."

"What kind of question?"

"I asked her if she was happy. She said no. We talked and decided it was best for both of us if we just made a clean break."

"Sorry, man. That had to sting."

It had. "It's been seven months, so the sting is gone. Now, I just mostly have regrets that we didn't do it sooner." He paused. "She called me last week to tell me she's engaged to her brother's best friend."

Nolan let out a low whistle. "Ouch. Double sting."

"A little. The funny thing is, I'm actually happy for her."

"You're a better man than I."

"I'm not sure that's possible."

Nolan laughed. "How's that crazy family of yours?"

"Still crazy, loud—and wonderful. They've been incredibly supportive even though I haven't asked for it. The truth is, I don't know what I'd do without them."

"I know what you m—"

The radio cut him off. While Nolan answered the call, Derek shook his head. While he'd been honest about his feelings where Elaine was concerned, he hadn't admitted what really bothered him. The truth was, he felt like the odd man out in his family. Every one of his five siblings had found their soul mate and were starting families.

Over the last few years, he'd watched his siblings fall in love and marry—and knew his relationship with Elaine was just settling. It was comfortable. And while he wanted to marry and have a family, too, he wouldn't do it just because he wanted to fill a void. The breakup *had* hurt, but it had also been a relief. He'd meet someone eventually. Until then, he'd spend his days enforcing the law and helping those who couldn't help themselves.

After he spent his two weeks of vacation relaxing in the quiet town of Tanner Hollow, North Carolina.

The squad car lurched forward and Nolan hit the lights. "What's up, man?" Derek asked, his pulse picking up speed.

"Someone broke into Claire Montgomery's home and is attacking her. Glad you're a cop because you're going on this call with me. You have your piece?"

"Always."

"Consider yourself Tanner Hollow's newest deputy."

Acknowledgments

Thank you as always to Wayne Smith and Drucilla (Dru) Wells, retired FBI agents. I couldn't do this without your invaluable input. Thank you for fixing all my mistakes!

Thank you to the fans for buying my books, which allows me to keep doing what I'm doing.

Thank you to my family for your unwavering support!

Thank you to all my fabulous people at Revell. This wouldn't happen without you, and I thank you, thank you, thank you for all your hard work at getting my books out there.

Thank you to my agent, Tamela, who always has my back! I love you, my friend. You're the best!

Thank you to my critique buddies who helped me plot out this story: Lynn H. Blackburn, Edie Melson, Linda Gilden, Emme Gannon, Erynn Newman, and Alycia Morales.

To more brainstorming buddies who helped me come up with the opening scene: Colleen Coble, Robin Miller, and Carrie Stuart Parks.

And last but not least, my "sister twin" who gave me even more ideas for this story and never fails to answer my "help me!" emails—DiAnn Mills. I love you, my friend, and I'm honored to share a birthday with you!

If I forgot anyone, please blame it on my poor, overworked brain. It wasn't intentional!

Lynette Eason is the bestselling author of *Oath of Honor*, *Called to Protect*, and *Code of Valor*, as well as the Women of Justice, Deadly Reunions, Hidden Identity, and Elite Guardians series. She is the winner of three ACFW Carol Awards, the Selah Award, and the Inspirational Reader's Choice Award, among others. She is a graduate of the University of South Carolina and has a master's degree in education from Converse College. Eason lives in South Carolina with her husband and two children. Learn more at www.lynetteeason.com.

Connect with
LYNETTE

Sign up for Lynette Eason's newsletter to stay in touch on new books, giveaways, and writing conferences.

LYNETTEEASON.COM

 Lynette Eason | LynetteEason

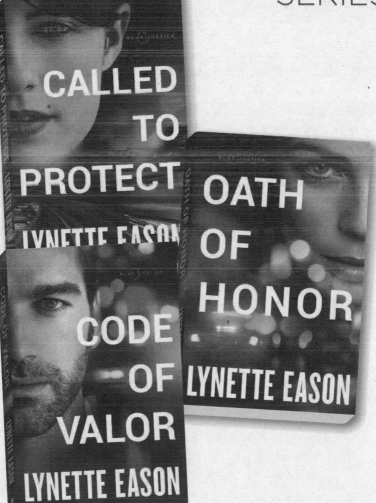

INTENSITY. SKILL. TENACITY.

The bodyguards of
Elite Guardians Agency have it all.

Want to know more about the
Carrington Dive Team?

Catch all their adventures here!